A Matter of Trust

Steve Schach

Wandering in the Words Press

Requests for permission should be sent to Wandering in the Words Press: 2131 Burns St, Nashville, Tennessee, 37216
www.wanderinginthewordspress.com

All characters in this book are fictitious, and any resemblance to real persons, living or dead, is coincidental.

PUBLISHED BY WANDERING IN THE WORDS PRESS

WANDERING
IN THE WORDS

ISBN-10: 0990919307
ISBN-13: 978-0-9909193-0-8
First Edition

To Sharon

Oh what a tangled web we weave,
When first we practise to deceive!
— Sir Walter Scott, *Marmion*

CHAPTER ONE

I unlocked the door of Room 1507 of the Mikado Hotel in Kyoto, turned on the light and stepped inside. The first thing I saw was Yoko Azuma's body lying in my bed. She was still wearing her navy blue bellhop's uniform, including the perky cap, but her blood had flowed all over the pillow as well as the sheet and floral bedspread that covered her. Even her cap was smeared with blood. I rushed out of the room as fast as I could. As I reached the bank of four elevators, one arrived. The doors opened, and two elderly Japanese women, resplendent in silver and peacock blue kimonos, slowly exited. I pushed past them into the elevator and slammed my fist on the button for the lobby. The women didn't even glance back at me.

As the elevator began to descend the fifteen floors, I realized that this would mean a third interview in a week with Inspector Watanabe. I didn't relish the prospect.

***

Before I go any further, I'd like to introduce myself to you. I'm Oliver Thompson, and I'm an accountant, a CPA. If you want to know more about me, you only have to look at a cartoon depicting an accountant or listen to those late-night comedians on TV describing their CPA. For some unknown reason, accountants are always depicted as short, fat and balding. To be perfectly frank, my height is below average. I'm somewhat overweight—okay, I'm fat. And I started losing my hair ten years ago, when I was twenty-eight years old. Now I have a strip of hair about two inches wide stretching from one ear to the other—the rest of my head is very bald indeed.

Cartoonists always seem to depict accountants as short sighted, wearing wire-rimmed spectacles with thick lenses that look like the bottoms of Coca-Cola bottles. I'm so myopic that I can't wear contact lenses, and, yes, my glasses look exactly as in those caricatures. Finally, comedians always seem to describe accountants as being unmarried. After all, who would go on a date with a CPA, let alone marry one?

Hold it! That's the one and only area where I leave the unfunny cartoons and so-called comedians behind me. I'm a married accountant, believe it or not. Here's how it all happened.

One morning last year I was sitting at my desk in my office in a prestigious office tower on Fifth Avenue in New York City, feeling particularly sorry for myself. The previous morning I'd met with Edwin Reilly, a long-standing client. Edwin made a huge fortune in Texas oil and an even huger one in Dallas real estate. I was about to explain the various clauses of a legal document to him when he said, "Look, Oliver, I really don't want to hear all this. I know you won't feel too hurt when I tell you that all this is boring me to tears—I'm sure everyone tells you that. Just let me sign the document. I trust you." Horrified at the idea of anyone signing a forty-seven-page legal document without my first having explained every single clause in detail, I ignored his request and started going through the document with him.

In the middle of clause 2.1(b)(ii) on page four, Edwin passed out, and I couldn't bring him round. First, I tried gently blowing in his face. Next, I said his name, louder and louder, until I was almost shouting. Nothing helped. Then I tried slapping his face, softly at first, then more firmly. Edwin remained unconscious.

Good grief, I've bored him to death!

In a panic, I called 911. The EMTs came within a few minutes, and I quickly explained the situation to them. They carefully placed Edwin on the gurney and wheeled him into the elevator. I accompanied them down to the street. While they were loading him into the ambulance, a cab drew up and deposited a passenger in front of the building. I grabbed the taxi, and told the cabbie to follow the ambulance to the emergency room. Edwin remained comatose for more than four hours. During this time, I sat in a cold sweat in the waiting room, only getting up repeatedly to buy junk food from a vending machine in the hallway. The more nervous I became, the more I ate. Finally, a harassed-looking resident physician came up to me and assured me that Edwin was in perfect health. Edwin, it appeared, had been sleeping badly for some weeks now, for a reason that the physician wouldn't divulge to me. Apparently, all attempts to get a good night's sleep had failed, until I started explaining the document to Edwin. Clause 2.1(b)(ii) on page four had proven to be the perfect trigger, and he'd plunged into the deep sleep he'd craved for so many days.

Needless to say, the episode did very little for my self-esteem. In addition, I was scared that I might actually kill some future client. While I was sitting in the hospital waiting room, the expression "he bores me to death" had kept going through my mind. As a result, I hardly looked up the next morning at 10:30 when my secretary, Miss Dixon, ushered a Ms. Stenqvist into my office.

Fearing that possible fatal consequences could result from meeting this new client, I continued to study the balance sheet directly in front of me on my desk until I heard a cough. I looked up and gasped, audibly. The first thing I noticed were her legs, which seemed to go on forever. I stared at those legs, and my stare also seemed to go on forever. Reluctantly raising my eyes, I saw a soft black leather briefcase, and then a little black dress that even I realized must have cost thousands of dollars. The dress clung to a perfect slender body. There's absolutely no need for me to try to describe that body—just use your imagination. Raising my eyes still further, I saw an exquisite neck, and then an oval face graced with baby-blue eyes, shoulder-length strawberry blonde hair, two rows of impossibly even white teeth, a straight nose and a look of adoration. That's right, adoration. I shot to my feet to greet my visitor, but found myself totally unable to speak.

Ms. Stenqvist obviously knew that she had this effect on men because the expression on her face didn't change in any way.

"I'm Nikki Stenqvist," she said. "You're Oliver Thompson?"

Her voice was low, her accent was clearly Scandinavian, but from those few words I couldn't tell if she if was Swedish, Norwegian, or perhaps Danish. I waved a hand in her direction to indicate that she should sit down, because I was still totally incapable of speech. As she settled into the plush brown leather armchair on her side of my desk and arranged those endless legs in a way that best displayed them, I felt my knees go weak, and I collapsed into my chair. Profuse perspiration poured down my face.

Ms. Stenqvist spoke again. "I understand that you're an expert on trusts?"

It was more a statement than a question, but I nodded my agreement.

"Elisabièta said that I should consult you," she continued.

During the eight years that the Archduchess von und zu Eckwitz und Böderheim has been my client, never once did it cross my mind that anyone had ever called her Elisabièta, not even her parents, but it seemed perfectly natural coming from Ms. Stenqvist. I nodded again.

"I've just inherited about $65 million from my stepfather. The money is in an offshore trust, and Elisabièta said I should talk to you about it."

For the third time I nodded. Yesterday I'd assumed that Edwin Reilly would never emerge from his coma, and today I was equally certain that I'd never be able to speak again. I was also concerned about my eye muscles. They seemed to be paralyzed because I was now totally unable to move my eyes away from those legs, no matter how hard I tried. But with legs like hers, willpower alone wasn't enough.

Ms. Stenqvist put her brief case onto the desk, opened it and took out a forty-page document. The briefcase now appeared to be empty.

"I want you to go through this trust and explain it me," she said.

At this point, I panicked. The worst that could happen to me for putting Edwin Reilly into a coma by explaining a legal document to him was being prosecuted for assault with a deadly weapon, namely, my boring voice. But if I inflicted any damage on this gorgeous creature in front me, I'd be so mortified that I'd have to kill myself on the spot.

Looking up at her, I was stunned to see the look of adoration still on her face. In fact, I was so shocked that the power of speech came back with a start. I said the very first thing that came into my mouth, which was "Um, er, um," after which I was promptly totally struck dumb again.

Ms. Stenqvist pushed the document in front me and said, sweetly, "Here."

I looked down. The first page bore the four words *The Dragonhead Family Trust.*

"My mother was once married to James Dragonhead," she explained.

I nodded yet again. Dragonhead, I knew, was a playboy who had inherited a vast fortune from his industrialist father. I don't usually read *People* magazine; in fact, I almost never read anything other than balance sheets and legal and financial documents. But I remembered seeing a report on James Dragonhead's sixth or seventh wedding relatively recently on CNN; he'd married an anorexic supermodel. I also recalled that only a few days later he'd died—apparently from an overdose of cocaine—on his yacht while it was moored off his private island in the Bahamas. I also seemed to remember reading somewhere that high living plus unending alimony payments to numerous ex-wives had driven Dragonhead to near poverty. I was therefore somewhat surprised when Ms. Stenqvist said, "The trustees tell me that the trust contains about $65 million."

Then she added, "They also tell me I can't spend any of it until I'm fifty."

If the trustees were right, Ms. Stenqvist would have to wait about twenty-five years. The very idea that this most beautiful of all women would have to wait even a nanosecond for her money overcame my instinctive fear of boring her to death.

"Based on my experience," I said, "it seems unlikely that you'd have to wait that long to get any money. Let's go through this trust deed of yours."

With any other client I'd have carefully studied the document on my own, then met later with the client to discuss my findings, but the thought of asking Ms. Stenqvist to leave my office was unthinkable to me. Accordingly, stumbling and stammering, I slowly went through the first few pages of the trust deed. From the second page I learned that Ms. Stenqvist's mother had been James Dragonhead's third wife. Dragonhead had no children of his own, and Ms. Stenqvist was his only stepchild, and he'd consequently made her his heir.

The key clause was in the middle of page four. Yes, Ms. Stenqvist had to wait until age fifty to obtain any of the capital, but she was entitled to all the income from the trust until then. Even if the assets of the trust were relatively conservatively invested, Ms. Stenqvist could have an annual income of about $2 million while the value of her trust continued to grow steadily year-by-year. Having explained this to her, I asked her if she'd like me to go on to the second section of the trust deed. To my dismay, she replied, "I want to be quite sure. Would you please go through that first section again."

Clearly I hadn't done a good job of explaining the provisions of the trust to her. So I spent fifteen minutes repeating the key points of the first part of the trust deed, all the time feeling guilty that my initial explanation had been inadequate.

Before I tell you what Ms. Stenqvist said next, I need to explain something so that you don't misunderstand her remark. It's customary for very rich people to invite their advisors to a meal to show their appreciation of the advice that they've received. For example, a rich entrepreneur will ask his tax lawyer to lunch with him at his club to acknowledge the fact that the entrepreneur feels it's inadequate merely to pay the lawyer his fee of $75,000 (for one hundred hours of work), when the lawyer's clever legal stratagems have saved the entrepreneur more than $2 million in taxes. It's a gesture of thanks that's clearly understood as such by both parties. A handful of my clients will take me to lunch once a year, but most prefer to show their appreciation of my services by taking me to a hit Broadway musical. The reason they prefer a theater to a restaurant is probably because that way they don't have to be bored to death by my conversation over a lengthy meal. I don't really like musicals very much, but I always accept their invitations because to turn them down would be interpreted as a deadly insult. Soon after *The Book of Mormon* opened on Broadway, a number of my clients wanted to express their appreciation for my services as well as display their clout at being able to get the best seats in the house for the hottest show in town at a moment's notice. I saw *The Book of Mormon* no fewer than seven times in four weeks. Those were four long weeks.

When I'd finished explaining the key provisions of her trust to Ms. Stenqvist for the second time, she smiled and said to me, "Thank you. Everything is really crystal clear. And now I'd be honored if you'd join me for lunch."

From the conventional viewpoint there wasn't anything unusual in her remark. After all, I'd told her that just one Letter of Wishes from her to the trustees would ensure her an income of millions of dollars every single year, and for learning this fact she'd have to pay me $1,125 for ninety minutes of my time. Accordingly, it would indeed be appropriate, in terms of the code of the ultra-rich, for her to invite me to lunch. Also, this was certainly not the first time that a client had asked me to a meal after only a single consultation. The unbelievably rich have a code of ethics of their own, and one unbreakable rule is the necessity of showing gratitude by giving the only thing that money can't buy: their time.

However, there was another side to her invitation to lunch. Had Ms. Stenqvist been a seventy-year-old dowager, without a moment's hesitation I'd immediately have escorted her to luncheon—as she would have put it—at whichever restaurant she wished. You may accuse me of being old-fashioned, you may even accuse me of male chauvinism, but what was going through my head was that, even today, it's unusual for a stunningly beautiful young woman to invite a short, fat, bald man to lunch.

In the midst of the ensuing silence, Ms. Stenqvist seemed to sense what was bothering me. She looked me straight in the eye and said, "Have you been to Guido's? The food is absolutely fabulous."

This remark made it clear that she wished her invitation to be interpreted in one way only; that is, strictly as a meal to thank me for what had been strictly business, so I warmly accepted. I rose from my desk and opened the connecting door to allow Ms. Stenqvist to precede me into the waiting room where Miss Dixon was seated in front of her computer.

Even though I always carry a BlackBerry, I also tell Miss Dixon where I'm going. Accordingly, as we walked past Miss Dixon's desk, I turned to her and said, "Ms. Stenqvist is taking me to lunch."

Then, just in case Miss Dixon was as old-fashioned as I am, I quickly added, "Ms. Stenqvist wants me to go to Guido's. She tells me that the food is absolutely fabulous."

When we arrived at Guido's, the maître d' rushed up to Nikki, beamed at her, and purred. "Ms. Stenqvist, it's wonderful to see you again. Would you like your usual table?"

We were taken to a corner table from which we could watch the comings and goings of what I assumed was the fashionable lunch crowd. The restaurant looked like a hothouse, so profuse were the plants. In addition to exotic species against the walls, there were flower boxes on stands between the tables. The sound-deadening ability of plants made it hard for diners at one table to eavesdrop on the conversation at the next table, an unfortunate practice at many top restaurants.

After we were seated, I looked around the room. Not surprisingly for a social recluse like myself, I didn't recognize anyone, so I just sat back and waited for the waiter to bring the menus. But I certainly was not relaxed. My all-too-real fear was that I'd say something that would bore this truly gorgeous woman, so I decided to simply keep quiet. We sat in silence for a few moments. Then Ms. Stenqvist spoke.

"Mr. Thompson, tell me all about yourself."

"I've been doing most of the talking today. Why don't you tell me all about yourself? And by the way, please call me Oliver."

"I will, Oliver, but then you must call me Nikki. I don't want to hear 'Ms. Stenqvist' any more. Okay, here's the story of my life."

By now you're probably wanting me to get back to telling you what happened in Kyoto—yes, I know, I bore all of the people all of the time—so I'll just very briefly summarize what Nikki proceeded to tell me over the next two hours. Her grandfather was Roald Stenqvist, *the* Roald Stenqvist who had started a clothing shop in the Swedish town of Uleå that was the starting point for Stenqvist Department Stores, now the largest department store chain in Europe by far. Roald married the daughter of an army colonel who had retired from an artillery regiment after a particularly bad fall from his horse during a steeplechase. Only one child survived past infancy and that was Berta, Nikki's mother. From the time she was born, Berta was groomed to take over Stenqvist Department Stores from her father. She obtained a degree in economics from the prestigious University of Lund. She worked in the family business for two years and loathed every minute of it, so her father sent her to Harvard to get an MBA, in the hope that a deeper understanding of the world of business might change her attitude. And it was at the Harvard Business School that she met Carter Prescot, III, the scion of the Chicago meat packing family.

"Most children are taught to say Mama or Dada as their first word," said Nikki. "My father was taught to say 'pork bellies.' He grew up hating the meat business with the same loathing that my mother felt for Stenqvist Department Stores."

At Harvard they were kindred spirits: tall, blond, handsome, rich, and looking forward with dread to an endless future of running their respective family businesses. People say that opposites attract, but Carter and Berta were drawn together by what they had in common. They sat together in class and worked together on projects. They sat at adjoining carrels in the library. They spent every minute of the day together, incessantly sharing their thoughts with one another.

The professors at the Harvard Business School encourage their students to think creatively about money and what it can be used to achieve. One day Carter and Berta sat down to think the unthinkable: What would happen if they dropped out of

Harvard, eloped, and lived on the trust funds set up years prior by their rich parents? The computations were quick and easy, the answers irrefutable—they each had more money than they could possibly spend together for the rest of their lives.

Three days later they were married in Harvard Chapel. They then mailed two letters, one to Sweden and one to Chicago. Nikki told me that her mother often wondered what happened when their letters were received. Berta never found out, because neither she nor Carter ever had contact with their parents again. The Prescots were so furious at the way that their son and heir had spurned the family business that they cut all ties with him. The Stenqvists were equally horrified by Berta's action and disowned her, too, although Roald Stenqvist later set up a trust fund for Nikki, his granddaughter, whom he never met before he died.

Carter and Berta, as creative as always, invented a new occupation—jet-setting. The private jet had just become a fashionable form of transportation, so they jetted from Aspen to the Riviera, from Venice to the Hamptons. Every minute of every day they lived for one thing and one thing only—namely, their mutual pleasure. They were a unit, two people who agreed on everything. In particular, they agreed that the very last thing either of them wanted was a child, because a child would interfere with their twenty-four hours of fun every single day.

But the maternal instinct in Berta was much stronger than she knew or was prepared to admit.

One day she found out she was pregnant. "To this day," Nikki said, "I don't know whether my mother forgot to take the pill for a few days or whether it was a deliberate omission on her part. Either way, that was how I came into the world."

Carter was furious. He begged Berta to have an abortion. When she refused, he immediately divorced her and continued his jet-setting life with a series of beautiful women. Shortly after Nikki's thirteenth birthday, Carter was returning to his hotel from a charity ball in Jackson, Mississippi, in a borrowed red Maserati Ghibli II. Having overindulged in mint juleps, he took a bend about forty miles an hour too fast, and was killed when he wrapped the car around a one hundred-year-old Southern magnolia tree. His girlfriend survived the crash, but was horribly disfigured.

After the divorce, Berta resumed her jet-setting existence just as soon as she could. This meant hiring a series of nannies to look after Nikki while Berta was pleasure-bound. Then when Nikki turned eight, her mother sent her to boarding school in Switzerland.

"As I'm sure you know, some of the finest schools in the world are in Switzerland. If my mother had chosen wisely, I could have had a truly superb education. Unfortunately, she chose the school that her jet-setting friends with their own children had recommended. As a result, at the age of eight I became a JSIT, that is, a jet-setter-in-training. The school was to all intents and purposes a year-round baby-sitting service for fabulously wealthy parents. They could leave their daughters there with the knowledge that they would be well looked after.

"If the parents wanted to see their daughter for a few days at Christmas, the school would make all the arrangements. If the child was too young to travel alone to Rio or Hong Kong or wherever the parents were going to be that Christmas, one of the teachers accompanied her, stayed at the destination for two or three days (which was usually the maximum length of time that the parents would want to be with their daughter), then flew back with the child. For jet-setters with children, the school was a godsend.

"However, the school was a lot less satisfactory for us students. The academic standards were utterly abysmal. The major subject in the curriculum seemed to be learning how to order servants around in four or five different languages. I left that school at age sixteen to spend two years at a Swiss finishing school. But the finishing school was just as bad; I never really understood what that school was trying to finish. We spent half the time playing sport, and the other half gossiping.

"When I left finishing school at eighteen, I did the only thing for which I was qualified. I became a regular dues-paying member of the jet-set. For the past seven years, I've lived a life of pleasure. Until I turned twenty-five a few months ago, I had a steady income from one of my grandfather Roald's trusts, and now I'll live off the Dragonhead Family Trust. But I've decided to leave the jet-set."

Nikki paused for effect. Despite my promise to myself not to say a single word, there was absolutely no way out. I had to ask the obvious questions: "Why? What happened?"

"Nothing happened. That's the whole problem."

She paused, took a deep breath and asked, "Have you ever seen pictures of jet-setters?"

"Sure. Nowadays you can't read the *Times* or turn on CNN without seeing them."

"And how would describe them?"

"Tanned and good looking."

"And what else?"

The conversation was suddenly starting to get just a little too personal. Had I been talking to someone other than Nikki, I might have been candid and said that what characterizes jet-setters more than anything else is that they're all slender, thin and skinny. Also lean, bony and slim. But I couldn't bring myself to say this to Nikki. First, she herself was as about fat-free as any jet-setter I'd seen on TV or in a newspaper photograph. But more significantly, I'd be drawing attention to my 350 pounds. There was no way I could do that.

"Oliver, haven't you noticed that jet-setters are paper thin, both the men and the women? And that's why I want to leave the jet-set."

She paused for a second. Then looked down at her hands, which were lying on her lap, and said in a small voice, so softly that I first thought I'd misheard her, "I go for brilliant fat men."

I was utterly bewildered and speechless for the second time in a few hours. But Nikki was equal to the occasion—her years of expensive Swiss education had instilled in her the techniques for handling every social situation, no matter how difficult or uncomfortable. She continued in her soft voice, almost a whisper.

"As I think most people realize, intelligent people are generally too smart to be jet-setters. Also—and I'm sorry I embarrassed you—I think you know that very few jet-setters are fat. You're the first supremely intelligent fat man I've met. And I could really go for you."

I remembered reading somewhere that there are surprisingly many men who are attracted to grossly overweight women. From Nikki's last remark I'd just learned that there are women who feel similarly about fat men, and it was my extreme good fortune to have met one. But Nikki isn't just any woman. She's truly one of the Beautiful People, in every way.

I used my BlackBerry to call my secretary.

"Miss Dixon, please cancel all my appointments for this afternoon."

"You don't have any," she said. "You asked me to keep the entire afternoon clear for you to redraft the Corelli Irrevocable Trust."

"Fine. I won't be back this afternoon." I pressed the red button and put the phone back in my pocket.

"Miss Stenqvist, or rather, Nikki, I'd be deeply honored if you'd spend the afternoon with me. I have an apartment on the top two floors of a building on Park Avenue, and I think we'd be more comfortable there than sitting here in Guido's."

I then waved to the waiter to bring me the bill. Nikki protested that I was her guest, but I insisted.

"You said you were inviting me for food. This has turned into a date. And I'm old-fashioned enough to insist that the man pays for dates."

"But I invited you for food, and you ate it. Surely *I* should pay for the meal?"

"I was so engrossed in what you were saying that I never even realized that I was eating. What did I eat?"

Nikki just smiled.

When we got to my penthouse, I invited Nikki to sit on the red plush sofa in the living room. She turned down my offer of a drink and invited me to sit beside her. I did.

Again she smiled. Then she asked, "Instead of a drink, do you know what I'd like?"

"No, what?"

The next thing I knew Nikki had embraced me in a grip that she could have learned only through hours of work in the gym every day under the ministrations of a ruthless personal trainer with the vicious outlook of a drill sergeant in the Marine Corps. She proceeded to kiss me in a way that I'd never previously been kissed, probably because the only other woman who had ever kissed me before was my mother, and she always kissed me with marked reluctance.

The kiss went on for quite a while and got quite adventurous. Even though I had no previous experience of that sort of thing, I knew that it was customary to go further than just kissing. And I tentatively touched her left breast with my right hand.

Nikki froze. She put her left hand on my right hand, and gently put it down onto my lap. "Darling, please don't ever touch me above the knee or below the shoulders until we're married," she said softly but firmly. "Now kiss me again."

Then I realized what she had just said. Yes, Nikki had dropped the M-bomb.

Despite the effects of the kiss, I was able to stay at least partially rational. On the one hand, I understood that Nikki was attracted to fat, intelligent men and, in all modesty, I am vastly overqualified on both counts. However, in my experience, there's one and only one reason why a stunningly beautiful young woman would want to marry a considerably less than stunningly handsome older man, and that's for his money. Many of my clients have dumped their loving wives after twenty or twenty-five years of happy marriage in order to marry what's euphemistically termed a "trophy wife." The term "gold digger" is also sometimes used to describe the second wife, generally by the first wife. But a woman with $65 million in an offshore trust doesn't need to marry the likes of me.

But even while Nikki was kissing me I was still able to think like an accountant, albeit at less than two percent of my full capabilities. And an ugly thought crossed my mind: What if there was no money in her trust? I only had her word for it that the Dragonhead Family Trust was worth $65 million. The rumor that Dragonhead had died nearly penniless bounced around in my brain. The conclusion was obvious: This beautiful woman was just another gold digger. Nikki was after my money!

I eased Nikki away as gently as I could and retreated to my side of the sofa. I stared straight into those unforgettable blue eyes, and said, "Ms. Stenqvist, you're a wealthy woman, and the Archduchess has no doubt informed you that I'm a wealthy man. Neither of us needs the other's money. Consequently, I'm sure that you'd have no objection to signing a prenuptial agreement to the effect that during our marriage we'll each maintain ownership of our own assets. Furthermore, in the unlikely event of a divorce, neither of us will receive anything from the other."

"Of course!" Nikki said. "How could you think otherwise? Now come back here, Oliver, I haven't finished kissing you yet."

Our courtship was brief but intense. I met her on a Tuesday. For each of the next three evenings we went out for a lengthy dinner. Each time she turned down my invitation to come to my penthouse. Instead, after the meal we took a cab back to her hotel. During the ride, Nikki sat primly in her corner of the seat. When the taxi arrived at its destination, she kissed me chastely, and then walked into the hotel. She didn't allow me even to escort her into the lobby.

Saturday at noon I called her.

"Nikki, how would you like to hire a car and drive into the country? We could stay at a country inn. Separate rooms, of course," I added.

When I arrived at Nikki's hotel I discovered that the concierge had organized everything for us. A powerful-looking yellow sports car was waiting in the hotel parking garage. I took one look at the car, and said to Nikki, "Would you like to drive?"

She just smiled that smile that I so love. Nikki knows that there are some things that men with my build can't do, and one of them is to fit behind the steering wheel of a sports car. But I managed to get into the passenger seat, and off we went in what Nikki told me was a Lamborghini Aventador LP 720-4 50° Anniversario. And apparently the paintwork wasn't simply yellow, but rather *giallo Maggio* (May yellow).

Two hours later we arrived at the inn that the concierge had chosen for us. Fortunately, he'd provided a map and detailed directions, as well as location coordinates for the GPS, because the country inn was literally in the middle of nowhere— I hadn't realized that there are such utterly rural areas so close to the city. The building looked old, very old, and I hoped that the plumbing and wiring had been redone at least once in the last two hundred years.

There was no need for me to be concerned. The owners, Tim and Margie Bernard, were a young couple who had rebuilt the entire interior while doing only the most essential repairs to the outside walls and the roof. Then they had furnished the place with love, good taste and genuine antiques. The result was superlative. At all times we had the feeling that we were staying in a house that had been untouched from the time that it was built early in the nineteenth century but nevertheless had all the modern comforts of a luxury hotel.

We asked our hosts to recommend a restaurant for dinner, and they suggested that we drive to a town some fifteen miles away. The restaurant there was as superbly decorated as our inn. The dark oak beams supporting the ceiling seemed genuine, as did the antique wooden cabinets that lined the walls. The china and glassware stored in those cabinets were reflected in the gleaming brass fittings.

The appearance of the restaurant, for some reason, looked vaguely familiar. When we asked him about the beautiful room, the manager told us that the Bernards had earned some of the money to purchase and reconstruct their inn by redecorating the restaurant some four years before.

The food was as excellent as the ambiance. As always, Nikki just ate a few mouthfuls while I polished off everything placed in front me. After all, if I lost even a pound or two, Nikki might just decide to marry someone else.

After dinner we returned to the inn and took a walk in the garden. It was a perfect September evening, warm and still, with low humidity—early fall at its best. The moon was just bright enough to light the path. We sat on a wooden bench under an apple tree, and kissed. The kissing went on for a long time.

Then I touched her breast again. This time Nikki's reaction was more emphatic.

"Oliver, I've told you not to touch me there. I've no intention whatsoever of going any further until I'm married. If you really love me, show me your love by respecting me."

The magical moment was lost. We went into the house to our respective rooms.

The next morning Nikki acted as if nothing untoward had happened the night before. She was her usual sparkling self. After breakfast, she suggested that we take a drive to a nearby waterfall that our hosts had suggested we see. It was only about twenty minutes away by car. She parked the Lamborghini and, after a short walk, we arrived at the waterfall. It wasn't spectacular, but it was quite pretty. We sat on a rock and watched the water tumbling into the pool below.

"About last night," Nikki said.

"I'm sorry about what happened, and it won't happen again," I said. The last thing I wanted was to fight with Nikki.

"I know it won't happen again. But that's not what I wanted to talk to you about. Oliver, I want you to know that I'm a virgin. No one has ever been allowed to touch me the way you wanted to touch me, let alone go any further. I've determined to save my virginity for the man that I marry, even though all my friends think that I'm insane. But sex is something very important and special to me. And you're equally important and special to me."

I was so touched by her words that I nearly cried. We drove back to the city in the Lamborghini Aventador in companionable silence.

Five weeks later, Nikki and I were married. The ceremony took place in my penthouse apartment on Park Avenue. A completely recovered Edwin Reilly was my best man. One bridesmaid was the Archduchess von und zu Eckwitz und Böderheim; even after all that's happened, I still can't think of her as Elisabièta. The other bridesmaid was supposed to be Miss Dixon, but when I asked her, she pointed out that for the past four years she'd been Mrs. Charlie Thackeray—no, I hadn't observed the wedding ring on her finger. Instead, I asked her to be matron of honor, and she readily agreed. Three of my clients who live in New York plus Charlie Thackeray were the only guests. I have no friends, and Nikki assured me that there was no one other than Elisabièta whom she wanted to be at her wedding.

CHAPTER TWO

The image of the dead girl in my bed haunted me. As the doors of the elevator opened, I could see that the lobby of the Mikado Hotel was crowded. I rushed toward the front desk as fast as I could. On my left, a line of dozens of smartly dressed men and women waited for an elevator to take them to a wedding reception in one of the ballrooms. I pushed through them, and also through the line of businessmen waiting patiently to check in. I caught a glimpse of the general manager of the hotel, Mr. Mori, about to enter the room behind the check-in counter, and I shouted across to him.

"Yoko Azuma is dead—her body is in my bed!"

The Japanese highly prize the ability of not showing any emotion. Mr. Mori had demonstrated that skill to me on a previous occasion, and now had no problem in demonstrating it again.

"Why, Mr. Thompson, how good to see you again. How are you today?"

I repeated, "Yoko Azuma is dead—her body is in my bed!"

Mori didn't bat an eyelid. "Come," he said, "Let's go up to your room and see."

He walked around the check-in counter, put a friendly arm on my shoulder and firmly walked me to the bank of elevators. The long line of waiting wedding guests moved back, making room for Mori and me at the head of the line. After a few seconds, an elevator arrived. The doors opened. Out walked two American tourists, draped with cameras. Behind them, pushing a laden luggage trolley, came Yoko Azuma.

There was no sign of blood anywhere on her bellhop uniform, even her perky cap was clean and crisp as always. And the happy grin was back in place.

***

I don't want to bore you with the history of my life. Instead, let me just say that I was born in Brooklyn, New York. My father was a bus driver, my mother worked as a cashier in a small restaurant near where we lived. Both died in their early forties of heart disease, aggravated by obesity—yes, it's hereditary. They passed away within weeks of one another in the year after I had graduated from college.

I had a lonely childhood and, for that matter, a lonely adult life until I met Nikki. No one likes a fat person, not even my sister, Eloise, who, unlike her parents and brother, wasn't cursed with the fat gene. Seven years older than me, Eloise studiously ignored me from the day I was born and made sure that her many friends treated me like a pariah.

Eloise married the first of her several husbands when she was seventeen and moved to Philadelphia.

School was a nightmare. I was always the last one to be chosen for any team. Even if the team was for an intellectual contest, such as a spelling bee, I was always chosen after everyone else. I didn't go to the high school prom, or to any other social events, for that matter. Surprisingly enough, the other students never bullied me, probably because I was so low on the social totem pole that no bully would dare hurt me, for fear of losing the esteem of his fellow bullies.

On the basis of my SAT scores, I was fortunate enough to win a full scholarship to Deighton College, where I earned a degree in accounting. During those four years, I lived with my parents, taking the train and bus to and from Deighton. My contact with my fellow students was restricted to the classroom.

I studied hard and was rewarded with excellent grades. But despite my outstanding academic performance, all the Big Four accounting firms turned me down. Eventually, I was offered a position in the New York offices of Copeland, O'Neill, and Copeland, a medium-sized New York City accounting firm. They assigned me to the Trust Department, probably because that was where I'd have minimal contact with clients.

For six years, I labored as hard at my job as I had at my studies at Deighton College, and my supervisors praised me for my work. Each year, I received a substantial salary increase and a generous annual bonus. Then, one day, Dr. Colleen Kogan, the newly elected managing partner, called me to see her.

I'd never before been in her giant corner office with a breathtaking view of Madison Avenue. The room was a mass of gleaming brass. There were brass bowls and brass candlesticks on brass tables, and large brass plates on the wall. Even the coffee table in the corner was made of brass.

Dr. Kogan repeated what I'd heard many times, namely, that my work was technically superb. However, she went on, unfortunately I'd never be promoted to partner because of my poor interaction with my clients. They, too, were uniformly delighted with my work from a technical viewpoint, but the vast majority preferred to discuss their affairs with anyone but me. She went on to say that the partners had unanimously agreed that they would welcome my staying on as an associate as long as I wished and, in fact, they all hoped that I would, but it was only fair to inform me that a future partnership was out of the question.

Her remarks came as a bombshell. After all, I'd never realized just how socially inept I was. Despite the kind way she'd spoken and the effort she'd made not to hurt my feelings, I felt as if I'd been hit on the head with an 18-pound steel mallet. I said nothing, clambered out of my chair and rushed out of her room as fast as I could manage. I took the elevator down to my floor, fortunately meeting no one else on the way. As I walked into my office, I was embarrassed to see that Edwin Reilly occupied the other chair—when Dr. Kogan had summoned me, I'd completely forgotten that Edwin had set up an appointment to see me at that time. My forgetfulness was truly surprising in view of the fact that Edwin was one of only a handful of clients who ever wanted to meet with me in person when a face-to-face discussion was needed to resolve an issue.

Edwin slowly rose to his feet. As always, he looked as if he'd come straight off the set of *Dallas* without changing out of his costume or removing his make-up; his heavily lined face was tanned year round. We shook hands. Edwin took one look at my appearance and asked me what was wrong. For some reason I told him everything—perhaps the kind look in his eyes overcame the instinctive wariness of friendless people. I explained that the partners unanimously felt that my work was technically superlative, but that my interpersonal skills left a lot to be desired. Edwin smiled in a fatherly way and then assured me that he knew both components of my life extremely well indeed.

"How old are you now?" Edwin asked.

"I'm twenty-eight. My birthday was two weeks ago." Needless to say, I'd celebrated my birthday on my own.

"Have you any idea what you're going to do now?" he asked.

"No, I've absolutely no plans. For the past six years, I simply assumed that I was going to become a partner. Today's news came as a total shock to me. As I told you, the partners want me to stay on as an associate for the rest of my working life, but my pride won't allow that. I must find something else to do, but what?"

"How about going into a consulting practice on your own as a trust expert?"

I rolled my eyes. "That's the very last thing on earth that I'd consider. I'd have no client base, and, if some unfortunate individual were unlucky enough to find his way to my office, how long do you think he'd stay?"

"Oliver, if you went into solo practice, I can guarantee you one client: me. The *only* reason that I deal with Copeland, O'Neill, and Copeland is that you're the star of the Trust Department. If you resign, and that seems likely from what you've said, I'm willing to set you up as a consultant. I'll guarantee you a minimum income for three years. I'll tell all my friends and business associates about your incomparable skills. In the unlikely event that my work plus that of my friends doesn't bring in this guaranteed minimum, I'll make up the difference out of my own pocket."

"That's an unbelievable offer. But what do you want from me in return?"

"Nothing. As you well know, I'm an extremely wealthy man. Thanks to you, I'm a lot wealthier than I was before I met you. All I'm doing is betting that you'll make a success of your practice, and you know very well that, when it comes to business, I almost always win my bets. If you earn more than the guaranteed minimum, this isn't going to cost me one cent, and I'll continue to have the benefit of your sterling advice. Now, do we have a deal?"

We shook hands then and there. Two days later Edwin was back with a contract. The terms astonished me. First, Edwin required me to set up a practice on Fifth Avenue. I'd intended renting a hole-in-the-wall office in Brooklyn near where I still lived in my late parents' home, an area where the cost per square foot of rental space was a fraction of the cost of the prime Manhattan real estate that Edwin had stipulated. Another clause specified that I'd have to hire a secretary, something that hadn't crossed my mind for one minute. After all, if I had just one client, surely I could answer the telephone myself.

Edwin was equally concerned with the physical appearance of the suite. The contract included an advance of $150,000 to have my rooms professionally decorated, and stipulated that the entire sum had to be spent that way. Most amazing of all was that Edwin had guaranteed me a minimum annual gross income of $500,000. I signed enthusiastically, but at the back of my mind, I suspected that Edwin had finally made a business mistake that was going to cost him more than a million dollars.

I was wrong. Edwin knew me far better than I knew myself. After only seven months in my new business, I'd earned a total of $500,000 in fees, and I've never looked back. My specialty is legal offshore trusts. There are a number of extremely wealthy individuals who feel the need to guard their money by storing it offshore, in banks situated in places like Belize or the Cook Islands. No, they aren't drug dealers trying to hide their ill-gotten gains, but honest taxpaying citizens who are concerned that, if their considerable fortunes were stored here in the United States, someone might be able to get their greedy fingers on their money. Who that *someone* is varies from individual to individual. Some of my clients are worried that the government might try to confiscate their wealth. Others fear vengeful spouses or future creditors. For example, many of my physician clients are terrified that some day an unhappy patient will successfully sue them for malpractice and they'll have to pay damages far in excess of their malpractice insurance. As a consequence, they would have to hand over all their shares in the restaurants in which they've invested their money.

To protect them financially, I suggest to these wealthy individuals that they set up offshore bank accounts. That is, they choose a territory like Nevis or Lichtenstein that has asset-protection laws, and they put their assets into a bank account there. If a creditor or ex-spouse tries to get hold of the money, the offshore bankers invoke the asset-protection laws. This forces the party trying to get hold of the assets to hire an expensive local lawyer to file a suit in the offshore country. Foreign lawyers, and especially lawyers who specialize in offshore banking, don't take cases on contingency. Instead, they insist on a large up-front payment and equally large regular monthly installments.

Very occasionally the local lawyer will be successful. For additional protection against that possibility, I advise my clients to set up an offshore trust rather than just an offshore bank account. Now their assets belong to the trust, not to them. If, as rarely happens, it seems that the local lawyer for the creditor or ex-spouse is on the point of possibly being able to attach the assets of the trust, the trustees invoke a clause that allows them to move the jurisdiction of the trust to a different country with equally strong asset-protection laws. The chase then continues with a new local lawyer in the new forum raking in the considerable shekels. All the money paid to the original local lawyer is now lost with nothing to show for it.

For the privilege of having offshore trustees to protect their money, each year my clients pay about two percent of the value of their trust to the trustees. Some clients want even more protection against their real or imagined enemies—almost invariably the latter. When that happens, I add a protector to their trusts. This results in an additional annual charge, of course. The trustees now can't do certain things—like pay money to the "wrong" people—without explicit permission of the protector, and the protector always says "no." As a result, my clients' assets are safer in an offshore trust than onshore here in the United States, but at a cost. Surprisingly, in the ten years I've been in this business, not one client has needed the protection of an offshore bank account, let alone an offshore trust, but they're happy to pay out hundreds of thousands—if not millions—of dollars each year to trustees and protectors. They even tell their friends about it, and my clients are so enthusiastic about their trusts that their friends sometimes end up putting their money into an offshore trust, too.

Setting up totally legal offshore trusts is my specialty. Even though I'm not a lawyer, I know more about offshore trusts than any lawyer I've ever met, and I charge my clients accordingly. Of course, I don't want to get arrested for performing legal work without a law license, a heinous crime in all fifty states—the lawyers have made things extremely cozy for themselves. Instead, if I need a legal document, I draft it and send the draft to J. Frederick Wagoneer, my no-good brother-in-law. After marrying a string of just average no-goodniks, my sister Eloise hit the jackpot and married Fred, a Philadelphia lawyer both literally and figuratively. Fred has no clients. Even when he worked pro bono for indigent criminal defendants, they indignantly told the judge that they would rather defend themselves than be defended by Fred. In his entire legal career, Fred has had exactly one real success. A yakuza gangster named Matsuko Hirohito was arrested at Kennedy Airport with two kilograms of heroin. Owing to a series of mistranslations and misunderstandings, the head of the crime syndicate retained Fred to defend the drug smuggler instead of a leading defense lawyer with a somewhat similar-sounding last name. By some miracle, Fred found an obscure legal loophole that enabled his client to get off scot-free. Fred used to boast unendingly about his *tour de force*, until one day I cruelly enquired, "And what successes have had you since then?" I could have been even crueler and asked him: "What clients have you had since then?"

To keep my sister out of the poorhouse, I email encrypted drafts of legal documents to Fred. Fred passes them off as his own work, and I then bill my clients for his "legal services." Fred knows better than to change a single word of my drafts. This way I ensure that all documents are the way I want them to be, my sister has a reasonable income and the legal fraternity can't sue me for attempting to break their monopoly.

You're probably wondering why I didn't invite Eloise and Fred to the wedding. The very last person in the whole wide world whom I wanted at our wedding was Fred. If any of my clients ever met their "lawyer," I'd be out of business, permanently. And Fred would be out of a job, too. And Eloise would be in the poorhouse. Accordingly, three weeks before the wedding I phoned Eloise in Philadelphia. What I wanted to say to her was that, as my only close relative, I very much wanted her to be at my wedding, but without Fred.

This was going to be a truly difficult phone call. Eloise unfortunately suffers from paranoia. For example, every so often she'll call me up and accuse me of stealing from her. The fact of the matter is that the "legal fees" I send to Fred on a regular basis are her sole source of income, but reality isn't the issue for someone who is paranoid.

When a second cousin of ours died in New Orleans and I flew there for two days to help wind up his affairs, she kept calling me to tell me that I had stolen a silver and platinum sculpture of a dove that our cousin had left to her. I couldn't take the dove from his home and deliver it to Eloise in Philadelphia because the estate had to be probated before any of the assets could be distributed. No amount of reassurance on my part or on the part of the executor of the estate could convince Eloise that the sculpture was safe and waiting to be delivered to her just as soon as the law permitted. My sister called me in New York at least twice a week to accuse me of stealing it, and the poor executor received his share of phone calls, too, until the estate was finally probated some weeks later and the executor personally delivered the artwork. What I've described to you are just a few of many examples of paranoid behavior that she's exhibited over the years. The challenge was: How could I invite her and not Fred to the wedding without Eloise coming to the conclusion that this was part of some vast conspiracy against her?

I began by telling her that I'd met someone and we'd decided to get married in three week's time. Her immediate reaction was not to congratulate me and wish me every happiness, but rather to accuse Nikki of being after my money—regrettably a typical response from Eloise. I assured her that Nikki had signed a prenuptial agreement that precluded her from receiving even one penny of my assets in the event of a divorce, and Eloise finally calmed down. Then came the tricky part, having to tell her that Fred was unwelcome. I decided that the only way to handle the situation was to take the bull by the horns. Accordingly, I invited Eloise to the wedding, but asked her not to bring Fred, and I explained why.

I'd expected one of Eloise's usual flaming outbursts, but, much to my amazement, she readily agreed. Then she told me that Fred had been acting a little strangely for the past year or so. In the interests of sibling harmony I didn't say that—in my opinion and in the opinion of just about everyone else who has ever met him—Fred has always acted very strangely indeed. Instead, I asked for details. It appeared that Fred was busy negotiating some really big deal in New York and flew to New York and back at least once a week. Fred usually shares everything with Eloise, including on one occasion some highly confidential information about one of my clients that he gleaned from papers that I'd sent him. But this time, Fred refused to say one single word about what he was doing. Eloise was sure that Fred would have no objection to her attending our wedding without him, because it would give him time to work on this secret deal.

Five minutes later she phoned me back. Contrary to what she'd thought, Fred was absolutely furious and had given Eloise an ultimatum: Either they would both come to the wedding or neither of them would come. I managed to convince Eloise that this meant that neither of them should come, which was a real pity because, as

I told you, Eloise is my only close living relative. But under the circumstances, there was no alternative.

After Eloise had hung up the phone, I briefly wondered about Fred's "really big deal" that he was working on here in New York. Then I became sidetracked with the details of the wedding and I forgot about it.

There's another aspect to my practice. It's not tax returns—I never do those, not even my own. No, it's money management. About six years ago, Edwin Reilly asked me to set up yet another offshore trust for the anticipated profits of yet another megadeal he was about to pull off. After his huge profits were safely offshore, he came to see me again.

"I want you to manage my funds," he said.

"I'm a CPA, not an money manager," I said. "I've never invested funds on behalf of a client."

"Nonsense," Edwin said. "You're one of the smartest guys I've ever met. I want you to determine the best way to invest my money. But, mind you, I'm not prepared to pay you one penny more than two percent of the value of the trust per year."

I thought quickly. Edwin's new trust contained $125 million, and two percent in fees would earn me two and half million dollars each and every year. Nevertheless, I still hesitated. I had no idea how to invest the money in a way that would keep Edwin happy, and I certainly didn't want him to sue me for mismanagement of his funds if, in his opinion, I made an unwise investment decision. But before I could protest further, Edwin spoke again.

"Of course, according to our contract you, and only you, will be responsible for all investment decisions—you can invest the money any way you wish. And the reason I'm paying you such large fees is because I want you to use your brilliance to increase my wealth. But I do like Chilean railway bonds."

Here was a man who over the years had single-handedly made more than two billion dollars, but who nevertheless wanted to pay me what I later discovered was about twice the going rate for financial advice to invest in what I would tactfully call an unusual investment.

Over the years, as more and more of my clients began to make the same request that I manage their money, I've come to learn that offshore investors are an unusual breed, and most of them want their money to be invested in unusual ways.

First, there are the Edwin Reillys of this world. They want to invest their money in something exotic, like lion-breeding farms in Tanzania or, for that matter, Chilean railway bonds. All I have to do for them is find a lawyer in the target country who is prepared to handle the transaction. Next, I put the offshore trustees in touch with that lawyer and I sign a few papers. Then I sit back and do nothing while the investment in question slowly loses its value. My clients, meanwhile, think that I'm the smartest financial adviser in the world because I chose to invest their money in the identical vehicles that they would have chosen if they'd had the courage to manage their own investments.

Then there are the gold bugs. Because they're concerned about inflation, they want their money in gold bullion or gold coins or the like. In fairness to them, many of my gold bugs have personally experienced hyperinflation, and they therefore feel the need to have the bulk of their assets invested in gold. Again, this is easy for me to implement, because there are any number of precious metal brokers all over the world. A major problem for gold bugs is that their investments don't pay dividends. On the contrary, gold investors have to pay for the storage and insurance of their gold bullion or coins. In addition, each year they have to instruct their trustees to sell two percent of the holdings of their trusts to pay my fees and another two percent to pay the trustees' fees, and another one percent goes to the protector. Clearly, gold doesn't grow on trees!

The third category consists of clients who want the money in their trusts to be invested in guaranteed investments. That usually means United States Treasury notes and bills. Anyone can buy these investments directly from the U.S. Treasury. In fact, the U.S. Government has set up a website called TreasuryDirect for that very purpose, and there's essentially no charge for this service. Instead, my clients put their funds into an offshore trust and pay their investment advisor (me) two percent of the value of their trust each year to advise them, and their trustees a further two percent each year to invest their money in Treasuries. And if their trust has a protector, there goes another one percent each year. Go figure.

Two of my clients, however, have told me that they want me to invest their money exactly where I put my own money. They don't want to know my secret—although I may tell you about it later—they just want my assurance that their money is with my money.

I manage the funds of about a hundred clients. The smallest trust has just over $2 million; the largest contains over $250 million. Given that the average trust is worth about $50 million, you don't have to be a CPA to calculate that my fees as an investment advisor total about $100 million each year. Unfortunately, the value of investments in Tanzanian lion-breeding farms, Chilean railway bonds and gold bullion almost invariably decreases steadily each year. But my current clients enthusiastically recommend me to enough new clients every year for my annual income to stay roughly constant.

CHAPTER THREE

Exiting the elevator at the Mikado Hotel, Yoko Azuma bowed deeply and respectfully to her boss. Mr. Mori returned her bow. Then she saw me and bowed, not quite so respectfully. She then put her arm against the door of the elevator to prevent it from closing to allow Mori and me to enter. Despite the long queue, no one else joined us in the elevator.

We rode in silence to the fifteenth floor. We walked to my room, and I inserted my card into the electronic lock of Room 1507. I walked in. Mori closely followed. The room was exactly as I'd left it, but with just a few important differences. The bed was empty, there was no blood on the pillow, there was no blood on the sheet and there was no blood on the floral bedspread.

***

Not knowing very much about weddings, I left every aspect of the ceremony in Nikki's capable hands and, as it turned out, this was a really wise decision. She organized everything down to the smallest detail. As I came downstairs about twenty minutes before the time at which the guests had been asked to arrive, I heard a string quartet playing *Eine kleine Nachtmusik*. Nikki had hired a fashionable caterer, and a butler was on hand to ensure that everyone had plenty to eat and drink. Nikki's favorite food, she'd once told me, was caviar and champagne, so it didn't surprise me that the sideboard in my dining room was laden with bowls of Beluga and magnums of 1985 Dom Pérignon on ice. The whole penthouse was decorated with flowers; my living room, where the ceremony was to take place, looked like a hothouse filled with exotic white blooms. The butler made sure that the guests were liberally plied with caviar and champagne before the ceremony. Then, at the request of the butler, we moved into the living room and waited for the bride and her attendants to appear.

The ceremony itself went very smoothly indeed. Despite my extreme nervousness, I was able to say, "I do" at the right time. After Nikki had replied identically to the corresponding question, the elderly Lutheran minister whom Nikki had chosen to perform the ceremony pronounced us husband and wife, and instructed me to kiss the bride. I needed no second bidding.

We then repaired to the dining room for more champagne and caviar. Then the caterer made a multi-layer wedding cake mysteriously appear. Nikki invited me to cut the cake with her, and the butler handed around the generous slices. For some reason, the guests interpreted the serving of the cake as a signal that it was time to leave. As a result, soon after the guests had eaten their fill of chocolate-raspberry génoise with white fondant frosting, they left together, with the exception of Edwin.

He apologized to Nikki, but assured her that he just wanted to bend my ear for five minutes. Edwin then took me aside and told me that he was uncomfortable with having all his money in Chilean railway bonds and he wanted to diversify his portfolio. I thought that he was perhaps considering blue-chip stocks or investment-grade bonds, or even bank certificates of deposit. Much to my bewilderment, Edwin's idea of "diversification" was selling half his Chilean railway bonds and investing the money in Bolivian railway bonds.

I almost never laugh, and for that reason I've had very little practice in trying to suppress guffaws. Nevertheless, I somehow managed to disguise my hysterical laughter as a fit of coughing. Finally I regained control of myself. I realized that I'd have to contact the trustees in Jersey in the Channel Islands and instruct them to tell the lawyer in Santiago, Chile, to sell half the Chilean railway bonds and wire the money to Jersey. Then I'd have to locate a lawyer in Bolivia to buy Bolivian railway bonds on behalf of the trustees. All in all, I wouldn't have to work very hard to earn my $2.5 million from Edwin's trust this year.

Then I realized that Edwin was speaking again.

"… but I don't know the first thing about Bolivian railway bonds. I want you to go to Lima and find out everything to enable you to make an intelligent choice of investment for me."

I didn't, of course, remind Edwin that he'd originally asked me to invest in Chilean railway bonds without first checking whether I knew anything about them—I didn't then, but I certainly do now! I also didn't inform Edwin that Lima is in Peru, whereas the capital of Bolivia is La Paz. Instead, I pointed out to him that I'd married Nikki only a few minutes before, and we were about to go to Paris for a two-week honeymoon. As is typical with my clients, Edwin wanted instant action, but even he was prepared to concede the sacredness of the honeymoon, albeit reluctantly. I promised Edwin that I'd organize everything by fax from our Paris hotel the first afternoon that Nikki went shopping. I told him that my Santiago lawyer would give me the name of an equally reliable colleague in La Paz, and that the transaction would be speedily carried out.

"Why do you want to fax them from Paris?" Edwin asked. "Why not use your BlackBerry to send out emails while you wait in the First Class Lounge for your flight to Paris to be called?"

I pointed out that emails are easily forged, and that offshore bankers and lawyers want everything in writing. They would like all documents to be notarized and to bear an apostille, but some are prepared to accept faxes signed by people they know well.

Reassured that I'd handle his investments to his complete satisfaction, Edwin left. I then thanked the string quartet for their services and they left, too. (I forgot to mention to you that the quartet had been playing without a break from the time that the marriage ceremony was over.) Nikki and I nervously paced the floor, waiting for the butler and caterer to go. More accurately, I paced the floor with an extreme case of nerves while Nikki sat on the red plush sofa as calmly as ever. As I previously mentioned—when I described what happened when I was sitting in the hospital waiting room—when I'm nervous, I eat. Of course, when I'm not nervous I eat, too, but I eat without ceasing when I'm nervous. As a result, first I had some caviar, which I washed down with a glass of champagne. Then I had a hefty slice of wedding cake. Then I looked at my beautiful bride, sitting so calmly in the living room, and I became even more nervous. That meant another round of caviar and champagne, which was followed, of course, by an even heftier slice of wedding cake. All this time Nikki sat there with that adoring look on her beautiful face.

Finally, we were alone. With regard to what happened next, let me simply say that our wedding night was everything I'd anticipated and much, much more. As I'm sure you've realized, this was my first sexual experience and you know that Nikki was a virgin, too. I'm extremely shy when it comes to discussing this sort of thing, so I'll just mention that in Nikki's case, there was no doubt whatsoever that she was a virgin. In fact, for a while I was wondering if surgical intervention would be required in order to deflower her. However, despite the fact that I was her first lover, Nikki demonstrated unbelievable sexual expertise. Perhaps she'd learnt all about it in her Swiss finishing school. To this day I wonder whether I was imagining some of the things she did on our wedding night.

The next day we flew in the A380 to Paris. Jet-setter that she was, Nikki had flown many times in an A380, but this was my first time. In fact, our honeymoon was my first trip abroad. I felt somewhat embarrassed that almost every page of Nikki's Swedish passport was covered with immigration stamps from exotic locales, whereas my recently acquired passport was still totally bare.

We stayed in a large suite at the Ritz. Those two weeks in Paris were my first holiday in ten years. I determined to turn over a new leaf and forget my work during our honeymoon, other than Edwin's Bolivian railway bonds, of course. I even tried to forget that I'm an accountant. But somehow I found myself reading the closing prices on Wall Street while Nikki paraded around in a negligee that probably was illegal to wear in any country other than France—and even there almost certainly required prior written permission from a judge.

On our first night in Paris, Nikki introduced me to *haute cuisine*. Until my marriage I had very little idea about fine food or fine wine. As I told you, I come from a working-class family, and, even after I suddenly became very rich indeed, my idea of a big evening was sitting alone at home with a six-pack of beer, a delivered pizza—with all the toppings and extra cheese—and a movie. Yes, a few of my wealthy clients were in the habit of inviting me once a year to lunch in fine restaurants or at their clubs. But although the food I was served there was certainly better than what I was eating at home in Brooklyn, I'd never eaten the most superb food of all, *haute cuisine*.

That first evening in Paris Nikki somehow managed to get reservations at La Poule d'Argent, arguably the top three-star restaurant in Paris, and accordingly the best restaurant in the world, if not the entire universe. Nikki phoned down to the concierge to organize a limousine. Then we spent nearly an hour getting dressed. Nikki insisted that I wear a dark suit, just as I would when dining with a client in New York. I was aware that my wife knew all about fashionable restaurants, so I didn't make a fuss and simply followed her instructions to the letter. When I was ready, I took a look at Nikki. Her silver-white evening gown seemed to defy the law of gravity. As we rode down in the elevator to the waiting limo, I simply couldn't work out how that strapless creation stayed in place.

I was in my usual worshipful daze in her presence, but after ten minutes in the Paris traffic, I began to get nervous. It wasn't that I was concerned about making a fool of myself—really fat people have no shame, of course—but I was truly worried that, out of ignorance and inexperience, I might do something that would humiliate Nikki in the eyes of the society in which she moved. After all, Nikki wouldn't like people to talk about her behind her back as the beautiful woman who married that short, fat, bald, ignorant CPA. As if she was reading my thoughts, Nikki took my hand in hers and whispered, "Darling, don't worry, everything will be fine."

The limousine finally pulled up outside La Poule d'Argent, and the uniformed doorman opened the door for Nikki. I followed her into the restaurant. Standing near the entrance was a shortish, gray-haired man in a perfectly tailored evening suit.

"*Bon soir, Madame Thompson, bon soir, Monsieur Thompson*," he said with a broad smile followed by a bow.

Nikki replied, in English for my benefit, "Good evening, Alfred, it's good to be back again." I wondered how Alfred had known our name. After all, this was the first time he'd seen me and the first time he'd seen Nikki in her new capacity as Mrs. Oliver Thompson, so how had he known that we were Mr. and Mrs. Thompson? However, once I realized that Nikki was a regular diner at La Poule d'Argent, I managed to work it out. The way she'd managed to get the reservation must have been to ask Alfred for a table for Miss Stenqvist, and then she'd told him her new name and marital status.

Feeling pleased that I'd been able to solve the puzzle, I followed Nikki as Alfred escorted her through an archway to a table in a smaller room on the far side of the large room we had entered. Standing at the table were two waiters who pulled our chairs back for us, helped us to sit comfortably, then took the ornately folded napkins that had been placed at exactly the precise spot on the table in front of us, unfolded them, and placed them carefully on our laps. A third waiter arrived. He had a heavy chain around his neck to which was fastened a shallow brass cup, ornamented with grape motifs.

"Ah, our sommelier," Nikki said, to let me know that this was a wine waiter, although I might have guessed that from the inlaid grape design on the cup. The sommelier asked us if we would like an aperitif. Nikki asked for a Dubonnet, and I followed suit. I'd never drunk Dubonnet before, but I'd seen it advertised in the *Wall Street Journal,* my source of all wisdom and knowledge.

When the menus arrived, I quickly realized that my one year of high-school French wasn't going to be of much use in trying to understand any of the items on the menu. As by now you know, when I panic, I lose my voice, so I couldn't ask Nikki for advice. In any event, just when I tried to speak to her, the sommelier arrived with the two hundred-page wine list that every three-star restaurant has to have. Nikki, however, carried it off beautifully. As the sommelier handed me what seemed like a wine encyclopedia and strode away, she said, "Oliver, darling, what year is their Château Margaux?"

I had no idea what she meant, but she went on, "Look in the Table of Contents for red Bordeaux wines."

I recalled enough French to know that *vin rouge* meant red wine, and I was quickly able to go to the right page in the wine list. Nikki then repeated, "What year is their Château Margaux?" pronouncing the name of the wine in such a way that I could easily locate it on the next page.

I found the page with Château Margaux, and discovered, much to my surprise, that the wine list contained multiple entries of Château Margaux, all produced in different years and all astronomically priced. Scanning the many vintages on offer, I noticed that the 1990 Château Margaux cost all of $2,750, whereas the 2005 vintage was a comparative bargain at only $1,600. To my even greater surprise, the 2009 vintage cost $250 more than the 2005; the age of the wine was not a sole determinant of its price.

Allowing myself to forget for a few seconds that I am an accountant, I threw caution to the winds. I waved the sommelier over and pointed at the 1990 Château Margaux.

"*Ah, oui,*" said the sommelier, followed by a string of rapid nasal French that I correctly guessed meant "an excellent choice of wine, *monsieur.*" I later discovered that, no matter what you order in a three-star restaurant, it's always an excellent choice. After all, when customers can afford to pay $2,750 for a bottle of wine and not less than $250 per person for food, the staff can afford to stroke their egos.

As the sommelier strode away, Nikki quickly muttered under her breath, "Darling, don't worry about the menu. The woman always orders first, so just tell the waiter you'll have the same thing I ordered, and I'll order food that I know you like. Now, here's the drill with the wine. The sommelier will come back with the bottle and show it to you. Nod, to show that he brought the right wine."

"But how do I know if it's the right wine?" I asked.

"Even if it's wrong, it doesn't matter, it will still be a wonderful wine. Just nod. The sommelier will then open the bottle and hand you the cork. Examine it carefully, then put it on the table."

Again I had a question. "But what am I supposed to look at when he gives me the cork?"

"I don't know—nobody knows. He gives you the cork, you look at it carefully, you can even sniff it if you like, then you put it on the table, and that's it. Now stop interrupting, darling, there's lots more for me to explain before he comes back.

"He'll go over to that wooden table over there, pour a small amount of wine into the cup fastened to that chain around his neck and put the wine bottle on the table. Then he'll smell the wine in the cup, taste it and spit it out in that bowl on the table. Ignore all that, he's just checking that the wine is perfect. Then he'll take the bottle, come over to our table and pour a small quantity into your glass. You pick up the glass, swirl the wine around a bit to allow the smell of the wine to permeate the air in the glass, then you smell the aroma, taste a little wine, and nod to the sommelier to indicate that the wine is satisfactory and he can pour a glass for me and then fill your glass."

Yet again I had what I thought was a reasonable question. "But how do I know if it's satisfactory? I've no idea what it's supposed to taste like—this Chatty Margaret or whatever it is that I just ordered."

Nikki hissed back, "Of course it will be fine. That's why the sommelier tastes it first, to prevent the customer's delicate palate being injured by a wine that's only 99.99 percent perfect. Darling, now just do what I said."

I asked her to go through the many steps again. Despite my extreme nervousness, I nevertheless had the presence of mind not to comment that I'd never had any trouble in the past opening a chilled Budweiser and drinking it directly from the can or bottle.

When the wine arrived, everything went according to Hoyle until I had to swirl the wine in my glass. In my nervousness I somewhat overdid the swirling. Three waiters instantly materialized to clean up the mess. But by now I'd cottoned on to the way the game is played in top restaurants—the customer is always right. Instead of apologizing to the sommelier, the three waiters, and to Nikki as I'd have done had I spilled beer in Jimmy Dean's Irish Pub two blocks from my penthouse, I simply pretended that nothing had happened and went on with the wine-drinking ritual, exhibiting what the French call *sang-froid*.

The meal that Nikki had ordered was the best I'd ever eaten. I won't bore you with the details. The wine tasted like liquid gold—both bottles. Four hours after I'd nervously sidled into La Poule d'Argent terrified that I might commit a faux pas, I strode out like a lion with a smile on my lips. As always, Nikki just nibbled at her food and barely sipped her wine, but I ate and drank everything that was placed in front of me.

For the next week we ate lunch and dinner at two- and three-star restaurants. More precisely, for the next week Nikki pecked at and I gorged on the finest food and wine in the world. By the end of the week I'd achieved two major breakthroughs. First, I could order food and wine unaided in any top restaurant. Second, my clothes no longer fit me. Nikki was delighted at the progress I'd made, and rewarded me by taking me to buy a complete new wardrobe. Surprisingly, there was no shortage of high fashion clothing in my new extra-extra-large size.

The second week was devoted to teaching me about Art, with a capital A. I'm sure we must have visited every single museum and art gallery in Paris, some of them more than once. Although it would have taken me years to acquire her knowledge and appreciation of art, Nikki at least started to transform me from a CPA into a caring, sensitive human being. And the first step in her plan was to accustom me to Great Art.

I wanted the honeymoon to go on for forever. After all, I'd amassed enough wealth to be able to retire then and there on an income of over $10 million a year. But I knew myself too well. A glorious two-week honeymoon in Paris was one thing, but spending the rest of my life doing nothing but eating, drinking, and indulging myself in life's pleasures would soon drive me crazy. Worse, it might lead to a break-up with Nikki, the only person in my life. So I told Nikki that we'd have to return to New York because I had unfinished work to do.

As always, Nikki instantly agreed. That look of adoration had almost never left her face since that first meeting in my office eight weeks before. Had it been only eight weeks? It seemed like a lifetime.

The first item that required my attention after we got back was sorting out Nikki's trust. I pointed out to her that, in view of my enormous annual income, we didn't need any money from her trust, and I suggested various investments for her that would steadily grow in value while yielding more than enough in earnings to pay her trustee's fees. We agreed that Nikki would think about it and then she'd send a Letter of Wishes directly to the trustees on Grand Cayman. The last think I wanted was to turn Nikki into an investment advisor junkie. She'd have to learn to manage her trust by herself.

Married life turned out to be wonderful in every way. As soon as we got back, Nikki sprang into action. On the advice of her best friend Elisabièta, Archduchess von und zu Eckwitz und Böderheim, Nikki contacted a team of interior designers. When they came to see the penthouse for the first time,

Pat and Alex turned out to be down-to-earth and really friendly, much to my surprise. Not even once did either of them indicate that the way my penthouse was decorated left a lot to be desired.

You're probably wondering why my penthouse looked that way. Here's the story. Once the financial management fees from my offshore trust clients started pouring in, I bought the two-story penthouse on Park Avenue. It wasn't the case of a once-poor boy buying an exclusive and expensive home to impress people; I bought it because I felt that the penthouse was a good investment that would appreciate considerably in value over the years. Okay, I lied to you again; it was *precisely* the case of a once-poor boy buying an exclusive and expensive home to impress people.

I then hired an interior designer who had advertised in the *Wall Street Journal* and asked him to decorate the penthouse. Unfortunately, I didn't know enough about decorating to know what I wanted, but the designer knew more than enough about decorating to know a rich sucker when he saw one. After months of work and more money than I care to admit to you, the final result looked like a cross between a European palace and the way I imagine a really exclusive bordello would look. The designer hired a painter to cover the walls and ceilings with frescoes of big-breasted bare goddesses in the style of the old masters, and the gilt furniture was covered with red plush velvet. When they saw all this, Alex and Pat said nothing. There were no smirks or secret looks; they were as professional as a priest in the confessional who has just heard a pillar of society admit to stealing from the poor box.

After the trip to Paris I knew exactly what I wanted in the way of decorating, although it was hard for me to express this in words. The good news was that Pat and Alex were able to understand my somewhat incoherent requests and could translate them into English. The bad news was that what I wanted and what Nikki wanted were very different, so after two sessions of trying to arrive at a meeting of the minds, I told Nikki and the designers that we had to compromise. My study and the billiard room were to be decorated according to my tastes, and the rest of the penthouse was entirely up to Nikki. Alex and Pat immediately saw the wisdom of this compromise, and the result was that all but two of the rooms are absolutely stunning but can't be lived in, and my study and the billiard room are extremely comfortable in every way. Best of all, the nude goddesses and gilt plush furniture were gone for good.

Soon after we got back, Nikki hired a maid, Christobel, and an *haute cuisine* chef named Alexandre. Then she bought a large black limousine and hired a driver whose name I can never remember. The limo and driver surprised me. I'd expected Nikki to buy a high-powered European sports car, but she was more concerned about the practicalities of trying to find parking in Manhattan. Limousines, like taxis, can wait almost anywhere. The limo purchase showed me a pragmatic side of

Nikki that I hadn't previously observed. Up to now, I'd viewed her as a spoiled, intelligent, unbelievably beautiful woman whose main interest in life was pleasure, hers and mine. Now I was delighted to see that she had a more practical side, as well.

Life for me went on extremely smoothly. My day started with a huge breakfast prepared and served by Christobel. At the front of the building my driver waited each morning to drive me to my office on Fifth Avenue. At noon the driver waited outside the office building to drive me home for lunch with Nikki. Breakfast was lavish, but lunch was a positively Lucullan feast. Most people have one big meal a day; I have three. This gave Alexandre an opportunity to exercise his considerable skills on a grand scale. Until Nikki hired him, he was accustomed to preparing a light lunch and a two course dinner, but my uncontrollable appetite gave Alexandre the opportunity to create two major culinary productions every day, gargantuan meals consisting of multiple courses accompanied by the appropriate wines. As a result, I barely managed to stay awake back in the office each afternoon, and I soon acquired the habit of doing as much important work as I could before lunch. At 5:30 p.m. our driver drove me home for cocktails and dinner with Nikki.

Alexandre, Christobel and the driver were all off on weekends. Occasionally Nikki and I would rent a sports car and spend the weekend at a luxurious inn in the country. Most weekends, however, we'd walk in Central Park, visit an art gallery or a museum, and go to a movie or the theater. Occasionally we'd eat in a fashionable restaurant, but most of the time Nikki would heat meals prepared in advance by Alexandre, and I'd open the bottles of wine specified by him to accompany that meal. Life for me was unending domestic bliss.

While I was working hard at the office, Nikki spent her days with her inseparable chum, Elisabièta. The two of them were together between breakfast and lunch and again between lunch and dinner. They spent the time shopping, enjoying a massage, shopping, visiting art exhibitions, shopping and more shopping.

One evening during dinner I asked Nikki why she never invited Elisabièta to our penthouse for a meal, or why the three of us never went out together.

"Darling, haven't you noticed that you scare Elisabièta?"

"Scare her? That's impossible! I'm a great big friendly teddy bear. I've never scared anyone in my entire life, not even little children or pedigree cats."

"You scare Elisabièta every time you open your mouth. She and I were at school together in Switzerland from the age of eight and we went on to finishing school together. We were roommates from start to finish. You know her as Archduchess von und zu Eckwitz und Böderheim and you're extremely respectful to her because she's a member of the German nobility. I love Elisabièta as a sister, you're the only person in the world who's closer to me than she is, but I sat in the same classroom as

Elisabièta for ten years, and I can tell you that she isn't too bright. That school we went to was a disgrace to the superlative Swiss educational system. I'm sure it wasn't accredited, because academic standards were totally nonexistent. Yet, even at that school, Elisabièta had trouble with every subject. Because I love her I used to believe that she was very smart but suffered from a learning disability that our teachers were too stupid to diagnose. The truth of the matter is that darling Elisabièta is very sweet, but she's as thick as two planks.

"You, on the other hand, are the smartest person I've ever met. And when it comes to advising people about money, you're in a league of your own. Remember, the only time that Elisabièta ever interacts with you is in connection with her trust. Even a highly intelligent person is somewhat cowed when they discuss investment strategies with you. Poor, dear Elisabièta is totally frightened. She has absolute faith in you because you've provided her with a steadily increasing stream of income. The reason that she asked you to invest her money where you invest your own is because she has absolutely no idea about investments. And the reason that she doesn't ask you any questions is because she doesn't know what to ask and wouldn't understand your answers even if she did ask. She meets with you once a year because you insist on meeting with every client at least once a year to be sure that he or she understands exactly how you're investing his or her money. Elisabièta doesn't understand, she doesn't want to understand, she can't understand. She meets with you because she has to. She smiles politely and really tries hard to understand what you're saying, praying all the time that she won't say something stupid. She's terrified for two months beforehand and for at least a month afterwards.

"Haven't you ever wondered why she never invites you to a meal or to a show? She was rich before she met you, but now she's fabulously wealthy, and she knows that it's all because of you. Nevertheless, she consistently breaks the gratitude rule because you scare her out of her wits.

"She was my bridesmaid because I told her I'd never speak to her again if she didn't agree to do it. She knows that I never make empty threats and she gave in. Didn't you notice during the wedding that she smiled at you the whole time but didn't say a single word before or after the ceremony? She was terrified all the way through, and as soon as she'd eaten her last forkful of wedding cake, she kissed me, wished me well for the wedding night, and fled.

"And you want me to invite her to dinner or ask her to go to a show with us? I think that she'd rather have extensive root canal work without Novocaine. If you had any feelings at all for Elisabièta, you'd write her a note stating that clients who have their funds invested where you invest yours don't need to meet with you unless they would prefer it. She'll be eternally grateful and will mention you in her prayers every night. As her former roommate I can tell you that, yes, she kneels at her bed and prays every night long and hard, and it can do you no harm to be added to the list of people for whom she regularly prays."

This speech quite overwhelmed me. My wife had never spoken this vociferously before or at such length. I assured Nikki that I'd release the Archduchess from any obligation to meet with me ever again. Loyalty to her friend is just one of Nikki's many, many sterling traits. Nikki is for me the perfect woman in every respect save one—she just can't understand that the telephone is a medium for two-way communication.

For example, I'd be seated at my desk at the office trying to understand a complex financial statement when the landline I'd installed for Nikki's exclusive use would ring.

"Darling," she'd say, "Elisabièta and I've bought the most beautiful dresses this morning. I can't wait for you to see them when you come home for lunch. I have to go. Bye!"

And she'd hang up.

That sort of call was no problem, of course, but occasionally the phone would ring and Nikki's voice would say, "Darling, Alexandre wants to know if you want the Maine lobsters as a starter or as the main course. I love you so much. Bye!"

Then I'd have to ask Miss Dixon to call my home to tell Christobel to tell Alexandre that I bowed to his superior wisdom when it came to food and would abide by his decision.

There was one humorous aspect of our life in New York. Nikki often didn't wait for the person she'd phoned even to say, "Hello." The moment that the other party picked up the phone, Nikki would launch into what she had to say. In her excitement to indulge in the one-way communication she adored, she frequently dialed the wrong number. I'm sure that at least half of her Nikki-grams, as I call them, went to the wrong recipients, and that all over New York there were people who innocently picked up the phone when it rang and then wondered for days about what they had just heard. But I loved her for it.

In contrast to her eagerness to deliver her Nikki-grams, her self-control with regard to food never ceased to amaze me. Despite the endless plates of superlative cuisine that were placed before her, she ate hardly anything. She'd try a mouthful of each item. Then, while I proceeded to devour every tasty morsel in front of me, she chased the remaining food around her plate with her fork, rarely actually eating much more than that exploratory mouthful. She was similarly abstemious with alcohol. She'd take one or two sips of a wine for which one of my clients, a noted Denver wine lover, would sell the souls of both his grandmothers to the devil. Then she'd leave the rest of the glass untouched, for Christobel to throw out at the end of the meal. After dinner, she'd occasionally ask for Napoleon brandy and take a mouthful of the fine cognac that Christobel poured into a large snifter for her. As an accountant, I was concerned about the vast sums of money we were wasting on discarded luxurious food and drink, but as a member of the *nouveau riche*, I thoroughly enjoyed the conspicuous wastefulness.

Much to my surprise, Alexandre almost never appeared. Just about the only time I saw him was the Thursday evening two weeks after we'd returned from Paris when I invited Eloise and Fred to dinner to meet Nikki. Eloise enjoyed her meal so much that she absolutely insisted on meeting Alexandre. I dispatched Christobel to lever him out of his kitchen. He came to the table in a very bad grace; in fact, I thought he was going to quit on the spot. But when Eloise started discussing the meal with Alexandre in a way that indicated that she knew nearly as much about food and wine as he did, he calmed down, and accepted her praises. From then on, the only time I saw Alexandre was on those all-too-rare occasions when we had Eloise to dinner. Other than that, Alexandre stayed out of sight in his kitchen. On payday I ended up giving Christobel a sealed envelope containing Alexandre's check and asking her to hand it to him. For some reason, Alexandre wouldn't meet with me.

There was only one flaw in our otherwise perfect life. Two weeks of uninhibited lovemaking in Paris were followed by total sexual abstinence. I'd simply lost the urge to make love to Nikki. No, it wasn't impotence—Viagra would have helped me with that. For some reason, I just had no sexual urge at all. At first I thought it was overindulgence in Alexandre's culinary triumphs and accompanying memorable wines. To solve the problem I markedly reduced consumption of both the next night, much to Nikki's surprise. "Darling, what's wrong?" she asked with great concern in her voice.

I was now doubly mortified, first at my lack of sexual activity for the past few days, and then at her amazement that I was eating and drinking so little. However, I felt extremely close to Nikki and therefore I was able to explain the problem to her.

She quickly reassured me. "I waited twenty-five years to make love for the first time, and if we have to wait a while to make love again, that'll be no problem at all. I just want you to be happy. I doubt that food has anything to do with the problem, just stop worrying about it, and everything will be as it was in Paris."

I had my doubts, but I took her advice. The result: no improvement whatsoever. So, two weeks after I'd mentioned the problem to Nikki, I went to see my physician, Arthur Buller, MD, who has a practice about three blocks from my office. Arthur took one look at me and then blurted out, "Last time I saw you, you were about 150 pounds overweight. Now you're at least 200 pounds overweight. We need to discuss this very seriously."

The next fifteen minutes proved to be acutely embarrassing for me. After hearing the facts, Arthur decided that my problem was a deeply seated psychological one. Food and sex were intimately connected, he declared, and I needed to consult a psychiatrist who specialized in these matters to help me decrease my appetite for food and increase my appetite for sex. The world's expert in this field, Arthur went on, was Professor Magda Emmersford whose office was in an adjacent building. He wrote her name and telephone number on a piece of paper and then handed it to me along with a brief letter of referral to Professor Emmersford, and the consultation was thankfully over.

CHAPTER FOUR

"Please repeat what you saw when you entered the room, Mr. Thompson," said Inspector Watanabe. Mr. Mori had called the police and they had received instructions to take me to the inspector. We were once again in the small interview room at Kyoto Police Headquarters. I'd been sitting there for over an hour.

"I've already told you twice what happened."

"Please tell me again."

"I unlocked the door of this room, I stepped inside, and saw Yoko Azuma's body lying in my bed."

"How could you see her in the darkness?"

"I told you, I turned on the light."

"No, Mr. Thompson, you mentioned nothing about lights before."

"I unlocked the door," I said through gritted teeth. "I switched on the light. I walked into the room. I saw the body of Yoko Azuma lying in my bed. She was dead."

"How did you know she was dead?"

"She was pale like a dead person, and there was blood everywhere on the bed and on her cap."

"But you've just seen Yoko Azuma for yourself, here in this very room. She didn't seem at all dead to me, and I couldn't see any blood on her. Also, there's no blood anywhere on your bed. She also denied entering your room at any time other than the first day when she carried your luggage into your room. How do you explain this?"

"I can't explain it any more than I can explain the incident at the Kiyomizu Temple or the earlier incident on the Philosophers' Pathway. But all three incidents happened."

"Mr. Thompson," said Inspector Watanabe with exquisite politeness, "I understand from Mr. Mori that you're waiting for your wife to rejoin you. I'll have you driven back to your hotel, and you will stay in your room until your wife returns. You will then have twenty-four hours to leave Japan."

He gave the briefest of bows, then left.

***

One morning over breakfast in our apartment, I saw Nikki studying the advertisement for the Metropolitan Opera in the *New York Times*. I quickly realized that big trouble lay ahead. It wasn't possible for me go to an opera or a concert and stay awake after consuming a colossal meal prepared by Alexandre, and I certainly didn't want to embarrass Nikki by snoring in public. All overweight people snore when we sleep; it's got something to do with layers of fat distorting the shape of our palates. As a result, the plain and simple fact was that I couldn't possibly accompany Nikki to classical music events without first losing at least 150 pounds of fat, and that meant losing Nikki, as well. I thought rapidly, and came up with what seemed like an excellent plan.

As casually as I could, I said, "Nikki, did you enjoy our two weeks in Paris?"

Nikki somehow knew that I was up to something. Perhaps it was the tone of my voice. She replied rather more quickly and loudly than usual, "Yes, of course, you know I did," and waited for me to continue.

I'd never seen her like this before. Up to now, life with Nikki had been in every way an unending extension of that look of adoration that had appeared on her face during our first meeting. Now Nikki seemed suspicious. I felt most uncomfortable, but I decided to proceed with my ploy, regardless.

"I'll always be grateful to you for teaching me about art in Paris. Why don't we go away again somewhere else where you can teach me about music?"

I couldn't make out from her face whether Nikki thought that this was a wonderful idea, or whether she wanted to hear more in order to discover what my real intentions were. Her response to my suggestion was neutral.

"When and where shall we go?" she asked.

"Today is the fourth of March. I thought we could take another two-week holiday next month. Why don't we go to Kyoto for the cherry blossom season?"

Let me explain my stratagem to you. While we were in Paris I'd learned that Nikki had never been to Japan and had no Japanese friends. So I assumed that it would be safe to go to concerts, ballets and operas in Kyoto. If I fell asleep and started snoring, I wouldn't embarrass Nikki in front of her friends, as would be the case if I dropped off during an opera or ballet at the Met. However, as you've probably guessed by now, my clever scheme to go to Kyoto turned out to be a really bad mistake.

I asked our travel agent to arrange the air tickets and the hotel. I then bought some guidebooks on Japan and a map of Kyoto, and promptly forgot all about them until two days before we were due to leave. I was sitting at my desk at the office, trying to understand the balance sheet of an Indonesian spice factory, an investment of one of my clients. Although I quickly realized that the majority shareholders were cheating my client out of least two-thirds of what he was entitled, I just couldn't work out how they were doing it.

After half an hour of dead ends and meaningless computations, I suddenly remembered the guidebooks. After all, I'd told Nikki that I'd handle every aspect of the trip to Japan, and I quickly realized that the time had come to become an instant expert on Japan in general and Kyoto in particular.

I opened the first guidebook, *Japan for the English-Speaking Tourist*. On page two, the authors strongly recommended that every tourist should buy a Japanese phrase book with the phrases transliterated into English as well as printed in Japanese characters. In that way you have two chances at being understood by a Japanese person. First, you say the transliterated phrase as best you can. If that doesn't work, you show the Japanese characters to him or her. The adult literacy rate in Japan is over ninety-nine percent, so this second method is bound to work if the first one fails.

I called Miss Dixon into my office—I still hadn't learned to call her Mrs. Thackeray and probably never would—and I asked her to go out and buy me a Japanese phrase book. Twenty minutes later she was back with a small paperback book filled with about two hundred pages of phrases. The cover of the book depicted a typical beautiful Japanese scroll painting. After admiring the cover, I opened the book at random. The first phrase I saw was, "I have food poisoning." Not a good start. I threw the phrase book on the floor in disgust.

I returned to my work. Suddenly I remembered a favorite Monty Python sketch, the one about the Hungarian man who walks into an English shop armed with a somewhat unusual English–Hungarian phrase book. Corresponding to each Hungarian phrase is an English phrase that bears no relation to the Hungarian phrase, and is somewhat risqué to boot.

I quickly picked up the Japanese phrase book and tried to decide whether *Ryoshusho o kudasai masen ka?* was indeed the Japanese for "Can I have a receipt?" or whether it actually meant "Not only are you ugly, but your belly button is filled with greenish lint." After studying the corresponding Japanese kanji characters for a while, I realized that I wasn't going to get very far with this line of inquiry and threw the book into the far corner of the room.

Now my mind was filled with nineteenth century British travelers who had been informed by Thomas Cook that everyone everywhere in the whole world, even peasants on the plains of Anatolia, could understand English, provided you spoke it loudly and clearly. I wondered if that was really true. Of course it was. And even if it wasn't true, I could always explain what I wanted with sign language.

For example, if I wanted something to drink, all I had to do was mime picking up a glass and drinking from it. No problem there. But wait: How would the waiter know whether I wanted beer, mineral water, juice or wine? I struggled to my feet, walked slowly across the room to where I'd tossed the book, and laboriously tried to pick it up. My paunch got in the way of the small book, but eventually I succeeded. At my desk, I opened the book to the section on beverages. Beer was easy; I simply had to say *biru*. Mineral water was also a cinch; the Japanese phrase was *mineraru uota*. Juice was equally easy—it turned out to be *jusu*. And wine was *wain*. Then I discovered *shampen*, *koka kora* and *konyakku*.

Once again the book sailed across the room and landed not far from its previous site. This, however, it fell far more loudly because now I was really angry. I got even angrier when Miss Dixon walked in, picked up the book, deposited it on my desk and walked out again, all without saying a single word.

Suddenly a thought crossed my mind. How was I going to use sign language to indicate that I needed to go to the bathroom urgently? *Bathu rumu* didn't sound correct. With marked distaste, I opened the phrase book for the fourth time.

According to page twenty-three, if I wanted to ask, "Where is the bathroom," I had to say *otearai wa doko desu ka?* How could I possibly learn such a complex sentence? My first reaction was to pick up the phone, call the travel agent and cancel the entire holiday. Then I thought of how Nikki might react. She was already extremely suspicious about my motives for the trip. If I tried to cancel it two days before we were due to leave, who knows what might ensue. I turned to the guidebooks again.

If I'd read the guidebooks with the same care I devote to a legal document or financial statement, I'm sure that I'd have learned everything important about Japan. However, I read through the books with half my mind replaying the angry scenes with my Japanese phrase book, and the other half plagued with guilt over the minor deception with Nikki regarding my motives for the trip as a whole. As a result, by the time Miss Dixon knocked on my door to remind me it was 5:30 p.m. and time to go home, I'd learned only five items.

First, never shake hands with a Japanese person. Instead, bow. The depth of the bow, the number of seconds to bow, and how many times to bow are all measures of the relative importance of the other person. Fortunately, *gaijin* (foreigners) don't need to know these intricacies and can get away with a nod.

Second, never count your change. It's insulting in the extreme, because the change is never wrong—Japanese cashiers are superb at mental arithmetic.

Third, there's no crime in Japan, so don't worry about it.

Fourth, Kyoto has 1,700 Buddhist temples and three hundred Shinto shrines, many of them exquisitely lovely. The problem in Kyoto is to avoid temple overload.

Fifth, always take off your shoes before entering a temple or a Japanese home.

As my driver drove the few blocks through the rush-hour traffic toward the penthouse, I put Japan out of my mind and instead thought fondly about my beautiful Nikki waiting at home. Perhaps things would have turned out better if I'd taken the trouble to learn more about Japan before traveling to Kyoto.

CHAPTER FIVE

In the taxi back to the Mikado Hotel, I decided that I'd die happy if I never saw Inspector Watanabe, Mr. Mori or Yoko Azuma again. To that list I added the Mikado Hotel and the city of Kyoto. Unfortunately, I had to go back to the hotel to await Nikki's return from Stockholm.

Standing at the hotel entrance was Yoko Azuma, perky cap, happy grin and all. And behind the front desk was Mr. Mori. I put on the best face I could manage under the circumstances and returned to Room 1507. I tried to sleep but, for obvious reasons, sleep eluded me. I opened the refrigerator and liberally sampled the well-stocked bar. The only effect was that I got drunk, but remained wide-awake.

How I wished that Nikki would return.

***

We flew from New York to Osaka on Japan Air Services. The service and food were truly exceptional, even for First Class. The route of the fifteen-hour flight took us over the wilderness of

Alaska. Peering down at the frozen tundra five miles below us, we both agreed that Alaska would be the venue for our next vacation.

We landed at Kansai International Airport at three in the afternoon. For some reason it took us ages to get our luggage, but finally we wheeled our trolleys past the incurious customs inspectors into the terminal building. I turned to Nikki. "Do you want to take a taxi to Kyoto, or shall we take the train?"

Nikki had heard all about the fabulous Japanese bullet trains, so we decided to take the Shinkansen train directly from the airport building. The train arrived in Kyoto precisely on time—no surprise there—and we took a taxi to the Mikado Hotel. The doorman escorted us into the lobby, the lobby manager signaled crisply to a bellhop to take our luggage from the taxi, and indicated to us the way to the front desk. The receptionist had no trouble finding our reservation and quickly checked us in. She then asked us to wait briefly for a bellboy to escort us to our room. She pressed a bell, and the "bellboy" arrived. According to the badge pinned to her chest, her name was Yoko Azuma. She was wearing a navy blue uniform with a perky cap, and her face was one big happy smile. She wheeled a trolley containing our suitcases toward us, stopped, and held out her hand to me. I remembered Principle One:

First, never shake hands with Japanese people. Instead, bow.

I bowed.

Yoko bowed back.

Then she held out her hand again.

I shook it.

The world came to an end.

It seems that she wanted me to give her my hand luggage for her to put on the trolley and wheel it to our room. Instead I'd broken Principle One, in public, thereby humiliating us both. Yoko blushed bright scarlet, I blushed bright scarlet, and we both wished that the earth would open so that we could immediately disappear from the lobby of the Mikado Hotel, Kyoto.

At that very moment I heard an iPhone belting out the opening theme of Hugo Alfvén's *Swedish Rhapsody No. 1*—Nikki had received a text. She read it and gasped. She passed it to me to read. It was unintelligible, filled with ö's and å's and other strange vowels.

I handed it back to her. Nikki whispered, her voice quavering, "My mother is very ill. I have to fly to Stockholm at once."

"There must be a travel agent in the hotel. I'm sure they can organize things for us."

"No, you stay here, I'll be back in a few days. Love you!"

And she rushed out of the hotel into a waiting taxi, her handbag over her shoulder.

Were I not as deeply in love with Nikki, I might have rushed after her, jumped into the next taxi, shouted, "Follow that taxi!" and met up with her at Kansai International Airport. We could have flown together to Stockholm. Our luggage was no problem; the Mikado Hotel would have stored our suitcases until we returned to Kyoto, or air freighted them to Stockholm or New York, whichever we wished.

But as with everything else, I dutifully followed Nikki's wishes and stayed in Kyoto. Yoko indicated the direction of the bank of elevators, and we rode in silence up to the fifteenth floor. Our mutual embarrassment was palpable; although, in my case, it was overlaid with dismay at losing Nikki, if only for a few days. Selfishly, I didn't think for one minute about Nikki's mother, perhaps lying deathly ill in a Swedish hospital room waiting for her daughter to arrive.

Yoko used the card to open the electronic lock of Room 1507 for me. Without Nikki, the large and beautifully appointed room looked like a prison cell.

Wallowing in self-pity, I ordered a room-service dinner and went to bed. Thanks to the fact that I'd dozed only briefly on the plane, I fell asleep almost at once, but woke at 2 a.m. For some reason, I felt wide-awake. I turned on the bedside light and started reading the thriller that I'd bought at Kennedy Airport, but that didn't help me to get back to sleep. Then I did the crossword in the *New York Times* I had read on the plane, but that did not make me tired, either. I watched CNN International for a while, also to no avail. Finally I turned off the light but I simply couldn't get back to sleep again. I got up when the sun rose at 5:30, dressed, and took the elevator down to Le Lac des Cygnes restaurant on the second floor of the hotel for breakfast. I arrived as it opened at six o'clock.

The breakfast buffet was unending. In addition to everything one would find in a lavish American hotel restaurant, there were bowls containing Japanese-style salads at the far end of the buffet table. Returning to the portion of the buffet that was more familiar to me, I saw a large silver platter, containing apple danish, peach danish and corn danish. I added a corn danish to my already heaped plate, if only out of curiosity. I discovered that it was truly delicious, and I resolved to suggest to Alexandre on our return to New York that he add the item to his extensive repertoire.

After three more trips to the vast buffet table, I'd eaten my fill and I signaled to the waiter. To my surprise, instead of a bill he handed me a thick plastic card with a number on it. I took this to the cashier, who handed me the bill. Surprise number two was that he wouldn't let me charge the bill to my room. I took out a credit card. Surprise number three was that the cashier wouldn't take a credit card either. I opened my wallet and handed the cashier one of the ¥5,000 bills I'd obtained from an ATM at the airport the previous day.

The display on the cash register showed ¥2,400 (about $24). I remembered Principle Two: *Never count your change. It's insulting in the extreme, because the change is never wrong—Japanese cashiers are superb at mental arithmetic.*

But I'm an accountant, and I mentally computed that I should receive two ¥1,000 bills, a ¥500 coin and a ¥100 coin. Without thinking I glanced down at the money that the cashier had handed to me and saw one ¥1,000 bill and what looked like a random selection of about 20 different coins. The wildly wrong change was surprise number four.

My reaction wasn't that the cashier was trying to rip off the rich tourist. Instead, the CPA in me quickly realized that the cashier wasn't going to be able to balance his cash at the end of his shift, and I politely pointed out that the change was incorrect.

The cashier gave me a look that would have struck anyone but a used-car salesman stone dead on the spot. He proceeded to fiddle with some sort of electronic calculator. He kept keying in numbers and pressing buttons and levers, while furiously counting and recounting change. Finally, he handed me the precisely correct change and bowed, very stiffly. I bowed back, took my money, walked slowly out of the restaurant and returned to my room.

I called down to the front desk and wondered about phoning Nikki, but then I realized that Nikki couldn't possibly reach Stockholm for a few more hours. I was worried, not about Nikki, but about the incident with the cashier. I rechecked the guidebook, but there it was:

Never count your change. It's insulting in the extreme, because the change is never wrong—Japanese cashiers are superb at mental arithmetic.

A cashier might try to cheat a customer by "forgetting" to give him or her one or more notes, or by "accidentally confusing" one note with another. But to hand over 20 or more coins of a variety of denominations, including tinny ¥1 coins and those ¥5 and ¥50 coins with holes in them wasn't an attempt at subterfuge, it was something more. And try as I might, I was unable to work out what the cashier's game was.

Then I started wondering about the way that the cashier had refused to allow me to charge the bill to my room or pay by credit card. The Mikado is a world-class hotel, and this was truly bizarre. After all, most guests don't carry large amounts of currency with them. I puzzled about this for a few more minutes and then I called the front desk and asked to speak to the duty manager.

"Mori speaking," said a calm voice.

I asked Mr. Mori why the cashier at Le Lac des Cygnes restaurant wouldn't allow me to sign for my breakfast or pay with a credit card. Mori obviously had years of experience in dealing with eccentric guests because he didn't sound the least bit surprised as he replied in his calm, slow voice, "Mr. Thompson, all our cashiers in all our restaurants are trained to let our guests charge their meals to their rooms or pay by credit card. Do you recall what your cashier's name was or how she looked?"

"All that I remember about him is that he was a man."

"Sir," replied the manager, "Are you sure you had breakfast at our hotel? All our restaurant cashiers are women."

I hurriedly thanked him and put down the phone. Mentally I played over the scene. There was absolutely no doubt whatsoever in my mind that my strange cashier had been a man. He'd worn men's clothing, he had a man's face and hair, and his voice was that of a man. No, despite what Mr. Mori had said, the cashier was a man. The mystery had thickened—a male cashier who was supposed to be a woman had, contrary to instructions, not allowed me to charge my breakfast to my room or to a credit card. Why? Try as I might, I couldn't come with *any* answer, let alone one that made sense.

After a night's sleep truncated by early awakening and followed by a giant breakfast, I decided to try to put the problem out of my mind and take a short nap. Three hours later, the arrival of a text from Nikki on my BlackBerry woke me.

"Mother is not as ill as I had feared. She is out of the hospital. Please do NOT phone except in case of emergency—you may wake Mother. I will stay with her for a few days, then return to Kyoto to be with you, my love. Please do NOT sit in the hotel and mope. I want you to go out and enjoy Kyoto. Go to the Philosophers' Pathway today. I love you so much."

There were two positive aspects to this text. First, her mother wasn't too sick, and so Nikki would be back soon. Second, Nikki still loved me. I sent her an adoring text in reply and then, as always, I followed her instructions and prepared to stroll the Philosophers' Pathway.

I opened one of my guidebooks and looked up the Philosophers' Pathway. According to the book, a philosopher named Kitaro Nishida used to stroll alongside a two-mile long canal with his students, and priests and scholars have subsequently used the route for contemplative purposes.

The idea of a contemplative stroll certainly appealed to me. I packed my guidebooks and map into my messenger bag, added the supposedly invaluable Japanese phrase book that Miss Dixon had bought for me, and went down to the lobby.

I asked the doorman to get me a taxi. The taxis in Kyoto come in two sizes, large and medium (in the United States they would be described as medium and small, but American taxi drivers don't have to navigate the narrow alleyways of Kyoto). The doorman took one look at me and waved to the driver of a large black Toyota Crown. The driver sprang into action, drew up his car in front of the hotel and opened the curbside passenger door for me using the automatic door opening system with which all Japanese taxis are equipped.

I put my hand into my trouser pocket to tip the doorman, but remembered just in time that tipping is strongly discouraged in Japan. I quickly withdrew my empty hand from my pocket and levered myself into the Crown. Reading from my guidebook, I said to the driver, "*Tetsugaku-no-michi.*"

The driver looked puzzled for a few moments. Then his face lit up and he said, "Ah! Philosophers' Pathway!" and off we went.

We drove past tall office buildings with elegant shops at street level. Seeing a restaurant, I suddenly realized that I was hungry. Then I remembered the incident at breakfast, and I knew that I would need considerably more Japanese yen for the rest of the trip just to eat. After all, notwithstanding Mr. Mori's assurances, it seemed that cash was the only possible way to pay for meals in Japan, even in top restaurants. Seeing an imposing-looking bank building, I asked the driver to stop. I tried to get out of the door. Then I remembered that I wasn't in Paris, and that the traffic drives on the left-hand side of the road in Japan. Only the curbside door of a taxi opens, and that happens only when the driver activates the automatic system, which my driver duly did.

After asking the driver to wait, I went into the cavernous banking hall. It looked as if the architect who designed it in the 1920s wanted the bank's customers to forget that they were in Japan—the banking hall could have been in Paris or New York. There were hardly any customers, and I had no trouble using my American Express Centurion card to obtain $1,000 in yen from an ATM. I returned to the taxi, but for some reason the driver waved me away. Then I realized that I was standing right next to the automatic door and would have been injured had he opened it with me standing there.

The rest of the taxi ride was uneventful. For about half the trip we were in the Kyoto central business district. Other than the signs in Japanese characters, there was no way of telling that Kyoto is a major Japanese city; the buildings were as cosmopolitan as the bank I'd just left. This wasn't a consequence of a post-war American-sponsored rebuilding effort. Kyoto—consisting mainly of temples—wasn't considered to be of sufficient strategic importance to be bombed in World War Two. In fact, I believe that Kyoto is the only major Japanese city that was left totally unscathed. Many of the international-style buildings appeared to me to date from the 1930s or 1920s, if not earlier.

Gradually we seemed to be leaving the business district, because the buildings got smaller. Then I noticed smart dress shops with English names on one block, and somewhat shabby homes and shops built in the traditional Japanese architectural style on the adjacent block—Kyoto didn't appear to be laid out uniformly. Finally, we reached a neighborhood that seemed to be more suburban than urban. The driver deposited me next to a tree-lined canal, pointed to his right and said, "Philosophers' Pathway." Remembering not to tip the driver, I paid him, and then climbed out of the taxi.

First things first, however: Food comes before philosophy, even in the dictionary. Accordingly I crossed the road and walked toward a restaurant that displayed noodle dishes in the window. Almost every Japanese restaurant has a window display of plastic models of all the dishes served there. When faced with a menu that's in Japanese, all the foreign diner has to do is to walk outside with the waitress and point.

As I entered the restaurant I noticed that there was a piece of cloth hanging from the ceiling just inside the doorway. A taller person would have had to duck his or her head in order to enter the restaurant. I never found out why many restaurants and shops had this cloth.

A waitress showed me to a table. The restaurant was sparsely decorated. In fact, other than the wooden tables and chairs, which were well made, the room was essentially bare. Then the waitress handed me a menu. It didn't surprise me in the least that the menu was handwritten, and entirely in Japanese. I got up from my chair and indicated to the waitress that I would like her to accompany me outside. When we got there I pointed to one of the dishes, the waitress nodded, and we went back inside the restaurant.

The white noodle dish I'd chosen turned out to be drenched in a spicy sauce. I washed the delicious food down with a truly wonderful Japanese lager beer. In fact, the meal turned out to be so superb that I asked the waitress for an encore. She seemed taken aback—perhaps she thought that she'd misunderstood my sign language. But I reassured her, and the repeat performance, which arrived a few minutes later, was equally delicious.

When she'd cleared the second dish, the waitress immediately returned with the bill; there was no way she was going to bring me a third version. She put the saucer containing the bill in front of me and pointed at the cashier. I got up to pay. When I reached the till, I saw that it bore decals for Visa, American Express, and MasterCard. Hesitantly I proffered my American Express Centurion card and was amazed when the cashier took it and treated the whole transaction totally nonchalantly, even though it was unlikely she'd ever seen a black anodized titanium credit card before. But if this simple restaurant with main courses costing around $12 took credit cards, why had the cashier in Le Lac des Cygnes restaurant of the five-star luxury Mikado Hotel refused to accept my credit card that morning?

Still baffled, I crossed the street back to where the taxi driver had dropped me about an hour before, and entered the Philosophers' Pathway. The slightly curved canal that I'd seen when I arrived ran southward; because of the curvature, I couldn't see how far it went. On the right hand side of the canal there was a gravel path, the Philosophers' Pathway. Both sides of the canal were lined with trees, many of them the famous cherry trees of Japan now resplendently in bloom. Fallen petals were strewn on the path and many also lay on the surface of the water in the canal. The combination of bright sunlight, blue sky, water, foliage and blossoms was breathtakingly lovely. I began to understand the symbolism of the cherry blossom, exquisitely beautiful but short lived, the Japanese version of *carpe diem*.

As I walked along the gravel path, the canal lay to my left. Beyond the canal was a fence, and on the other side of the fence were houses and the occasional shop or temple. It was difficult to see too much on that side because of the dense foliage and frequent high walls, but every few hundred yards there was a bridge over the canal, and when I was alongside a bridge I could see the houses and temples on both sides of the street that ran from the high hills on my left, across the bridge, and continued on to the other side of the path.

To the right of the path was a similar fence, and beyond that fence there was a road running parallel to the canal. On the other side of that road were more houses and shops, as on the left hand side of the canal. And, as on the left hand side, the only place where there was a break in the fence was where there was a bridge over the canal.

I was surprised that I was almost the only person walking along this exquisite route. Everyone knows that cherry blossoms are short lived, and I couldn't work out why hordes of Kyotans weren't making use of the opportunity to experience this truly glorious sight.

I continued to walk along the Philosophers' Pathway, immersed in my own thoughts, now mainly about food, I have to confess, when suddenly I felt something hard and round pressed firmly into the small of my back. A voice that sounded like a Japanese man trying to talk with an American accent whispered, "Don't turn around, don't move, or I will shoot you."

I froze, not moving a muscle. From movies and TV shows I knew that, in order not be killed, it's imperative to obey a gunman's orders. Then I felt a hand snake into my right hip pocket and remove my wallet. The gun didn't move from the small of my back.

The voice whispered again, "Don't turn around until I've left the area or my friend will shoot you."

Utterly terrified, I obeyed. I heard running footsteps in the gravel growing softer and softer behind me. Then there was silence. Drawing on my last reserves of courage, I slowly turned around. The area was totally deserted. The "friend" had been a trick to prevent me from looking round at the gunman while he made his getaway.

The ambush area had been carefully chosen. There were no bridges to be seen either behind me or in front of me, and thus no gaps in the fences. They stretched, unbroken, for as far as I could see on either side of the canal in both directions. In order to get help, I would either have to walk back some hundreds of yards to the previous bridge (and I couldn't recall how far back that was), or go forward to the next bridge, and I'd no way of knowing how far ahead that would be.

The gunman had run back, so I decided to go forward—I let my inherent cowardice determine in which direction I should walk. As I turned around to head south again, I saw my wallet lying on the edge of the gravel path. Completely forgetting that it might bear the fingerprints of the robber, I rushed to pick it up. My credit cards all seemed to be there. Only the money was missing, both what was left from the ¥100,000 in yen bank notes I'd just obtained at the bank and the $300 in dollars that I'd brought with me from New York.

I advanced along the path as fast as I could. As I passed huge trees on both sides, my overactive imagination conjured up legions of armed bandits lurking behind them, all waiting to rob me. The distance to the next bridge was probably only about three hundred yards, but the Philosophers' Pathway seemed like the endless wide street lined with high walls that I see in my terrifying recurrent nightmare. In my dream I struggle hopelessly to wake up but can't, and I'm forced to continue on and on, pursued by nameless terrors.

But my living nightmare finally stopped. A bridge lay ahead, the fences on both sides eventually came to an end, and I rushed into a nearby pottery shop on the right hand side of the canal. I was incoherent, but the shopkeeper seemed to understand that something awful had happened to me.

A few minutes later, a police car drew up at the pottery shop, and a uniformed officer stepped out from the driver's side. I pantomimed a gun, but couldn't make him understand what had happened. He returned to his car and spoke on the radio. After a few minutes he indicated that I was to sit in the front passenger seat. From the loudspeaker I heard a heavily accented voice speaking English, asking me to identify myself. I gave my name, and then explained what had happened. I was still not totally coherent.

"Please take the officer to the place where it happened," said the disembodied voice.

Accompanied by the policeman and the owner of the pottery shop, I walked back along the Philosophers' Pathway. Everywhere there were large trees. As a result, try as I could, there was no way I could distinguish the place where the hold-up had taken place from dozens of similar looking areas. The thief had chosen his spot extremely well.

We walked back to the pottery shop and the waiting police car. The uniformed officer indicated that I should get into the car. I was driven for many miles. Eventually we arrived at an imposing building similar in style to the bank in which I'd changed the money that the gunman had stolen from me, only considerably larger. The policeman parked the car, and we walked up the wide staircase to the front portal.

The building turned out to be Kyoto police headquarters, although it seemed to me that, when it was built around the end of the nineteenth century, it had been constructed for some other purpose. The officer escorted me along a maze of corridors and staircases—there didn't seem be an elevator anywhere. Eventually he left me in a small room that contained a card table, two folding chairs, an ashtray filled with cigarette butts, and a strong smell of smoke. On the opposite wall there was a wanted poster with four badly reproduced heads, three men in the top row and a woman below them. So poor was the quality of the pictures that I doubted that even their own mothers could have recognized them.

I sat on one of the chairs. It was most uncomfortable. I stared at the wanted pictures opposite me, wondering if my assailant had been one of the three men—the voice I'd heard was definitely not that of a woman.

I suddenly remembered the third item I'd gleaned from the guidebook I'd read in my office back in New York in what now seemed to be a previous existence.

There's no crime in Japan, so don't worry about it.

I consoled myself with the thought that the four faces on the poster opposite me were surely pictures of wanted recidivist jaywalkers.

After about ten minutes, the door opened. A short, dapper man entered. He wore a houndstooth sports coat, a beige shirt and a brown silk tie decorated with pictures of stylized cormorants. His trousers looked as if they had just been pressed, and his shiny brown wing tip shoes were polished to a high gloss. His face was nondescript in every way except for a pencil moustache that seemed to come straight from a "Late Late Movie" made in the 1930s.

He bowed and then sat down opposite me.

"Mr. Thompson, I am Inspector Watanabe. May I see your passport, please?"

I handed him my passport. He looked carefully at every page and then handed it back to me with another bow.

"Mr. Thompson, please explain in detail exactly what happened on the Philosophers' Pathway." Watanabe spoke perfect English with what sounded to my American ears like an Oxford accent. However, I didn't feel comfortable enough to ask him where he'd learned the language. Instead, I took a deep breath and described, as clearly as I could, what had occurred.

When I finished, Watanabe said, "I'm sorry to hear this. Japan is largely crime-free, but occasionally unpleasant things happen. Armed robbery is especially unusual because anyone committing a crime with a weapon is particularly severely punished."

He paused for a moment, and then asked, "By the way, how do you know he had a gun?"

I was totally surprised by the question. I told Inspector Watanabe that, when I felt a round protuberance pressed firmly into the small of my back, the thought had never crossed my mind that my assailant had had anything other than a loaded gun in his hand. Also, the gunman had threatened to shoot me.

"However, it perhaps could have been a metal tube?" asked the inspector.

"It's possible, yes," I said.

"Now, may I please look at your wallet?"

I stood up, took my wallet out of the right hip pocket of my trousers where I keep it, and handed it to Watanabe.

"Most men keep their wallet in their back pocket, much to the delight of pickpockets. Do you always keep your wallet in your right hip pocket?"

"Yes. Why?"

"Did the thief try the back pocket first?"

"No, he went straight to the right hip pocket."

"Did you see the thief at any time?"

"No, he snuck up behind me."

"If he snuck up behind you, how did he know that your wallet was in that pocket?"

I was totally thunderstruck and couldn't think of anything to say. Then suddenly I realized what had happened. "He was hiding behind a large tree and saw me walk past him. I was daydreaming and as a result I didn't observe him. As I walked past his tree, he saw where I keep my wallet from the bulge in my trousers. He waited for a few seconds, then stepped behind me and stuck his gun in my back."

Inspector Watanabe rose to his feet and handed me back my wallet. "Please put it where you usually keep it."

I returned the wallet to my right hip pocket.

"Now walk up and down."

Puzzled, I obeyed, while Watanabe stared intensely at my trousers. Finally, he spoke.

"Mr. Thompson, forgive my forthrightness, but your trousers are wide at the waist but short in the leg. The way that your trousers are cut makes it impossible for anyone to see a bulge in your hip pocket."

That was easy for me to answer. "My wallet is empty now—the thief took everything except my credit cards. But when he robbed me, my wallet was filled with yen notes and dollar notes."

Inspector Watanabe didn't seem to be convinced. He left the room, returning shortly with a newspaper and scissors. He proceeded to cut a sheet of paper into pieces approximately the size of a dollar bill, and then piled them up. "Is that the height of the stolen money, both Japanese and American?"

"Probably."

I took out my wallet once more, inserted the newspaper "money," replaced the wallet, and strolled around the room again. Even I could see that no bulge was visible.

Inspector Watanabe suggested that we sit down again. He took out a pipe and went through the ritual of emptying the bowl into the already full ashtray, adding fresh tobacco from a pouch in his pocket, and lighting match after match until the pipe finally took. The smell of his tobacco was unusually pungent.

"Mr. Thompson, let me see if I understand what happened. A man snuck up on you from behind while you were walking on the Philosophers' Pathway. He stuck a metal object sharply into the small of your back, telling you to keep silent and not to move. Despite the fact that he'd no way of knowing that you keep your wallet in your right hip pocket, his hand went straight there and nowhere else.

"He drew out your wallet. He warned you not to look back or his friend would kill you. You then heard retreating footsteps on the gravel behind you. You found the wallet lying on the ground. All your money was missing, but nothing else. That means he must've taken out the money while he was telling you not to look back. He then threw the wallet away and ran. Is that correct?"

I nodded.

"Mr. Thompson, as I told you, crime is rare in Japan, armed robbery is almost unknown, and armed robbery where the gunman knows exactly where his victim keeps his wallet even though he's never seen him before is unheard of. You couldn't identify the place where the robbery took place. And the story about the 'friend' wouldn't have fooled a child. If you had to wait until the gunman was gone for fear that his friend would shoot you, how was the friend going to get away without you seeing him?"

My mouth fell open. I was totally stunned.

"Are you suggesting the armed robbery never happened?"

"I'm not suggesting anything. All that I'm saying is that your story is extremely hard to believe."

I rose to my feet. "Inspector Watanabe," I said as coldly as I could, "Just suppose for one minute that you're right and that I made the whole thing up, which I most definitely did *not*. What possible motive could I have? There's no way I could claim on my insurance for the money I withdrew at the ATM at the bank."

The inspector narrowed his eyes. "At which bank did you withdraw the money?" he asked.

"I've no idea. I asked the taxi driver to stop when I saw a bank on the route he chose from the Mikado Hotel to the Philosophers' Pathway. But I have the ATM receipt in my wallet, of course. Accountants never ever throw any pieces of paper away."

Once more I reached into my right hip pocket and took out my wallet. I opened it and took out the newspaper, which I stiffly returned to Inspector Watanabe. I then looked for the receipt from the

ATM. It didn't seem to be there. I looked again. Nothing. Finally, I emptied the contents of the wallet onto the table. The receipt wasn't in the wallet.

The Inspector's eyebrows rose. "The thief took nothing but your money and, for some reason, the receipt from the ATM which would've proven that the missing money existed, at least at that time. He then returned your wallet to you." As he finished speaking, his eyebrows rose even higher. Had he flatly called me a liar, his expression couldn't have been more insulting.

I couldn't indignantly rise to my feet because I was already standing. I bowed to the inspector and, with as much of my dignity as was left, strode to the door, opened it, and walked out. Then I realized that I'd no chance whatsoever of finding my way out of that rabbit warren of a building without assistance. I turned back to see Inspector Watanabe still seated at the table. He was peacefully puffing on his pungent pipe and smiling sardonically.

CHAPTER SIX

Getting back to my hotel posed a problem, because I had no money to pay for a bus, let alone a taxi. I decided to take a chance. I hailed a passing taxi and asked the driver to take me to an ATM, showing him my American Express Centurion card. He took me to the Kyoto Tower, where I withdrew ¥50,000, returned to my cab, and the cabbie drove me to the Mikado Hotel.

I rode up to the fifteenth floor, inserted the electronic key card in the lock and opened the door of my room. Lying on the floor in front of me was an article cut out of a newspaper that had been pushed under the door. Affixed to it was what seemed to be a purple Post-it note. I picked up the piece of newspaper. On closer inspection it turned out to be part of a page from *This Week in Kyoto*, a magazine that's widely distributed free of charge to all tourists. The clipping carried a small advertisement, surrounded by a heavy printed frame, for the Kyoto Noh Theater. Stapled to the clipping was a purple piece of paper entirely in Japanese that I assumed was a theater ticket. There was no accompanying note.

My initial reaction was puzzlement. Why on earth would anyone give me a ticket to a Noh performance? And in any event, who knew that I was staying in Room 1507 of the Mikado Hotel? Then a frightening thought crossed my mind—if the gunman knew exactly where I kept my wallet, he probably knew my hotel room, too. That meant that the ticket must have something to do with the hold-up earlier that day.

First things first, though. Before going any further, I needed to be sure that the purple piece of paper was indeed a ticket to the Noh Theater. I rode down in the elevator and showed the purple paper to the concierge.

"A friend of mine gave me this. What is it?" I asked.

She smiled. "It's a ticket for tonight's performance at the Noh Theater. It starts at 6 p.m. I don't suppose you'll stay for the full six-hour performance."

"Why ever not?"

"How much do you know about Noh?" she asked, somewhat hesitantly.

"Well, it's traditional Japanese theater, just like Kabuki, isn't it?"

"No, it isn't at all like Kabuki, that's the whole point. Kabuki is really fun. The costumes and stage settings are as fancy as on Broadway, the plots are like soap operas, and you'll have no trouble following the action, because there is an English program that explains everything. Also, like many others, our Kyoto Kabuki Theater provides a simultaneous English translation via headphones, as well. You'll find that the audience at a Kabuki theater is noisy, with the crowd thoroughly enjoying the comedy bits, and sometimes even shouting out comments during the action."

"And Noh isn't like that?"

"Noh isn't like that in any way. Just about the only thing the two have in common is that all the actors are male in both Kabuki and Noh. Kabuki is popular entertainment; Noh is considered high culture. Kabuki is for the masses; Noh is for intellectuals.

"Noh is very slow moving and restrained," she went on. "For example, if an actor portrays a woman or a spirit, he wears a mask. But if he portrays a man, his face must appear to be mask-like no facial movement of any kind is permitted. Then, as I said, even a foreigner can understand a Kabuki play, but most Japanese can't understand a Noh play."

I was taken aback. "But isn't the play in Japanese?" I asked.

"Yes, but in a six hundred-year old form of Japanese that's so archaic that almost no-one today can understand it. And don't expect an English program or headphones. Noh theater has not changed in any way in the past six hundred years. I'm pleased that you're interested in Japanese traditional theater, but you might consider going to the Kabuki Theater tonight, rather than the Noh Theater."

"Thank you for your frank advice, but I suspect that my friend who gave me the ticket will be hurt if I don't go." The truth, of course, was that I was sure that the Noh theater ticket was somehow connected to the hold-up, and I was determined to attend the performance. After all, what could happen to me in a crowded theater? The possible gain far outweighed the small risk.

Having made up my mind, I asked the concierge, "Could you please arrange for a taxi at 5:30?"

"It would be wiser to leave much earlier than that. In addition to the usual rush-hour traffic, you need to know that the theater is in an old part of town where the streets are very narrow. The traffic congestion is really bad, even by Kyoto standards. I would suggest that you leave here no later than five o'clock."

I thanked her and went up to my room to change into a suit—it was clear from what the concierge had said that this would be a formal occasion. I also followed her advice regarding the taxi and was glad that I did. The ancient streets in the geisha district of Gion were as narrow as she'd described, and the traffic was all but at a total standstill. At two minutes to six, my taxi finally stopped in front of the Kyoto Noh Theater.

I joined the stream of other theatergoers who were trying to find their seats before the performance began. Every man was wearing a suit and almost every woman wore a kimono. This made sense to me. Although a woman in a kimono is a rarity on the streets of Kyoto, people who attend a Noh production are extremely tradition-minded.

An usher in a pink and gold kimono led me into the theater. The front two-thirds of the auditorium was reasonably full; the seats in the rear third were all empty. I was therefore taken aback when she showed me to the first seat in the back row. As I sat down I realized that, seated all by myself, I was unprotected; the incident with the armed robber on the Philosophers' Pathway was still very fresh in my mind.

But before I could move to another seat, the house lights dimmed and the performance started. As with a Broadway musical, the play began with the overture. However, there was no orchestra pit. Instead, the orchestra sat behind a screen on the left side of the stage. I found the music to be exceedingly monotonous and was greatly relieved when the overture finally ended. Next, the members of the orchestra came out from behind the screen, filed very slowly onto the stage, sat down in a row at the back of the stage, and struck up a new melody. There were four men. One played a reed flute; the other three were drummers. Two of the drummers played their drums with their hands, one with the drum on his hip, the other with a differently shaped drum on his shoulder. The third had yet another type of drum, placed on the floor in front of him, which he struck with drumsticks.

Next, in came the six-man chorus. I'd hoped that the chorus would bound onto the stage singing,

"There's Noh business like show business, like Noh business I know," but no. They filed in very, very slowly—even more slowly than the orchestra—then sat on their legs on the right side of the stage. The orchestra then played and sang a lengthy number with two words that I heard clearly, namely, "Yo ... Ot!" There was no way to modify the sound of any of the drums; the only variations in the music came from the almost otherworldly reed flute and alterations in the rhythm of the drums.

Then an actor came onto the stage. He was wearing a mask, a large orange wig and a bright orange costume. He walked slowly, very slowly, onto the stage, and then he did a dance consisting of a lengthy sequence of slow, formalized movements. After about ten minutes, I began to feel very tired indeed. This was partly due to tiredness from the long air journey and partly to the repetitiveness of the performance. To be blunt, I became extremely bored, mainly because I'd no idea what was going on, nor had I had any previous exposure to this traditional art form.

I found myself starting to nod off, and became terrified that the other theatergoers would hear the resulting snoring, even though they were seated far from me. I needn't have worried. Just as I was about to fall asleep, a white envelope dropped onto my lap. I snapped my head to the left to see who had delivered it, but I saw only a small part of the back of a man as he walked rapidly out of the auditorium.

I snatched up the envelope and rushed after the man as fast as I could, but when I reached the foyer, it was completely deserted. If the man had gone out into the street, I would never be able to catch him, and there was no way I was going to try to search the theater building. Instead I decided to open the envelope. Inside was a half a page cut from the same issue of *This Week in Kyoto*. On the one side was part of an article about shops selling traditional Japanese crafts. This didn't seem very promising, so I turned over the page. On the other side was an advertisement for a club named GoGoGo.

It was clear that, if I wanted to discover more about the hold-up, I would have to go to the GoGoGo Club. I walked out of the foyer to the place where the taxi had dropped me and waited patiently for a cab.

Ten minutes later, I was still waiting. Then a man came out of the foyer. He looked at me, shook his head and said, "No taxi." Then he held up the fingers on both his hands.

I immediately understood that no taxis would bother to drive along the narrow lane past the Noh Theater until ten o'clock when weaker members of the audience with only minimal *sitzfleisch*—I couldn't find the equivalent Japanese word for the ability to sit still for many hours anywhere in my phrase book—would be ready to go home only four hours after the performance had started.

He then pointed around the corner, and said, "*Basu.*"

I went around the corner to the bus stop. Fastened to the pole was exhaustive information about the bus route, as well as a detailed timetable. The bad news is that everything was in Japanese, in contrast to the bus stop I'd seen near the Philosophers' Pathway, a significant tourist attraction. In other words, the city of Kyoto has gone to a lot of trouble to make it easy for English-speaking visitors to move from one of the many excellent tourist attractions to the next, but it would have been totally unreasonable of me to expect bus information in English at bus stops used almost exclusively by Japanese speakers, such as this stop next to the Noh Theater.

I was now faced with a dilemma—I had no idea where the bus would take me. If the stop outside the theater were on an in-bound route, I would be able to alight in the city center and hail a taxi to the GoGoGo Club. But if the bus were headed out of town, the route would end at some distant suburb. If the terminus turned out to be relatively deserted, this might well put me at the mercy of the armed robber again. The potential risks were just too great even to consider taking a bus.

Instead I decided to return to my seat in the Noh Theater and try and stay awake for three hours until it would be possible to get a cab. But as I started to walk from the bus stop back to the entrance to the theater, a taxi bearing two late theatergoers drew up. As soon as the couple got out, I got in.

I exultantly shouted "GoGoGo!" to the taxi driver, not realizing that this could be somewhat misinterpreted. However, when he turned round with a quizzical expression on his face I understood his confusion. I showed him the newspaper clipping, and off we went.

In New York, a fashionable club doesn't even open until eleven o'clock, and nothing really happens until well after midnight, or so I understand—I'm not exactly a regular club goer, as you know. But here in Kyoto, the GoGoGo Club was in full swing when the taxi driver dropped me there soon after seven. The line in front of the building seemed unending. Between where I stood and the entrance to the club were dozens and dozens of young people beautifully dressed in casual clothing. Not only did I stand out because I was the only non-Japanese, I was the only person who was formally dressed. In fact, I was probably the only person ever to visit that club in a tailored navy blue pinstripe suit and power tie.

After what seemed a lifetime (but was probably only about 15 minutes), I reached the end of the line, paid the exorbitant cover charge and walked into the club. In front of me was an archway leading into a dimly lit hallway with a low dome-shaped roof. After I'd taken a few tentative steps in the dark, the hallway veered to the right, and I found myself at the entrance to a cavernous room, probably a converted warehouse.

In fact, this was the first time I'd been in a club, but I'd seen many clubs in movies and on TV shows and had some idea of what to expect. What I didn't expect was that the designers of this club had seen the exact same movies and TV shows that I'd seen, and had incorporated everything they had seen into this one club. The ceiling was mirrored. Just below the level of the ceiling were enormous television screens showing rock videos, and suspended some ten feet above the floor were gold cages holding go-go dancers. The lighting effects were eclectic. A spotlight raked the ceiling, and strobe lights, ultraviolet lights, flickering candles and mirror balls added to the chaos. White smoke billowed from the walls. Finally, despite the gigantic size of the room and the noise from the dance floor filled with dancers, the sound of the music was deafening. No matter where I stood, speakers blasted my ears with rock music. In fact, it was so loud that I couldn't even make out if the words of the songs were in English or Japanese.

I wandered through the room, expecting to see someone who would tell me why I'd been sent to this place and could shed some light on the hold-up of that afternoon. However, every couple seemed intent on dancing frenetically; they all totally ignored me. After fruitlessly combing the vast dance floor at least twice, I decided to try the archways leading from the room. The first led back to the hallway through which I'd entered—that didn't help. The second archway led to the restrooms—again of little use. Next, I walked through the third archway and was amazed to find myself in a typical English pub or, more precisely, in a typical English pub as portrayed in those same movies and TV shows that I'd previously mentioned to you. I asked the barman for a whiskey on the rocks, and was pleasantly surprised to see him pour from a bottle of Chivas Regal 12 Year Old—I suppose I could have had a single malt Scotch if only I'd thought of it. The drink cost ¥4,500, but fortunately I still had the money I'd drawn from the second ATM.

The atmosphere in the bar was curiously restful, probably because the volume of the music was low enough to allow the servers to hear the customers' orders. That is, instead of being excruciatingly and unpleasantly loud, here in the bar it was merely loud. I sipped my drink slowly and planned my next step.

It seemed to me that the only reason I'd been sent to the Noh Theater was to receive the instruction to go to the GoGoGo Club. I had no idea why I'd not been sent directly to the GoGoGo, but at least I was at the club now. My first thought was that in this huge crowd nothing unpleasant could happen to me, but then I realized that the noise level in the main room was so high that an assailant could shoot me with a machine gun and no one would hear a thing. On the other hand, the dancers would probably see the killing, so the chances of being attacked in the GoGoGo were therefore small. That was encouraging. The challenge, however, was that I seemed to have been sent to the GoGoGo Club on a wild goose chase. Was it possible that the person I was supposed to meet had already left, or had he not yet arrived?

Outside the club I'd seen a sign stating that the club was open from six to midnight. The envelope had been handed to me around seven, and I couldn't have been expected to arrive at the club much before the time that I had. It was now around eight, and I was tired, very tired. The excitement of the hold-up, the frustrations of my interview with Inspector Watanabe, travel fatigue, the lack of sleep the previous night, and the boredom of the Noh performance all suddenly combined, and waves of exhaustion started to hit me. Mind-numbing tiredness overcame my desire to solve the mystery of the strange goings on. I drank the last of the whiskey in my glass and staggered to the entrance. A taxi was waiting, and surprisingly soon I was in bed in Room 1507 in the Mikado Hotel, fast asleep.

That night my usual nightmare returned, again and again. As always, I was running down an endless wide street lined with high walls. But this time there were three differences. First, the street was lined with cherry trees on both sides. Second, as I ran, I felt a gun in my back. Third, Inspector Watanabe's voice kept repeating, "Don't look back or my friend will shoot you," and then he laughed. Needless to say, I did not get a restful night's sleep.

CHAPTER SEVEN

Notwithstanding the heavy drapes that kept the room pitch black, I woke early. I hesitated before returning to Le Lac des Cygnes restaurant for breakfast because I didn't want a repeat of the previous day's problems. Then I had an idea. I called down to the front desk to ask if any other restaurant in the hotel was open for breakfast, but was told no. The choice was now Le Lac des Cygnes or a restaurant in some other hotel. Looking at my possessions laid out on the bedside table, I saw that I could make up the sum of ¥2,400 from my yen bank notes and coins. In this way I could avoid any unpleasantness with change if the same cashier was on duty.

Accordingly I went back to Le Lac des Cygnes. The buffet selection was as superb as ever, especially the corn danish. As the end of the meal, the server again gave me a thick plastic card with a number on it. I took this card to the cashier, who, this time, turned out to be a woman. On impulse I gave her a ¥5,000 yen note, and was almost simultaneously given two ¥1,000 notes, a ¥500 coin, a ¥100 coin, and a deep bow in return. I bowed back, and returned to my room in a daze.

Again I decided to sleep after breakfast, and again the arrival of a text from Nikki woke me. She told me that her mother was doing well, and that she would soon return to Kyoto from Stockholm. And again, she instructed me to see the city.

I was overcome with a fervent hunger to hear her voice, but I remembered just in time that phoning would wake her mother. Instead, I sent her a loving text in reply, telling her that I missed her so much and that I would tour Kyoto while I waited for her.

According to all my guidebooks, the two most memorable attractions in Kyoto are Ginkaku-ji and Kinkaku-ji or, in English, the Silver Pavilion Temple and the Golden Pavilion Temple. I decided to toss a coin to decide which one to visit by myself, and I would then visit them both with Nikki when she returned to Kyoto. I flipped the ¥500 coin that the cashier had given me as part of my breakfast change. The coin fell on the floor and rolled under the bed. I didn't even bother to try to retrieve it—the possibility of injuring myself far exceeded the $5 value of the coin, even assuming that I could somehow lay my hands on it.

Plan one having failed, I tried a different tactic. Given that the laws of probability were fatally biased against my visiting either pavilion, I opened a guidebook to find if there was something else equally worth seeing, and found that Ryoan-ji, a temple with a famous Zen rock garden, was highly recommended.

Outside the Mikado Hotel a black Crown was waiting. I asked the driver to take me to Ryoan-ji. I'd learned from one of my guidebooks that the Japanese word for a Buddhist temple is *tera*, and that the kanji character for *tera* is also pronounced *ji*—no, I don't understand that either. I'd already informed the driver that I wanted to visit a temple when I'd told him to go to Ryoan-ji, but just to be sure, I added the word *tera*. The driver said "*hai*," very loudly, and off we went. He took me along a series of byways, many of them narrow alleyways. Despite his attempts to bypass the usual heavy Kyoto traffic, occasionally we were stuck in a line of cars at a traffic light. Apparently wanting to make use of every second of his day, at each of these stops the driver used his cell phone.

Then we found ourselves in a traffic jam of gargantuan proportions. My taxi came to a total halt in front of a small pavilion three stories tall on an island close to the edge of an ornamental lake. The top two stories were covered with gold leaf. The driver pointed to the building and said, "Kinkaku-ji." This was the Golden Pavilion Temple that I had wanted to visit.

The road on which we had come to a standstill as well as the entire area in front of the ticket office was filled with hundreds, perhaps thousands, of schoolchildren. They were all in uniform. The girls wore sailor suits, all perfectly pressed, with every seam precisely correct. Some of the boys wore blazers and ties, but most wore jackets that buttoned up in front all the way to the neck. All the students had thick plastic name badges, with the letters etched from behind and colored black. The badges seemed to be about four inches by three inches, and contained two or three lines of Japanese characters—I assumed that the information displayed included the name of the student, the class and the name of the school. Each badge was mounted in exactly the same place on the left side of every student's chest, and each badge was perfectly straight. All the students were extremely well behaved, except for a few of the boys. I was pleased to see that. I didn't want to go home with the impression that all Japanese children are automata, and was delighted to observe that a handful, at least, were quite undisciplined.

The teachers accompanying the children were equally well dressed. Most of the teachers seemed to be men in mid-gray suits with white dress shirts and nondescript ties; many of the men were aged fifty or older. The women, too, were beautifully dressed. I wondered if it was always like this in Japanese schools, or whether everyone made a special effort for field trips. I was also amazed to see groups of just six or seven students with many of the teachers. Was this the standard staff–student ratio?

After what seemed an eon, the stationary traffic in front of the Golden Pavilion Temple started to move. We inched our way forward, and finally arrived at Ryoan-ji.

The host of signs at the entrance to the temple asking visitors to remove their shoes before entering made it unnecessary for me to remember Principle Five:

Always take off your shoes before entering a temple or a Japanese home.

On the left-hand side of the entrance was a group of wooden mats on which to stand and remove one's shoes. Behind those were dozens of partitioned racks for storing shoes. Several of the pigeonholes in the racks were occupied. I took off my shoes, placed them in a pigeonhole near the top of the area marked with a nine, and walked into the temple.

The major attraction of Ryoan-ji is the Zen Buddhist garden to the left of the entrance. The garden is about twelve yards by thirty yards in size. It consists of an expanse of small white stones into which are embedded fifteen rocks surrounded by moss—fifteen is the Zen Buddhist number of perfection. The rocks are arranged in such a way that, no matter where on the temple porch you stand, you can't see more than fourteen of them at the same time. The explanation printed on the back of the entrance ticket explained that, the longer you contemplate the garden, the more you understand what it means.

I contemplated the garden for about five minutes, but no enlightenment came. I simply couldn't work out the meaning underlying the three groupings of five rocks of different shapes and sizes embedded in a sea of small white stones, carefully raked. Instead I decided to think about the other puzzles in my life. First, I tried to discover the truth behind the currency-challenged male cashier at breakfast the previous day. I stared at the garden, concentrating my gaze in turn on each of the fourteen rocks that I could see from that position and tried fiercely to come up with an explanation regarding the cashier. My mind remained stubbornly blank.

I moved to a different place on the porch, sat down again, and now I concentrated on a different puzzle: *How did the gunman know where I kept my wallet?* Suddenly, enlightenment struck me like a lightening bolt. The statement on the entrance ticket was correct: The longer you contemplate the garden, the more you understand.

The explanation was simple. The doorman at the hotel who had summoned the taxi the previous day had seen me put my hand in my right hip pocket to give him a tip—before I remembered in time that tipping is frowned on in Japan. He'd used his cell phone to call a confederate. While I was eating my lunch of savory noodles, the confederate had had time to get into position behind the large tree and wait to hold me up and relieve me of all my cash.

I was about to jump up from the temple porch and call Inspector Watanabe, when I suddenly realized that I'd better contemplate the rocks in the garden a little longer, because there was a gaping hole in my explanation. I hadn't told the doorman at the Mikado Hotel where I wanted to be driven; I gave my destination to the taxi driver only after the car door was shut. This meant that whatever was going on was far more sinister. Someone had followed me all the way from outside the Mikado Hotel to the Philosophers' Pathway the previous morning. The good news was that my worries were over—no-one could possibly have tailed me to Ryoan-ji, because the route my taxi driver had followed had included many narrow roads and by-ways, and he would surely have noticed any attempt at tailing. But wait—the black Crown had been waiting for me outside the hotel. Maybe the driver was in cahoots with whoever it was who wanted to tail me, and had simply used his cell phone to alert the other party while we were en route to Ryoan-ji. After all, at every stop the driver had used his cell phone, and he certainly could have informed interested parties as to where I was headed.

Something was wrong, seriously wrong. In a state of panic, I rushed back to the entrance of the temple.

When I reached the shoe racks I saw that my shoes were gone.

***

My first inclination was to report the crime to Inspector Watanabe. Then I realized exactly what he would say.

"Your feet are far larger than those of most Japanese. Why would anyone want to steal your shoes? Did other people see you putting your shoes there? If not, how did the thief know that those were your shoes? Were any other shoes stolen today? Do you realize that stealing shoes from the racks outside a temple is sacrilegious, and no Japanese person would dream of doing it? Were you, in fact, wearing shoes today? Do you have a receipt for your shoes, or was that stolen, too?"

Yes, my imagination was running wild, but even when I calmed down, I realized that there was nothing whatsoever to be gained by contacting the inspector. Instead I asked the person who was selling the admission tickets if she'd seen anything. I think she understood what I'd asked, but she simply shook her head. No one else in the entrance area was prepared to admit that they understood any English, either. My feeling was that they were all exceedingly embarrassed by what had happened, and the easiest way to handle that embarrassment was simply to pretend that they didn't understand me.

There was no alternative. I walked back to the taxi area in my socks, and asked the driver of a waiting black Crown to take me to a shop where I could buy new shoes. He drove me to Ikeburuko Department Store, the largest and fanciest department store in central Kyoto. I was extremely embarrassed to have to walk into that grand store in my socks and ask for directions to the shoe department. The alternative, however, would have been to ask the driver to take me back to my hotel for another pair of shoes. The staff on duty would have had the pleasure of seeing me walk through the large lobby to the elevator in my shoeless condition. Ikeburuko Department Store was infinitely better. After all, no one knew me there.

The shoe department, like every department of Ikeburuko, had an enormous selection of high-quality products, often imported. As a result, I was able to replace my shoes with an identical pair. Sitting in the comfortable shoe department, I suddenly recalled Principle Four:

Kyoto has 1,700 Buddhist temples and three hundred Shinto shrines, many of them exquisitely lovely. The problem in Kyoto is to avoid temple overload.

With 1999 temples to go, I decided to buy an extra pair of shoes, just in case. Carrying one pair and wearing the other, I took yet another taxi back to the hotel. I rode up in the elevator to the fifteenth floor, as always.

When I reached my room, I saw my stolen shoes arranged neatly in front of the door.

CHAPTER EIGHT

I decided to console myself by having dinner at Yemyo, arguably one of the most expensive restaurants in the world, with meals starting at $500. Instead of asking the concierge to make a reservation for me I found the number in the current issue of *This Week in Kyoto* magazine and phoned the restaurant myself. The reason was that I wanted to be sure in advance that I could pay with a credit card, because I didn't have enough yen for the meal.

The receptionist assured me that I could pay with Visa, MasterCard or American Express. In fact, meal after meal I found that I could pay with credit cards, even in inexpensive restaurants. As the days passed, this made the behavior of the male cashier the previous morning at Le Lac des Cygnes restaurant in my hotel seem even more bizarre.

At Yemyo I tried to drown the day's woes in an orgy of kaiseki cuisine. I was lucky to get a table overlooking the Oi River with the densely wooded Arashiyama Mountains in the background. The waitresses wore traditional kimonos, and served the food on lacquered trays, in exquisite porcelain and lacquered bowls that seemed, to my untutored eye, to be of museum quality. The meal consisted of an unending series of courses, each served in a bowl or on a plate that matched either the shape or the color of the food, or both. It was a treat for the senses with one small drawback: I had absolutely no idea what I was eating, from start to finish.

Back in my hotel, I lay on my bed and tried to inject some sense into the nightmare that was overtaking me. Was there a rational explanation for what was going on, or was I becoming paranoid, like my sister Eloise? Was this an inherited condition? Did Eloise have a genetic predisposition to believing that the world was conspiring against her, that had affected her all her life, and was the same inherited mental condition starting to afflict me, too? Or was there some other way to explain what was happening? And if so, was there a real-life conspiracy at work, not an imagined one?

Unable to find answers to my questions, I was about to drop off to sleep when there was a knock at the door. Standing outside was a bellhop whom I hadn't seen before. He handed me an envelope on a silver tray, bowed and left. In the envelope I found a train ticket together with a letter from Inspector Watanabe. His written English was as impeccable as his spoken English, and his elegant handwriting was a pleasure to read.

Dear Mr. Thompson,

I am sure that you will find that the temples of Nara are even lovelier than the temples of Kyoto. I have enclosed a train ticket on the Kintetsu Railway (not Japan Rail) leaving Kyoto Station tomorrow morning at 8:30 a.m. Enjoy your day in Nara.

Respectfully,
Seiji Watanabe
Inspector, Kyoto Police

I immediately looked up Nara in one of my guidebooks. Nara, it seemed, was a small town some forty-five minutes by bullet train from Kyoto. And yes, it had temples, lots and lots of them. But why was Inspector Watanabe so keen that I should visit them? Was he trying to get me out of Kyoto for a day so that he could complete his work without interruption from a crazy American whose shoes had been stolen and then reappeared? But I hadn't reported the missing shoes to him, and that meant that the mysterious shoes had nothing to do with it. Could he have found out about my shoes some other way, and did he now want this troublemaker out of town for at least one day?

The more I went through the possible motives behind Inspector Watanabe's note and train ticket, the more disquiet I felt. It seemed that something truly serious was happening, a conspiracy of some sort. This conspiracy somehow involved the breakfast cashier, the hold-up, the stolen shoes that were subsequently returned and now the train ticket to Nara. And what about the Noh Theater and the GoGoGo Club?

One thing was certain. I absolutely, positively had to be on that train at 8:30 the next morning. I set the alarm on my BlackBerry to wake me at six, and the alarm clock built into the TV to five after. Then I called the front desk for a wake-up call at ten after. This was one trip that I was definitely not going to miss.

***

I arrived at the correct platform thirty minutes early. Kyoto station seems to have been designed to make life as difficult as possible for travelers—it's impossible to get from point A to point B without going up stairs and down stairs. I was carrying only a messenger bag with my guidebooks and my map, but all around me I could see travelers struggling to haul their baggage across the stair-laden obstacle course. I didn't see any physically handicapped passengers—it would have been impossible for them to reach their train without unending assistance.

At the platform I sat on a bench and waited. I carefully observed the other people in the vicinity. There was a grandmother with three unruly grandchildren under the age of six, a young couple obviously very much in love and a number of students in casual clothes. No one seemed out of place; perhaps I wasn't being tailed. Or possibly the tails were so skilful that I could not detect them.

At 8:20 the train drew into the station. I found the correct carriage, entered, searched for my seat and was delighted to find that the window seat reserved for me was almost large enough for my ample torso. I pressed the button to recline the seat, relaxed, and started to look forward to the trip through what I anticipated would be lush green countryside.

Through the window I watched the conductor signal the driver that the train could now leave. As he waved his arm, in the glass I saw the reflection of a man who was about to take the seat next to mine. As I turned toward him, he bowed. He was a tall, thin, gray-haired elderly man in a mid-gray suit, white shirt and nondescript tie. And then I realized that I was the only other passenger in the carriage. Given that he could have purchased a ticket for a seat next to a window in the otherwise unoccupied carriage, why had he chosen to sit next to me?

My initial fear was that he was going to kill me. Then I realized that, although it was possible, it was extremely unlikely. After all, he wouldn't be able to make his escape from the high-speed bullet train after murdering me. For the same reason I also excluded the possibility that he wished to become a member of that exclusive club of Japanese criminals whose major achievement in life was holding me up at gun point and stealing my wallet. In fact, he couldn't possibly do anything unpleasant to me while we were both on the Kintetsu Railway, and the expected crowd at Nara Station would definitely preclude any sort of antisocial behavior at our destination. If I felt the least bit threatened there, I would simply take the next train straight back to Kyoto.

I couldn't bear to look at my traveling companion—instead I stared out the window. I soon learned that the anticipated train ride through the glorious countryside wasn't going to happen. The whole area between Kyoto and Nara was built-up. Occasionally a patch of green turned out to be a paddy field, usually with a farmer tending the rice plants growing in the pools of water. I did see a small lake surrounded by open countryside, backed by mountains. And, at one point, we rode through a grove of huge trees, but almost all the time, the view from the train window consisted of houses, shops, factories, apartments and the occasional temple or shrine. I kept looking out the window to keep my thoughts off the thing that really concerned me. What was uppermost in my mind at that moment wasn't the fact that ninety percent of Japan is mountainous and hence uninhabitable, and as a result the population is squeezed into every square inch of the remaining ten percent. No, what bothered me was the fact that next to me sat a man who had deliberately chosen to occupy a cramped seat partially filled by my overflowing girth, when he could have sat anywhere in the otherwise empty carriage.

Then I realized something important. Inspector Watanabe had arranged this meeting. I had no way of telling whether my traveling companion was as surprised to find me sitting in the window seat as I was when I saw him taking the aisle seat, or whether he even knew that Inspector Watanabe had organized our meeting. But there was absolutely no doubt whatsoever in my mind that Watanabe had arranged for us to sit next to one another on the 8:30 express from Kyoto to Nara.

Thus reassured, I turned to my companion.

"Excuse me, do you speak English?"

He nodded, firmly. "Yes. Can I help you?"

"Are you traveling to Nara to see the temples?" I asked him.

"Yes, I am. Are you?"

"Yes, I am, too." The conversation was becoming positively scintillating. I was tempted to ask next if he came here often, but I quickly realized that if I was to discover the reason behind the many weird events in my life, I had to treat this meeting on the train with the utmost seriousness. Just one mistake could upset everything. The fact that I had been too exhausted to rendezvous with the unknown person in the GoGoGo Club meant that one opportunity had already been lost. Under no circumstances would I deliberately do anything to jeopardize this new opportunity to uncover the truth about the conspiracy.

The letter from Inspector Watanabe had spoken about temples and that meant that it was important to visit temples if I were ever to uncover what was happening. I turned to my traveling companion.

"Which temple are you going to see today?" I asked.

"I want to visit the Horyu-ji complex in Western Nara," he said. "It's a United Nations World Heritage site. Those temples are really important."

Aha, now we're getting somewhere.

My companion had just said, "Those temples are really important." Clearly the secret lay in those temples. But I was a stranger in a land with a culture and language utterly different to mine. How could I solve the puzzle when I didn't even know how to get to the temples, let alone understand what would be said to me there?

"In that case, could you please tell me how I can travel to those temples?" I asked, trying to keep my voice as nonchalant as possible. Now was certainly not the time to let him know that my heart was pounding in my chest and I was almost dizzy with tension.

"Of course. In fact, I would be delighted if you'd accompany me to Horyu-ji this morning."

"It would be my pleasure. Thank you very much indeed! By the way, my name is Oliver Thompson."

"And I am Suzuki." Remembering not to shake hands, I bowed my head. Back home in America, my next question would have been, "And what do you do?" but this was Japan, and I certainly didn't wish to offend the only person in the whole world who, as far I could see, might reveal to me the key to the riddles. Instead I just smiled, waiting for him to speak again.

Just as I thought that the silence would last forever, Mr. Suzuki asked, "Are you visiting Japan on business?"

"No, I'm in Kyoto on a two-week holiday. I understand that the temples in Nara are really exceptional." And as I spoke, I bit my tongue. The last thing I wanted to do was to let on to him how obsessively interested I was in the temples of Nara.

"I see," he said. I could not detect any guile in his voice or a hidden meaning. Was it possible that this man was just an innocent courier whose job it was to ensure that I traveled from Nara Station to the correct temple? Nothing would be gained by forcing the issue—I would have to wait patiently until we arrived at the temple complex. And in the meantime, it was imperative to keep off the subject of temples.

I desperately tried to find a neutral topic of conversation. Of course, the only thing that went through my mind was temples, temples and more temples. Finally, I had an idea for a perfectly innocent question that couldn't be misunderstood and couldn't possibly have a hidden meaning.

"Are you also on holiday?" I asked.

"In a way," he said. "I'm retired, so every day is a holiday."

His remark was obviously untrue. Mr. Suzuki—if that was his real name—was clearly working for Inspector Watanabe. I did not respond to his lie. I realized that, if I offended him in any way, he might refuse to take me the temple complex that was "really important." Even if I could find my own way to Horyu-ji without him, surely I would have no way to make contact with the person or persons who could reveal the secret of the putative conspiracy. I had to remain on the very best of terms with Suzuki until I'd learned everything. Instead I nodded and smiled, and pretended that I'd accepted his statement that he was a retiree.

"And what did you do you before you retired?" Again I bit my tongue. For all I knew, asking a retired Japanese man about his former job might be the height of bad manners.

Even if it was the sort of question that a well brought-up Japanese person would never ask, Mr. Suzuki gave no sign that I'd committed an indiscretion. "I was a civil servant," he said. I knew from his answer that I wasn't going to find out anything more about what he did or where he did it, so I just stared out the window until we arrived at Nara Station.

CHAPTER NINE

Mr. Suzuki was horrified when I suggested that we take a taxi to the Horyu-ji complex, even when I assured him that I would pay for it. The number fifty-two bus, he said, would take us straight from outside the station to the Horyu-ji bus terminus. From there, he assured me, it was just a short walk to the temples. I wasn't sure whether he was genuinely opposed to the extravagance of taking a taxi when a bus would do or whether, in his role as a retired civil servant, it was the appropriate attitude to assume. Whatever the reason, we stood at the bus stop across the road from the station for some ten minutes, after which the bus arrived.

We entered the bus from the rear door. Mr. Suzuki explained to me that this was a driver-only bus, or *wam man basu*. It took me a short while to work out that the Japanese words were essentially a transliteration of the English words "one man bus." Following Mr. Suzuki's lead, as I entered I took a ticket from a machine. In addition to the by now familiar Kanji script, the ticket bore the number one. We'd boarded the *wam man basu* at Stage One, as indicated on the ticket. As the journey progressed, Suzuki explained, the signs above the front window of the bus would indicate the fare for passengers who had boarded at each stage. When we were ready to alight, we would walk to the front of the bus and give the driver the exact change as indicated on the sign for Stage One.

"But what if we don't have the exact change?" I asked, panic finally revealing itself in my voice. I had visions of being thrown off the bus in the middle of the countryside, and never ever being able to return to Kyoto and my beloved Nikki. Mr. Suzuki was most reassuring. He explained that there are two change machines up front, one for changing notes, the other for changing coins, to enable the passenger to always make the exact change and then drop it in the slot. I accepted this explanation, and sat back to enjoy the ride.

For some reason, I'd deduced from my guidebooks that Nara was a small country town and that we would drive through open fields to the temples. In fact, Nara turned out to be the capital of Nara Prefecture; the city, a provincial capital, was substantial in size. The bus ride lasted nearly an hour. We first drove through the busy city center, and then the surroundings became more suburban. We saw almost no countryside, and virtually all of the limited unbuilt land was devoted to paddy fields.

Apart from an older woman who alighted quite soon after we'd climbed on the bus, and an American tourist with two large fancy cameras who got off after about ten minutes, we had the whole bus to ourselves. I found this disconcerting at first and then frightening. I was being driven into the western suburbs of a city I hadn't even heard of until the previous day, in the company of a "retired civil servant" who clearly wasn't. I kept trying to reassure myself that Inspector Watanabe had organized the whole thing, but the virtually deserted bus upset me and caused me to worry incessantly.

Eventually the bus reached the terminus. Suzuki was all smiles. He pointed toward some spires. "Now a short walk, and we'll arrive at the temples." After a short walk I was perspiring, and was relieved to see a shop selling souvenirs and ice cream. There were two flavors, vanilla and green tea. Mr. Suzuki suggested that I try the green tea flavor. Green tea is served with every Japanese meal, and the best I can say about it is that it's an acquired taste that I hadn't managed to acquire yet. I didn't want to upset my guide in any way, shape, or form, so we each purchased a cone of green tea-flavored ice cream. It was truly awful. It was bitter in an unpleasant way, and the added sugar didn't mask the taste. But in deference to Mr. Suzuki, I ate every morsel, and didn't let on that I was eating the ice cream purely for diplomatic reasons.

"Did you enjoy it?" asked Mr. Suzuki.

"Well, it certainly was unlike American ice cream," I said as politely as I could. He did not react to my tactful answer.

Another short walk led into an area of really narrow streets, with room for only one car to pass. Furthermore, there were several ninety-degree bends with metal mirrors mounted to enable motorists to see what was coming down the road. Occasionally a gate in the high wall lining the street was open and I could see a house that was surprisingly large and luxurious compared to what I'd seen in Kyoto. The gardens I saw looked like illustrations from a book on Japanese gardens—every leaf was in place. Many of the houses had parking areas. I don't understand how they could possibly maneuver their relatively large cars from their cramped parking areas onto the road, let alone how they could drive through the confined streets of that neighborhood.

As I mentioned, the narrow roads had high walls on either side, making the area ideal for another hold-up, but after several of Mr. Suzuki's "short walks" we eventually arrived at the Horyu-ji complex without incident. Wherever a mirror was mounted at a corner I peered into it to see if we were being followed, but the road behind me was empty every time. The only people I observed en route were an occasional homeowner tending her garden, and one woman taking her yellow Labrador Retriever for a walk. For the rest, the area was totally deserted. First the bus, now this neighborhood. Why was there no one else in this part of Nara? After all, from what I'd seen during the fifty-five-minute bus ride, greater Nara clearly had a population of hundreds of thousands, and we were in the vicinity of one of the world's greatest cultural heritage sites, the Horyu-ji complex. Why had the area essentially been evacuated? Was the whole set-up some sort of trap arranged by

Inspector Watanabe and, if so, why? Surely if Watanabe had some fiendish plot up his sleeve, his home base of Kyoto would be a more appropriate venue. It seemed crazy to drag me out here, to this deserted area of Nara. And what was the role of the Labrador Retriever? Surely an Akita or a Kishu Ken or some other dog breed originating in Japan would be more appropriate for this elaborate *mise en scène?* The yellow Labrador had seemed just as friendly as the ubiquitous retrievers of American suburbia. Did this have any significance? Was it an attempt to lull me into a sense of false security before the trap was sprung? And, most important of all, what was Suzuki's part in all this?

We passed a complex of three shops. First there was a hair salon, complete with a red, white, and blue striped rotating barber's pole. But the salon seemed to be totally deserted—I could see neither clients nor hairdressers. This was strange. Next to the hair salon was a small convenience store. One person stood behind the counter, shielded by the newspaper he or she was reading. The third shop was a souvenir shop. It was barred and shuttered. This was even stranger. Judging from the spires, we were within a hundred yards of a major tourist attraction, yet the souvenir shop was closed. Why? What was happening in this corner of Nara?

Finally we left the virtually deserted area and reached an open gateway, the entrance to the temple complex. There was a handful of other people, two ticket sellers in glass booths and four ticket takers, plus two tourists standing near the center of the large courtyard at the edge of which we now stood. I read the sign on the wall to our right. Mr. Suzuki had been correct; this was indeed a United Nations World Heritage site. The presence of two ticket sellers and four ticket takers implied that the Horyu-ji complex was a major tourist attraction. Yet the only tourists I could see were the couple now walking hand-in-hand toward the large brown pagoda in the center of the courtyard. Were they part of this painstaking masquerade? Why was the complex virtually empty of visitors?

Once we'd bought our ¥1,200 tickets and entered the complex, Mr. Suzuki suggested that we visit the eighteen sites shown on the map on the rear of our tickets in the order in which they were numbered. This seemed a methodical way to ensure that we didn't overlook any of the sites, and I readily agreed. The first stop was the brown pagoda in the middle of the courtyard. On each of the four sides, a short flight of steps led up to a screened opening. We walked up one of the flights of stairs, and I tried to peer through the screen into the interior of the temple, but the screen was totally impervious to light and I couldn't see anything. I didn't say a word to Mr. Suzuki, but walked down the stairs and around the pagoda to the next flight, Suzuki following me. The screen here was equally opaque; again I could see absolutely nothing.

I turned to Mr. Suzuki. "Can you see anything?"

It was as if I hadn't spoken. I thought of repeating my question, this time louder, but realized that, for some reason, Suzuki had no intention of responding to my query. Instead I said to him, "Let's go on to Site Two."

We walked to one of the temples at the side of the courtyard, only to find that the building didn't seem to have an entrance of any kind. It wasn't that it was barred to the public—there was simply no possible way in that I could see. Mr. Suzuki just stood there with a totally neutral expression on his face. I realized that, if I said anything, he would again ignore it.

What was Suzuki's game? It was clear that this aspect of the trip, at least, had nothing to do with Inspector Watanabe or Mr. Suzuki. After all, the Horyu-ji complex is over a thousand years old—in fact, the main temple is the oldest wooden structure in the world—and neither Watanabe nor Suzuki could have arranged for the pagoda screens to be opaque or for the next temple to be entryless. What was annoying, however, was Suzuki's clear determination to pretend that everything was hunky dory when it was obvious that the first two sites had proved to be disappointments at best.

I decided to continue to say nothing, and strolled slowly on to Site Three, which was the Dokaido or lecture hall, a massive building with two open sides, which contained some beautiful huge Buddhist statues. Together we admired the centuries-old artwork while Suzuki explained the religious significance of each piece and pointed out aspects of Buddhist religious art in a way that revealed a love and deep knowledge of his subject.

When we had finished, I suggested that we proceed to Site Four, a temple to the north of the Dokaido. But, try as we might, we could find no way to exit from the Dokaido to reach the next temple. We could see it through the open wall of the Dokaido, but there was no access route. In fact, the high grass on all sides of Site Four implied that no one had walked near the temple for a long time. Why then was that temple numbered on the map on the entrance ticket? It was clear that Suzuki (if that was indeed the real name of the self-proclaimed retired civil servant) wasn't going to tell me why, and I wasn't going to give him the satisfaction of asking him.

The next site was a temple that was accessible and even had a doorway. However, it was barred shut, and there was a sign indicating that visitors weren't permitted to enter. The following item was a temple that, according to my guidebook, contained a number of significant religious statues. There was a passageway encircling the temple, and from the passageway it was possible to peer through carved openings into the temple itself. However, the lighting inside the temple was so dim that it was impossible to see anything except large vague shapes. Again I didn't say anything, and again Suzuki didn't make any sort of comment.

On we strolled, through a gateway, past a small lake, and into the second portion of the temple complex. Next, according to the ticket, was another temple. Much to my amazement, this one was open to the public. In front of the temple was the notice regarding shoes that I'd expected to see all day but hadn't yet encountered, because we'd not yet been able to enter a single temple. Suzuki and I started to take off our shoes. I was certainly not going to let on about my fears that my shoes would be stolen once again. Instead I calmly and deliberately untied the laces, slipped out of my shoes—they were one of the two new pairs I'd just bought at the Ikeburuko Department Store—left them where indicated, and started to walk up the stairs to the temple with Suzuki.

Halfway up the short flight, however, something made me look back. My shoes were exactly where I'd left them. Suzuki saw me looking at my shoes. "You don't have to worry," he said. "There is almost no crime in Japan, and stealing of shoes from temples is totally unknown."

Had I not been so suspicious and, yes, apprehensive that something was about to happen, I would have made some remark about the hold-up on the Philosophers' Pathway as well as the mysterious disappearance of my shoes from Ryoan-ji, and their even more mysterious reappearance outside my room. But yet again I held my peace and acted as if all was well.

We walked into the temple. It contained two features, the usual prayer area and a stall selling souvenirs and items of a religious nature. We sat for a while on a bench. I couldn't make out if Suzuki was meditating, praying, just relaxing, or politely letting me recover from the exertions of the day. I'd heard Japanese people described as "inscrutable" but Suzuki seemed to turn inscrutability into an art form, if not an Olympic event. Try as I might, there was no way for me to fathom what he was thinking.

By common consent, after about five minutes we rose from the bench and returned to our shoes, which were exactly as we'd left them. I put my shoes on, and we walked together to the next place of interest to us. This was the Treasure Hall. We could enter it. It was well lit and it contained some superb art. The catch here was that to the left of the really important piece, a statue of the Buddha, there was a discrete card with the word "replica" on it.

Now we walked down a long lane with vendor's stalls on the one side and housing for the priests on the other side to reach the third area of the temple complex. I'm sure that I've already told you far more than you ever wanted to know about the Horyu-ji complex. Let me just say that the third area was just as disappointing as the first two had been, if not more so.

By now, competing emotions raced through my brain. On the one hand, I was just plain angry. It was clear that Inspector Watanabe had carefully orchestrated the visit. He and Suzuki had forced me to travel by train and bus to a temple complex that was, to put it mildly, a bitter disappointment in so many ways. They had compelled me to walk several miles, partly through an all-but-deserted quarter of Nara, partly through an equally deserted temple complex. Even the green tea ice cream seemed to be part of this charade.

On the other hand, I was eager to discover why "the temples are really important." One thing was certain: There had to be a reason why Inspector Watanabe had brought me to Nara and to this temple complex in particular. Strange things had been happening to me, and I desperately needed to find out why. So, surely the reason that Seiji Watanabe had sent me here was for me to discover the explanation of the weird events of the past few days. But nothing had happened in Nara to enlighten me. On the contrary, Mr. Suzuki had treated the whole expedition as pure tourism. The more eager I became for him to explain the strange events in my life, the more eager he became to explain why "the temples are really important" in terms of their historical, religious, cultural and architectural significance. He was extremely knowledgeable and explained everything clearly in nearly perfect English. Although I thought I could sense something underlying his façade, I simply couldn't uncover it.

Finally, we exited from the complex and walked back to the bus terminus, Mr. Suzuki once again refusing to countenance a taxi. We took a slightly different route through the neighborhood, which still proved to be deserted. When we finally reached the bus stop, I was sweating, partly from exertion and partly from fear—the whole situation was becoming frightening.

Suzuki had refused to consider taking a taxi from the Horyu-ji complex to the bus stop, and now he refused again even to consider taking a taxi from where we were back to the city center. During the second bus ride, I realized that from the economic viewpoint he was right. The lunch-hour traffic through the narrow streets of the Nara business district was almost at a standstill, and a taxi ride would indeed have been most expensive. But there seemed to be a reason beyond pure cost as to why Suzuki had insisted on the bus. I didn't argue with him because I was hoping that there would be someone else on the bus who would divulge the secret of my adventures. However, the bus eventually arrived at Nara Station and I alighted, still unenlightened.

Suzuki suggested that we eat at a restaurant in the station building. I'd agreed to his every suggestion up to now and saw no reason to change my policy, so I assented. We were lucky to get the last table in what seemed to me to be a workingman's café. He asked if he could suggest a dish I probably hadn't tried, a fish dish local to Nara. I agreed, and suggested that we drink Kirin lager with our fish.

First the beer came, and Mr. Suzuki explained to me that, in Japan, you never pour a drink for yourself. This seemed a friendly custom, and I told him so. Each of us then duly filled the other's glass, and I determined to ensure that his glass would remain full during the meal.

Then the food arrived. I was given a large bowl of dry rice topped with a small piece of fish over which had been poured a thimbleful of orange sauce. The fish dish was so disappointing in every way that the thought crossed my mind that maybe, just maybe, Suzuki was doing everything that he could to annoy me. Of course, there seemed no reason for him—or anyone else—to do that, but I decided to test this theory. If it seemed to hold, the next step would be to try to work out why he was doing this, and what Inspector Watanabe had to do with it.

After lunch I proposed taking the train back to Kyoto, but Mr. Suzuki appeared truly horrified at the very idea. We couldn't possibly go back, he insisted, without first walking to Nara Park to see the temples there. Tired as I was, I decided to play along. After all, he'd said, "walking" to Nara Park, not taking a taxi, or even catching a bus. It was clear that he was still up to his tricks. We left the restaurant, crossed the road and entered a pedestrian mall at least two miles long.

Soon after we entered the mall we saw a line of people standing outside a restaurant, an all-you-can-eat sushi restaurant. Clearly, a meal there would have been far preferable to the awful food I'd just eaten. Suzuki even told me all about the sushi restaurant—the signs were in Japanese, and as a result I had no way of knowing why there was a line in the mall at that place. This information was further evidence that he was deliberately trying to annoy me.

On the next corner was a street vendor cooking some sort of doughy item on a gas grill. She put the dough on a skewer, cooked it, dipped it in a syrupy sauce and then put the skewer on a stack containing perhaps a dozen she'd already prepared. "Would you like to try a typical Japanese sweetmeat?" Suzuki asked.

"Sure!" I answered. I never turn down food.

We each took a skewer, and I eagerly bit into my dessert. After all, lunch had been a grave disappointment, and there is nothing better than a gooey dessert covered in sauce. Bad mistake. This was the most repulsive food I'd ever eaten, making the green tea ice cream seem like ambrosia. It took every ounce of self-control to prevent myself from spitting my mouthful onto the sidewalk then and there in front of the middle-aged vendor and her friends, who were saying "Good, good," and bowing enthusiastically to me. I smiled with my mouth full of this abominable confectionery, and managed to walk two blocks to a trashcan where I emptied my mouth and disposed of the rest of the culinary disaster. All this time, however, Mr. Suzuki was munching contentedly away. He didn't say a word when he saw what I did with the food he'd recommended. Again, it was as if nothing at all had happened.

Finally we reached the southern entrance to Nara Park. The park contains dozens of temples, hundreds of tame deer that will eat out of your hands, and thousands of people—Nara Park and its temples was as crowded as the Horyu-ji complex had been deserted earlier that day. The temperature had started to rise, and it was becoming unpleasantly humid, but Suzuki apparently deliberately took me first to a temple on the northern edge of the mammoth park, thereby maximizing my discomfort by making me walk the entire length of the park, while deliberating avoiding the many paths that were fringed with shade trees on both sides. Bus lines run through the park, and I also saw many taxis on the roads between the temples. Consequently there was absolutely no reason for him to insist that I walk all the way unshaded from the sun, other than to discomfort me further.

We paid to enter the temple, but were then not allowed to go in because a Shinto wedding was in progress. Despite the heat and my rising anger, I found this most interesting. Four chairs were set out in the main entrance to the temple, two by two, with low tables in front of each chair. The bride and groom occupied the front two chairs; two older individuals, who I guessed were the parents of the bride or the groom, sat behind them. The two women wore the most elaborate kimonos I'd seen up to now; the two men were in European formal dress, the type of clothes worn by men at society weddings in Britain. Two young priests, a man and a woman, conducted the ceremony. After about five minutes, an older priest arrived. He gave a short sermon, then left. The younger priests served ceremonial food and drink to the four individuals. I was about to see what was given to them when Mr. Suzuki suggested that we visit a museum at the back of the temple area. Much as I would have liked to watch the rest of the ceremony, I went with him. I was certain that he took me to the museum at that time to annoy me further, and this feeling was reinforced when we found that the museum was closed. More precisely, *I* found that the museum was closed—I was absolutely convinced that Suzuki knew that fact before he dragged me away from the wedding ceremony that he could see I found fascinating.

We returned to the front of the temple to find the wedding over, and the wedding party of fifteen posing for photographs on chairs arranged in a circular arc below the temple area. As in America, a wedding consultant advised the photographer, but I was interested to see that a kimono consultant was also present. She spent at least five minutes adjusting the unbelievably elaborate white kimono of the bride, and a minute or two adjusting the kimonos of each of the other women. However, I was annoyed that Suzuki had first dragged me away from the wedding but now insisted that we stand in the heat to watch the kimono consultant at work. Finally, the kimono consultant nodded to the photographer who looked through the lens and began giving instructions to the subjects. As soon as the bride moved slightly, the kimono consultant rushed forward to make another micro-adjustment. While all this went on, there was no doubt in my mind as to Suzuki's game, but the questions still remained: Why was he trying to annoy me in every possible way? And was it Watanabe's idea?

Perhaps I should draw a merciful veil over the remaining sordid details of that afternoon's activities, but I think you really need to know about the rest of Suzuki's shenanigans. After we left the members of the wedding party, Suzuki dragged me around the corner to an exhibition of drums and seventeenth-century paintings that was utterly boring. A hall contained two large drums used in some ritual ceremony as well as some twenty scrolls containing paintings that even my inexperienced eye could tell were of poor quality. Why there was an exhibition at all and how anyone had the effrontery to charge ¥800 admission was beyond my comprehension. On the other hand, I'd forked over a total of about $50 in admission fees that day to visit temples that were closed, inaccessible, had impermeable screens, were too dark to see inside, or were disappointing in some other way, so paying $8 to see a truly lousy exhibition was really a bargain— at least I got to see *something*!

After an extended stop at a soft-drink vending machine, we pressed on to the far western edge of the park. This meant a lengthy walk in the hot sun and high humidity to the largest wooden building in the world, a building that contains the largest bronze statue of the Buddha. Strangely enough, I found both the temple and the statue to be really moving. The look of sheer peace and contentment on the gigantic face of the Buddha almost made the day's exertions worthwhile.

Suzuki then announced that, although there was at least another full day's worth of worthwhile temples to see, we'd seen the crème de la crème and could now return to Kyoto. I suggested a taxi or bus back to the station, but Suzuki insisted that we walk as there was something he wanted to show me. There were about forty stalls in front of the temple, and Suzuki took me to one that was selling T-shirts. He pointed out that truly pornographic T-shirts were being sold quite openly. I was too exhausted to even think about that.

Next, we walked from the park toward the station. On the left, Suzuki indicated the Nara National Museum. He explained that the museum contains exquisite Buddhist art and also archaeological finds from the area, and was well worth a visit. My control finally snapped.

"Mr. Suzuki," I said as calmly as I could, "I've no objection to your visiting the museum, but I'm far too tired to accompany you. I see the station ahead of us. I hope that you won't be insulted if I walk there and take the next train to Kyoto. I don't have the energy to walk anywhere other than straight to the nearby station." I was simply too tired to care. If the explanation of the incidents of the past few days lay in that museum, then I would have to live the rest of my life without finding anything out. Even if Suzuki had drawn a gun and ordered me to visit the museum, I would have told him to pull the trigger and put me out of my misery. And if my mild outburst had offended Suzuki, then so be it. Enough was enough.

Much to my amazement, my reply seemed to please Mr. Suzuki. He tried to keep his face as expressionless as it had been the rest of the day, but there was a definite upturn on both corners of his mouth. "I'm sorry that you're so tired," he said.

"We shall take the next train back to Kyoto." The thought struck me that he'd been trying the whole day to get a reaction of this sort out of me; now that he'd succeeded, we could both go home. If only I'd objected to the green tea ice cream, I would have been spared the rest of the torture!

The remainder of the afternoon was pretty much a blur. Having spent the better part of a day trying to exhaust me both physically and emotionally—and succeeding on both counts—Suzuki now solicitously insisted that I sit on a bench in the station while he bought the tickets for our return trip. He took my arm as we walked to the platform. The train soon arrived, and we climbed aboard. I fell asleep before the train left the station, and Suzuki had difficulty in waking me when the train arrived at Kyoto station. He then walked me to the taxi rank, made sure that my taxi driver knew my hotel, thanked me somewhat stiffly for a very pleasant day and walked off. I was too tired to say anything.

When I got back to my hotel room, the red light on the phone was flashing to indicate that there was a message for me. I called the operator to be told that, while I was traipsing from temple to temple in Nara in the company of Mr. Suzuki, my darling Nikki had called me, but had not left a message. I checked my BlackBerry. Nikki had tried to reach me while Suzuki and I were in Nara, but apparently there had been no connectivity at the time—perhaps we had been inside one of the many temples when she had called me.

Under normal circumstances I would have been furious at Suzuki—and Inspector Watanabe—for everything that had happened to me that day, and especially because their machinations had prevented me from talking to Nikki. But I was simply too tired to care. I hung up my phone and fell into a dreamless sleep of exhaustion.

CHAPTER TEN

The telephone woke me. A familiar sound, a whisper that had haunted me since that afternoon on the Philosophers' Pathway, the voice that had sounded like a Japanese man trying to speak with an American accent said, "Ginkaku-ji, the Silver Pavilion Temple, at 11 a.m." and hung up.

I looked at the clock that formed part of the radio built into the bedside table. It was just after four a.m., and further sleep was impossible. One reason was that I'd slept for more than ten hours. A second reason was that I hadn't eaten a thing since, at the suggestion of Mr. Suzuki, I'd tried that truly nauseating confection in the Nara pedestrian mall after lunch the previous day, and I can't sleep on an empty stomach. But the real reason, of course, that I couldn't possibly go back to sleep was the thought that I had to go to the Silver Pavilion Temple at 11 a.m. that morning to meet with the man who had robbed me at gun point on the Philosophers' Pathway.

I could have ignored the instruction and stayed safely in my room. But I had to learn the explanation for all the many strange goings on, and the robber was clearly a key player in the game. Just as I had to go the Noh Theater and then to the GoGoGo Club, there was no way that I could be anywhere other than the Silver Pavilion Temple at 11 a.m. that morning.

I could have called Inspector Watanabe and told him about the phone call. But the inspector didn't believe that the robbery had even taken place. Even if he did, he wouldn't be able to accept that it was possible for a stick-up artist to arrange to meet his victim a few days later in a public place; in fact, even I was wondering about that. No, Inspector Watanabe would have to be kept out of it. At best he would do nothing, at worst he would somehow prevent me from keeping the rendezvous, and once again I'd miss an opportunity to learn more about the conspiracy.

I called room service and ordered a meal. I don't recall if I ordered a late dinner or an early breakfast—to tell the truth, I don't remember a single aspect of that meal. All I knew was that at 11 a.m. I had to meet with the armed robber, and I was extremely scared.

Although there was nothing I could do if the robber decided to shoot me, at the very least it seemed prudent to try and find out as much as possible about the Silver Pavilion Temple before going there. If I had some idea of the layout of the place, I might be able to take reasonable precautions. I consulted my guidebooks.

First, I read that this two-story temple, originally built as a retirement villa, wasn't silver at all! The

Mikado who had constructed it some five hundred years ago had intended to cover it with silver just as his grandfather had covered the Golden Pavilion Temple with gold, but he had died before this could be done. This was a useful piece of information—it would save me going round in circles looking for a silver building, all the while being unprotected from the gunman.

Next I learned that the extensive gardens were designed for moon viewing as well as the usual admiration of nature during the day. There are accordingly two gardens. One is a large traditional garden that extends from the villa up toward the hillside to the east. The other garden, directly in front of the villa, is made of sand. There are two components within the sand garden, a large cone with its top lopped off that symbolizes Mount Fuji and a large triangular lower area marked with striations that represent the effects of moonlight. Having made a mental picture of the layout of the area, I tried to come up with a strategy that would keep me alive as long as possible.

After some minutes of intense thought, I finally came up with a plan that seemed foolproof. I'd arrive at the Silver Pavilion Temple at ten, a full hour ahead of time, and scout out the entire place. The whole area would be full of schoolchildren in their uniforms, of course, and I'd stick closely to a group of children as a form of protection—no gunman would possibly hurt a Japanese schoolchild. The protective cover of the children would allow me to investigate even the far reaches of the vast traditional garden, which, the guidebooks assured me, was among the loveliest in all Japan—although the admiration of beauty was extremely low on my list of priorities. Next, I'd find a place to sit and wait for the gunman to arrive. From then on I'd have to play it by ear, but one thing was for sure: even if the Silver Pavilion Temple were only half as full of schoolchildren as the area in front of the Golden Pavilion Temple had been, the sheer numbers of schoolchildren would ensure that I'd be safe.

In order to arrive at ten, I'd need to estimate how long it would take to reach the Silver Pavilion Temple by taxi. I opened my city map of Kyoto and, much to my horror, observed that the Silver Pavilion Temple was a block or two from the start of the Philosophers' Pathway. I began to get cold shivers up my spine—the proximity of the two sites was surely more than just coincidental. Kyoto is a large city, and the armed robber could surely have arranged to meet me at any public place. Why had he selected the tourist site closest to the Philosophers' Pathway? This question was as puzzling as all the other unanswered questions.

At 9:30 a.m. I asked the doorman to get me a taxi. For much of the ride I stared intently at the buildings on both sides of the road in the hope that I'd see the bank where I'd withdrawn ¥100,000 on my way to the Philosophers' Pathway. I could only conclude that we must have taken a different route, because none of the many banks we passed looked even remotely like the one I was trying to find again. My inability to locate the bank depressed me considerably. One of the many reasons that Inspector Watanabe didn't believe that I'd been held up was that I couldn't identify the bank where I had used my Centurion Card to withdraw the money at the ATM. If I'd only been able to locate that bank again on the way to the Silver Pavilion Temple, I'd have felt considerably more confident than I was feeling at that moment. Days later it suddenly occurred to me that all I had to do was call American Express and obtain full details of where I had made the cash withdrawal using my card. But, as you will see, the problem of the missing ATM receipt soon resolved itself, in a most unexpected way.

I'd estimated the driving time accurately, because promptly at ten, the taxi crossed the canal next to the Philosophers' Pathway, and a minute later I found myself at the entrance to Ginkaku-ji, the Silver Pavilion Temple. Before exiting the taxi I looked for the protective cordon of schoolchildren on a field trip and my heart skipped a beat—there wasn't a single student to be seen. Then it hit me: This was Sunday, and children don't go to school on Sundays. In fact, they don't go to school on Saturdays either, which probably explained why the area around the Nara temple complex the previous morning had been so empty the previous day. After all, hardworking people tend to take it easy on Saturday morning. Although this explained one aspect of the extraordinary day I'd spent in Nara, it didn't help me with the real problem, namely, that I was going to be an isolated, unprotected target once I entered the area of the Silver Pavilion Temple.

Being a craven coward, my initial reaction was to tell the taxi driver to take me straight back to the Mikado Hotel via the shortest possible route. But then I realized that solving the enigma had become an obsession with me, so I paid the driver and walked slowly into the Silver Pavilion Temple area, looking all around me with the greatest caution as I entered.

My carefully laid plan was now in ruins—there was no way that I could use innocent schoolchildren as human shields. I needed Plan B and I needed it fast, because I'd less than an hour to come up with a way to protect myself during the meeting with the gunman. One idea that came to me quickly was to buy a bulletproof vest. But Japan has such strict gun-control laws that it seemed unlikely that bulletproof vests were sold in shops. And even if they were available to the public, how could I find such a shop and get back to the temple in time? And finally, there was no chance whatsoever that they would have one in my size.

No, I'd have to meet the gunman unprotected, and hope for the best.

As I'd previously realized, my first step had to be a careful examination of the lay of the land. I bought a ticket and casually attached myself to a party of four elderly Japanese visitors as they walked into the temple area. They ambled down the side of the sand garden and stopped at a small Shinto shrine in the middle of the wooden veranda at the front of the villa. In turn, each of the two women put a coin in the receptacle and clapped her hands three times to attract the attention of the deity, the same way that the heavy bell rope is tugged three times to strike the gong mounted over larger shrines. Then they put their hands together and prayed. Their husbands, however, just stood idly by, tacitly accepting their wives' piety but not participating in the prayer ritual.

I looked around and realized that if I sat on one of the wooden chairs on the veranda, I'd be able to watch everyone as they entered the area. Behind me was the pavilion itself but it was closed to the public—like so much else in Kyoto—so I didn't have to worry about my back. Best of all, the veranda was a totally public area, so I was completely safe as long as I sat there.

For the first five minutes I intensely scrutinized every individual who entered the area. With my poor vision this wasn't too easy, but there were only a few visitors, and I was able to see that most of them were either senior citizens or young children and were therefore unlikely to be the gunman who had strode confidently away from the site of the hold-up on the Philosophers' Pathway—I could still hear his footsteps in the gravel getting softer as the distance between us rapidly increased.

Finally, a young boy of about fifteen accompanied by a much older couple, probably his grandparents, came by. He searched his pockets for a coin, couldn't find one and eventually borrowed a coin from his grandfather. Then he prayed long and intensely.

I soon lost interest in observing the visitors and started studying the site as a whole. In front of me was the sand garden. A gardener was carefully making a minor repair on the far left-hand side. His skill in manipulating the white sand convinced me that he couldn't possibly be the gunman in disguise. Beyond the sand garden and to the left stretched the most beautiful traditional Japanese garden I'd ever seen. In fact, the combination of water, trees, rocks, moss, and flowers was so exquisite that, for a few minutes, I forgot the purpose of my trip to the Silver Pavilion Temple and soaked up the loveliness that extended all around me. The high hillside on my left was a natural backdrop for this haven of artful beauty that crept halfway up the hill.

The loud caw of a bird suddenly brought me back to reality. Glancing at my watch, I could see it was now half past ten. The gardens were still only sparsely populated with visitors, and I couldn't see a single male aged between twenty and forty. The fact that my back was to the pavilion gave me further reassurance. In fact, from where I was sitting I could see a sign on the closed door of the pavilion that stated firmly, "Not Open to the Public."

Then I thought for a moment. A law-abiding citizen—and the Japanese are an intensely law-abiding people—would respect that sign. But would a gunman? Would such a notice put off someone who had demonstrated his flagrant disregard for the law by sticking a gun into my back and stealing my money? After all, the Texas Book Depository wasn't open to the public, but that hadn't deterred Lee Harvey Oswald from killing President John F. Kennedy from the sixth floor of that building.

Now I was starting to get really worried. At the very least I needed to wait for the mysterious gunman in a safe location. I'd assumed, wrongly, that the whole area of the Silver Pavilion Temple would be teeming with schoolchildren, and then I'd assumed that my back was safe because visitors couldn't enter the building behind me. Cold shivers started to travel up my spine again. I had less than thirty minutes to find a safe place from which to await the arrival of the gunman, and nothing looked promising in any way. I thought about standing next to the sand garden close to the gardener who was repairing the small breach in the sand, but in the interim, he'd finished his work and moved on elsewhere. Then I had a better idea. Suppose I followed the path up the hillside to my left. From that part of the gardens I could see not only the area in which I was now sitting but also almost the entire expanse of the gardens of the Silver Pavilion Temple. In other words, from that place I could observe everything that was happening in the area surrounding the pavilion. The only downside risk was that I'd be exposed to possible danger as I walked up the hillside.

As I was weighing up the risk I heard the shot.

Had I been experienced in combat, I'd have immediately noted that the shot seemed to come from behind me. I'd have jumped off the three-foot high veranda on which I was seated and thrown myself flat on the ground, pressing my body against the front of the veranda in order to shield myself from further bullets coming from the direction of the pavilion.

However, this was the first time I'd ever been under fire, and it took me some time to realize that the initial step I had to take was to work out the spot from which the gunman had fired the shot. Even when I'd appreciated that my worst fears had been realized and that the gunman was indeed inside the temple, the idea of throwing my 425 pounds onto the ground seemed absurd. I wondered what everyone else was doing. I looked around, and was utterly flabbergasted to see that not one single person had even reacted to the bullet, let alone taken cover. At the very least I'd have expected frightened stares in my direction from the few visitors within earshot of the temple. But it was as if nothing at all had happened.

Had nothing happened? Was I becoming paranoid to the point where I heard nonexistent gunshots? Had my earlier experience with the gunman also been a hallucination? Was that why Inspector Watanabe hadn't believed me—had my story seemed unreal to him because the hold-up had taken place in my mind?

Then I pulled myself together. Two thoughts were coming to the forefront of my brain. First, the bullet didn't seem to have hit me. I felt no pain, all my limbs seemed to be in full working order, and there was no blood on me anywhere that I could see. Second, I had to get out of there as fast as I could. It was one thing to have a gun stuck in my back, but dodging bullets was quite another. I leaped out of my chair as fast as I could, jumped to the ground and made for the exit as fast as my legs would take me. Fortunately, there was a line of three taxis waiting, and I was soon on my way back to the hotel.

What frightened me the most wasn't the idea of having being fired at, but the way that no one else had reacted to the gunshot. Then I remembered that I'd clearly heard the shot. However, I couldn't report the attempted murder to the police for the same reason that I couldn't tell Inspector Watanabe about the gunman's telephone call. In the minds of the police, the gunman didn't exist.

At the same time, I had to protect myself against future murderous assaults from members of the conspiracy. An idea came to me: Perhaps I should contact Inspector Watanabe and tell him what had happened, no matter what the consequences might be. After all, the police would surely be able to find the bullet, and that would prove the existence of the gunman. Once Inspector Watanabe had irrefutable proof that someone was firing bullets at me, his whole attitude would surely change.

While I was trying to decide what to do next, my taxi drew up at the Mikado Hotel. The elaborately uniformed doorman opened the door, and I entered the air-conditioned comfort of the lobby. As I was walking past the reception desk to the elevators, one of the receptionists called out my name. I turned to her.

"Mr. Thompson, your wife just called and said that she would call again later."

This was the last straw. Not only had the gunman tried to kill me, but his summons to the Silver Pavilion Temple had prevented me yet again from talking to Nikki and finding out when she was coming back to Kyoto. I thanked the clerk and resumed my walk toward the elevator bank. There was an elevator waiting, and I rode up to the fifteenth floor, as usual.

I opened my door using the electronic key and immediately noticed a large white envelope lying on the table near the window. The envelope was unsealed. I reached inside and drew out dollar bank notes and yen bank notes. I counted the money. It was the $300 and the ¥100,000 that the gunman had stolen from me. To add insult to injury, the receipt from the ATM was also there.

Now I couldn't possibly contact Inspector Watanabe. I could just see myself phoning him and saying, "Yes, he stole the money from me on the Philosophers' Pathway, but while he was shooting at me at the Silver Pavilion Temple, his confederate returned all the money, every last penny. And they also returned the ATM receipt. As a result, now I have proof that I actually had the ¥100,000 that he stole from me and then returned to me."

"Really?" the inspector would have said, with his eyebrows rising to the level of the top of his head. "They returned the receipt as well, did they? Have you ever heard of a gunman returning all the money he stole, let alone returning the money together with proof to convince me that the money actually existed?"

No, there was no way I could report any of the day's incidents to Inspector Watanabe. At best he would humiliate me again, at worst I'd face charges of filing a false police report. I suddenly appreciated what I was up against: a devilishly cunning enemy. Incontrovertibly there was some sort of evil conspiracy at work in Kyoto. I started shivering from sheer terror.

My instinctive reaction was to rush to Kansai International Airport and take the first flight home from Osaka to New York. But then my darling Nikki would come to the hotel and find me gone. And, if she were on her own in Kyoto, she might also become a victim of the conspiracy. I had no idea what to do—I was helpless with fear.

CHAPTER ELEVEN

The next morning another 4 a.m. telephone call woke me. Once again it was the armed robber/attempted assassin. Once again trying to sound like an American and once again failing abysmally, the voice said, "I call again at ten," and hung up.

And once again, further sleep was impossible. One of our greatest fears is fear of the unknown, and on this occasion I had it badly. At least the previous morning I knew that I was going to meet the gunman at the Silver Pavilion Temple. This time I'd no idea what was going to happen. The only positive aspect of this latest call that I could see was that it was now Monday, admittedly very early indeed on Monday morning, but nevertheless it was now Monday. That meant that all the sites of historic interest would once more be teeming with schoolchildren, affording me some additional protection against being killed in a public place. On the other hand, the meeting later that day—if there was to be a meeting—might conceivably be in a private home or even on a farm forty miles out of town. Consequently I had no guarantee that any

163

schoolchildren would be in the vicinity of the rendezvous. Nevertheless, I somehow felt hopeful that this time more people would be around than were present on the previous day at the Silver Pavilion Temple.

Somehow or other I had to pass the six hours between the wake-up call and the promised 10 a.m. communication. I turned on the TV. Surfing the channels, I found a Japanese movie and tried to work out what the actors were saying. This exercise kept my mind occupied and, to a certain extent, helped to calm me down.

After the movie ended, I showered, shaved, dressed and went down to Le Lac des Cygnes restaurant for the breakfast buffet. I took with me my copy of the *Japan Daily Bulletin*, the excellent English language newspaper that the hotel each morning thoughtfully placed outside the door of every room occupied by a foreign guest. I read the paper as I ate my meal, and this, too, helped keep my mind off what was to come. When I'd read everything of interest to me, I poured a third cup of coffee, ate a third corn danish and proceeded to solve the crossword puzzle.

After this lengthy breakfast, I decided to walk around the block. I'm not sure why I did this, but the change of routine also helped to reduce my anxiety. As I was about to re-enter the hotel I suddenly realized the purpose of the repeated 4 a.m. calls. The gunman surely knew that I was suffering from travel fatigue, like all travelers who have just endured a long-distance flight, and that as a result my sleep patterns were already disrupted. By calling me at 4 a.m. with a message that was certain to alarm me, the gunman would ensure that I'd be further sleep-deprived, thereby slowing my mental processes when I needed them the most, that is, when I met with him. Having worked this out, I triumphantly returned to my room, set the alarm on my BlackBerry for 9:50 a.m., lay down on the bed and actually managed to sleep for nearly three hours.

The alarm went off, and the telephone rang almost simultaneously. Either the gunman had called a few minutes early or I had set the alarm incorrectly. Deprived of the ten minutes I'd given myself to wake up properly, I had to battle to clear my brain. The telephone had rung at least three times as I attempted to force myself into a state of consciousness, but finally I picked up the receiver.

The voice said, "Big Bell Temple. Right now." And he hung up.

The name Big Bell Temple certainly didn't a ring a bell with me. I looked in the index of each of my guidebooks in turn. Nothing. Then I vaguely recalled reading somewhere that one of the temples in Kyoto had an enormous bell, and I called down to the concierge's desk. For the first time since I'd arrived at the hotel five days before, a man was on duty. He immediately told me that the Chionin Temple had the largest bell in all Japan and asked if he could arrange for a guide to show me round the temple complex that afternoon.

On the one hand, the idea of a guide was very attractive to me. It meant that I wouldn't be alone at the temple. I suddenly realized that if only I'd thought of taking someone along with me the previous day to the Silver Pavilion Temple, the gunman might not have shot at me. I was about to ask the concierge to arrange for a guide when I remembered that, in his latest telephone call just a few minutes before, the gunman had said, "Right now." Clearly there was no time to organize a guide. Instead, I thanked the concierge, grabbed my guidebooks and hurried out. Fortunately there was a taxi waiting outside the Mikado Hotel, and fifteen minutes later I arrived at the Chionin Temple.

In front of me was an enormous gateway. It must have been at least twenty-five yards high, if not higher. A row of successive purple, white, red, yellow and green flags decorated an upper layer of the gateway, giving it a festive appearance. I assumed that the five bright colors had some significance in the Buddhist religion. I passed through the gigantic gateway, and in front of me was a long flight of broad stone stairs. For someone of my bulk, stairs are not the preferred way to travel from point A to point B, and a massive flight that has been hacked out of the rocks centuries ago is even less desirable. The thought came to me that the gunman was well aware of the effect of serious physical exertion on someone of my girth, and was perhaps lying in wait for me near the top of the stairs, ready to pounce on me in my weakened state. To climb or not to climb, that was the question.

After weighing the pros and the cons, my unstoppable drive to uncover what was happening to me turned out to be stronger than my all-encompassing fear of what might occur as I clambered up the stairs. I rested every few steps, not just to get my breath back, but also to look around for the gunman. The area wasn't totally deserted, but I'd have felt a lot happier had there been more visitors in the vicinity.

I finally reached the top, unscathed, and looked around for the gunman. Instead I found an enormous courtyard, with buses and taxis driving in and out via a road to the side. I cursed my taxi driver for not having driven right up to the temple but instead leaving me to climb the massive staircase. Not only was I starting my search of the temple grounds in a state of near exhaustion, but also the fear I'd experienced while ascending the staircase had tired me still further. This was a singularly inauspicious beginning to an excursion that I'd hoped might lead to my uncovering at least part of the conspiracy.

Tired as I was, I looked carefully all about me. To my left was a huge Buddhist temple. In front of me were dozens of tour buses. Hundreds of schoolboys poured out of their doors, and teachers organized them into what at first sight looked like military formations in front of the temple. The hordes of students were excellent news for Oliver Thompson, lily-livered coward extraordinaire.

I decided to visit the temple first, because the caller had said "Big Bell Temple." If that didn't work, I'd next proceed to the large bell itself. A second reason for choosing the temple was that the area was filled with people—as far as I was concerned, there was security in numbers. I walked slowly toward the temple. I hadn't yet recovered from my physical exertions, and I was still breathing heavily.

In front of the temple was a sign over a large metal container telling visitors to take a plastic bag from the container and place their shoes in it and take the bag with them into the temple. What a great idea. Someone had come up with a sure-fire way to prevent shoes from being stolen. I didn't realize until much later that this wasn't a precaution against theft, but rather the only way to make certain that every worshipper in a large crowd could locate their own shoes when they left the temple.

Plastic bag in hand, I walked up the six stairs on the temple veranda and from there into the temple itself. The interior was vast. The dimly lit space was partitioned lengthwise into two halves. The half nearest me consisted of a wooden floor on which worshippers could sit; the other half of the huge hall was reserved for the monks. On the far side of the central partition were hundreds of low stools arranged in rows, and beyond them against the far wall was an elaborate altar. Although I'd never visited a Buddhist place of worship before coming to Kyoto, there was no doubt in my mind that I was now inside a major temple.

The area for worshippers was deserted—no gunman lurked. I took a step or two to my rear, then leaned against the back wall and waited. A few seconds later, six or seven elderly women wearing rather drab clothing walked in and arranged themselves in a group on the floor right in front of the doorway near me. They sat cross-legged, a position that was physically out of the question for me. Instead, I just stood by the door, waiting for someone who might be the armed robber to arrive. Suddenly hordes of schoolboys poured into the hall through three or four doorways. I looked back through the entrance next to me. Monks directed the schoolboys as they approached the temple. They herded each formation up the stairs and through one of the doorways. Then the monks instructed the boys in that group to sit in a line that stretched from the front of the temple to the back wall against which I leaned. The gray-suited male teachers stood next to their students. After a relatively short while, the entire hall was full.

While the side of the temple that was open to the public was filling up, I suddenly heard a rhythmic drum beat emanating from the far right-hand side of the monks' portion of the hall. Then what seemed to be an unending procession of monks started to file in from the far end of the building. They arranged themselves in such a way that each stood next to a stool. I noticed at least five or six different types of robes and hats, usually in bright colors. A group of fifty or sixty monks appeared first, all wearing the same set of robes and headgear, and then a group in a different style of robes and headgear came next in the procession. In retrospect, there must have been some 250 monks, but at the time there seemed to be many more.

The last person to enter was an older man in an orange robe; two younger men wearing golden robes accompanied him. I assumed that the older man was the abbot of the temple. He sat on a large couch placed next to the partition facing the altar, and the men in gold stood on either side of him. All the other monks sat down. By this time, the floor on my side of the partition was packed solid with schoolboys, and the pressure of the crowd forced the small group of elderly women outside. Other than the schoolmasters, there was still no sign of anyone who could possibly be the gunman.

The drumbeat continued, and a male voice started a somewhat monotonous chant. The two men in gold approached the altar. From where I stood I couldn't see what they were doing. After a minute they walked back to the abbot and each presented a lacquered box to him. Now the pressure of the schoolboys on the floor was so great that I found myself being forced outside, too. I walked through the doorway and saw the elderly women sitting cross-legged on the veranda outside the door and worshipping from there.

I immediately realized that the crush of students precluded any sort of rendezvous with the gunman inside the temple, at least until the service was over. So I walked down the stairs, put on my shoes and tried to find the big bell. Perhaps I'd meet the gunman there.

To the left of the temple another staircase stretched upwards, much narrower than the first, but at least twice as long and considerably steeper. There was a massive cast iron railing in the middle of the staircase. The left-hand side was packed solid with schoolboys; the right-hand side was empty. My heart sank—it didn't seem that I was physically capable of climbing those steps. But there was no other way to get to the big bell and, hopefully, the gunman. With the gravest of misgivings, I started to climb. On my left, the hordes of schoolboys stared at me. Some of them giggled as I passed. More of them giggled every time I paused to catch my breath and carefully look round for the gunman. Everyone on the staircase seemed to be a uniformed schoolboy or a teacher escorting a large contingent. As before, there was no possibility that the gunman was near me.

Eventually I reached the top. I had difficulty in breathing and my heart was hammering in my chest. I closed my eyes and rested for a few moments, hoping that the effects of the climb would soon pass.

I opened my eyes again and looked around. In front of me I saw many hundreds of schoolboys lining up to enter another temple situated in front of a pool of water—there was no bell to be seen anywhere on the level at which I now stood. I cursed again. This time I cursed myself for being so stupid as to assume that a lengthy line of schoolboys on a staircase meant that the big bell was to be found at the top of those stairs. Instead, I should have asked someone for directions. Then I realized that, unless I'd found the gunman standing at the big bell, in any event I would have had to clamber up to the temple by the pool; there was no alternative to my searching the entire area until I found the gunman.

I noticed a schoolteacher leading a group of boys. I asked him where the big bell was located. Fortunately he spoke English and gave me clear directions. He told me to go all the way back down the stairs, turn left, walk for about one hundred yards, then take the left fork. I thanked him, and then proceeded to follow his instructions, all the while looking around for the person who had telephoned and told me to come to the Chionin Temple. Again there was no one around who could possibly fit the bill. All I could see were schoolboys in their navy blue uniforms and their schoolmasters in medium-gray suits, a sort of uniform for teachers.

Walking down the lengthy staircase was easier than climbing up, but not by much. The stone steps were too high and too deep for me to walk down comfortably. I've no idea whether this was a deliberate design decision on the part of some long-dead abbot to ensure that the monks would stay alert, or whether the person who had built the stairway many centuries ago had no idea how to design stairs that were easy to walk down. But whatever the reason, I was extremely unhappy when I reached the bottom.

Following the directions that the teacher had given me, I turned to my left. After about a hundred yards, the path forked. There stood a monk in black robes and a black headdress. Just to be sure I asked him which path led to the big bell. He indicated the left fork, exactly as the schoolteacher had said. One hundred yards more and I reached the bell. It was mounted in a wooden building situated within a small thicket of trees; the building had no walls. Suspended from dozens of thick ropes fastened to the roof was a massive polished wooden beam that could be used to strike the gigantic brass bell. The beam didn't seem to be fastened down, and I wondered why playful schoolboys didn't go up and strike the bell. Then I read in my guidebook that 17 monks are needed to ring the bell. Bearing in mind the mass of the wooden beam, I was certainly prepared to believe that.

My fascination with the scale of the bell and the beam temporarily caused me to forget my extreme tiredness, as well as the real reason for my visit to the Chionin Temple. However, I soon returned to reality. Once more I looked intensely around me, but the only people I could see were one or two elderly women and a few schoolboys. Then, in the background, I noticed the monk in black who had confirmed the directions of the schoolteacher. No one else was in the vicinity.

I started to walk back toward the temple. I noticed a sign in front indicating that the way to the treasury was to the right. I had no idea what might be displayed there, but the only part of the complex that I'd not yet investigated was the treasury. I took my shoes off again, climbed the stairs to the veranda that surrounded the temple, and followed the sign in the hope that the gunman might be waiting for me in the treasury. My path led me around the large temple and behind it. Here I encountered a bridge linking the temple proper with the assembly hall situated to the rear of the temple. This bridge was a so-called nightingale floor. The nails and the boards are arranged in such a way that the floor squeaks loudly if anyone walks on it, thereby warning the monks of the presence of an intruder of any kind. I utilized the built-in alarm capability of the floor to determine if the gunman was following me. The total silence behind me was proof that I was alone.

Beyond the nightingale floor was the treasury. There was a sign advertising the Seven Treasures of Chionin, but I didn't bother to read the list. I was willing to pay $5 to enter the Treasury to try to meet the gunman, and there was no need to convince me that this would be money well spent. I paid the cashier and entered the treasury. The route took me past some pleasant painted screens, but nothing particularly special. Then I reached a large wooden board decorated with the Seven Treasures of Chionin. Each was illustrated and labeled. I suddenly grew suspicious and asked a guard standing nearby. His English was minimal but it turned out that my skepticism was fully justified. Visitors don't get to see the Seven Treasures, only the board depicting the Seven Treasures—the rest of the area is off limits! Through a gap between screens I caught a glimpse of monks and their guests eating lunch in one of the rooms. But nowhere could I find the person who had called me twice that morning in order to tell me to come to the "Big Bell Temple."

Utterly frustrated by the whole exercise, and unbelievably tired by the stair climbing I'd endured in my endeavors to meet the gunman, I retraced my steps, re-entered the courtyard and found a taxi waiting. I asked the driver to take me to a nice restaurant for lunch. He drove me to a small restaurant just outside the temple complex that served kaiseki cuisine. The superb food revived me somewhat, but I was suffering from lack of sleep, physical exhaustion and sheer frustration. For two days in a row I'd tried to meet the mysterious gunman. On the previous day he'd shot at me, but today he'd studiously avoided me. I still had no inspiration whatsoever as to what his motives might be. I was angry, baffled, defeated, perplexed, bewildered and confused. And I had no idea what to do next.

I sat at the table, utterly dejected. The only feasible alternative that I could see was to take the next plane back to New York. But what would happen to Nikki when she returned to Kyoto? I was starting to sink into a deep depression when I suddenly understood one part of what was happening to me.

The reason that I hadn't seen the gunman either at the Big Bell Temple or at the Silver Pavilion Temple was that the gunman didn't want me to see him. That was also why I didn't see him at the Noh Theater or the GoGoGo Club. In fact, I was suddenly totally sure that, no matter how long I'd stayed at the GoGoGo Club that evening, he wouldn't have appeared.

Of course, this didn't explain why he'd arranged for me to visit all these places. Perhaps he was some sort of control freak who got his jollies from ordering me to go to certain sites and then seeing me obey his commands. But whatever the reason, I firmly resolved that I would no longer follow the instructions of the gunman. Obeying his orders was a no-win situation for me.

I felt a new life force flowing through my body. Having paid my bill, I asked the restaurant to get me a taxi. I wanted to get back to the hotel as quickly as possible to plan my next move. Even though the taxi driver found an almost congestion-free route back to the Mikado Hotel, it still wasn't fast enough for me in my newly found optimistic mood. When the taxi arrived, I raced to my room as fast as I could and opened the door.

Lying on the floor was another clipping from *This Week in Kyoto*. This time it was a full-page advertisement for the Kyoto Craft Emporium, a six-story shop that apparently stocked everything the tourist might want to purchase as a souvenir. Specialties included kimonos, fans, armor, samurai swords, damascene jewelry, wood-block prints and ceramics. I quickly made up my mind that, wherever I went that afternoon, the one place that I would *not* visit was the Kyoto Craft Emporium because the one place where the gunman definitely would *not* show himself to me was the Kyoto Craft Emporium.

I decided that the best way to tell the gunman that I was up to his tricks was to go shopping at a totally different place. I decided that the Ikeburuko Department Store, where I'd bought my two pairs of shoes, would be the place to purchase a kimono for Nikki. When I arrived there and was directed to the kimono department, I suddenly encountered a snag. There were plenty of low-priced, ready-made kimonos, but they looked cheap, too. On the other hand, it wasn't possible to buy a ready-made $5,000 kimono. The department for best-quality kimonos sold what I can only describe as kimono kits, that is, the material for the kimono itself and for the other components of the complete outfit, including the obi or sash. The price included the services of a tailor who would then make the various pieces of the ensemble to fit the wearer exactly. But in the absence of Nikki, there was no way I could buy a really exquisite kimono, and I doubt if she would have been pleased to have a kimono kit waiting for her in our hotel room. I regretfully left the department store, mentally resolving to come back with Nikki in order for her to select a superb kimono as a memento of our trip.

Back in the hotel, I took great pleasure in the way that I'd finally realized the gunman's strategy, and how I'd stood up to him and ignored his orders. I stood up and walked to the full-length mirror mounted on the outside of the wardrobe. I looked into my eyes and asked, "Oliver, are you crazy?"

The answer came back loudly, clearly and quickly. It was a loud and firm, "No!"

It was time to fight back.

CHAPTER TWELVE

I called down to the concierge. "I need a private investigator who is discrete, efficient, speaks English fluently and can see me at short notice. Can you recommend someone?"

The concierge on duty replied at once, "We usually recommend a former detective in the San Francisco Police Department to our English-speaking guests. He emigrated to Japan some eight years ago and opened an office here in Kyoto as a private investigator. His office may already be closed for the day, but I have his home telephone number. Would you like me to try to set up something for tomorrow morning?"

"Yes, I'd like that very much. Please contact him and call me back."

Ten minutes later the concierge was on the line again. "I've set up an appointment for tomorrow morning at nine. The name of the company is Golden Gate Services. Their offices are in a building two blocks from here." He gave me directions and the exact address.

Then I phoned American Express Asia headquarters in Singapore, and was given the name and address of their affiliated bank in Kyoto. I took a taxi to that bank, showed the manager my passport and Centurion Card, and left the bank with $5,000 in U.S. dollar bills in my pocket.

That night I slept well, knowing that my affairs were soon going to be in safe hands. At 8:50 a.m. the next morning I walked the two blocks to the office building that housed the private investigator. The directory in the lobby was almost all in Japanese, but there was an English sign stating, "Golden Gate Services 7th Floor." With a feeling of complete confidence that my nightmare would soon be over, I rode up in the elevator.

A secretary ushered me into the somewhat Spartan office of a man who looked very familiar. "I'm Yoshio Goto—call me Yosh."

As we shook hands I tried to work out where I'd seen Yosh before.

Yosh smiled and said, "I've seen that puzzled look many, many times over the years. The clue is: *Goldfinger.*"

And I immediately worked it out. Yoshio Goto, with large closely-shaven head, large black moustache and huge muscular body, was virtually the split image of the villain Oddjob in the James Bond movie Yosh had mentioned. We both laughed politely as Yosh waved me to the chair on the other side of his desk.

"And how can I help you?" Yosh asked.

"I arrived in Kyoto six days ago. Since then a number of unpleasant things have happened to me. Some are relatively unimportant. For example, my shoes were stolen at a temple and then returned to my hotel room. Others are more serious. I've been held up at gun point and I've been shot at."

Yosh's face clouded. "You've come to the wrong place. You want the police."

"I've been to them. They say that there's no evidence that the hold-up took place. In fact, even *I* am starting to doubt that it took place.

Yosh seemed even less willing than before to take my case. I took out the wad of U.S. banknotes I had acquired the previous day. "I'll give you $5,000 as a non-refundable deposit. Hear me out, do some preliminary investigating. If by the end of the day you don't want to take my case, then fine. You may keep all of the unspent money."

Yosh seemed even more reluctant than before, if that was at all possible. There was a long pause. Then he said, "I'll get my secretary to type up a contract to that effect."

He left the room for a few minutes, returning with two copies of a seven-line paragraph. We both signed the two copies, he gave me one copy and put the cash I had given him in a drawer.

"Okay," said Yosh, "Fire away."

I started by telling Yosh what had happened at the Philosophers' Pathway. He listened in silence until I told him that I couldn't explain to Inspector Watanabe how the gunman had known that I keep my wallet in my right hip pocket and that I also couldn't provide proof that I'd changed the $1,000 into yen because the thief had taken the ATM receipt.

"In other words," Yosh said, "There was no proof that the hold-up took place, but there was also no proof that it didn't take place. Watanabe is a good cop, and I think I understand why he reacted the way he did. Unless there was some scrap of evidence about the hold-up, there would be no point in even opening a file. Furthermore, if there really was no hold-up, as he seemed to believe, an investigation could lead to an unpleasant international incident, which nobody wants.

"Don't get me wrong," he quickly added, "I'm not saying the hold-up didn't happen."

He paused for just a second or two and then asked, "What happened next?"

"Two days ago at about 4 a.m., the phone rang in my hotel room. The same voice as before whispered that I had to be at Ginkaku-ji, the Silver Pavilion Temple, at 11 a.m. He then hung up."

"And did you go?"

"Of course!"

"Why of course? He might have tried to kill you."

"Funny you should say that, that's exactly what happened. I was sitting on the veranda in front of the Silver Pavilion Temple at 10:30 a.m. when I heard a gunshot from behind me."

"From inside the pavilion?"

"Yes. At least I think I heard a gunshot. There weren't many people in the vicinity, perhaps because it was relatively early on Sunday morning, and no one acted as if they had heard a gunshot. Also, I heard the shot, but I didn't hear a bullet."

"Just a moment. Are you sure about those times? You said that the gunshot was at half past ten, but your appointment with the gunman wasn't until eleven."

"I went an hour earlier than specified in order to spy out the land, and the gunman probably arrived early, too."

"Why do you think he shot at you?"

"I've absolutely no idea. It makes no more sense than what happened next."

"Which was what?"

"I rushed out of the garden and into a waiting taxi. When I got back to my hotel room, there was a large white envelope on the table. It contained the dollars and the yen that had been stolen from me at gun point, as well as the ATM receipt."

"You found *what*?" Yosh almost shouted.

I repeated what I had said.

"But that makes absolutely no sense. Why return the money? Why return the receipt? And why shoot at you if his confederate had returned your money? You realize that I can make no sense of what happened yesterday morning."

"I can't either. That's why I'm here."

There was silence for a short while. Then Yosh spoke. "Tell me about the next incident."

"Inspector Watanabe sent me a note suggesting that I visit Nara and enclosed a train ticket."

"He did *what*?"

I had the feeling that Yosh would have been much more comfortable if I'd stated that the note and ticket had come from three little green men from Mars. He clearly didn't believe me, and I think he was about to return my $5,000 and bring the interview to a rapid end. I thought quickly.

"I have his note with me." I reached into the pocket of my blazer and handed it to him.

My production of hard evidence changed Yosh's whole demeanor. I got the impression that, for the first time, he started to believe that maybe, just maybe, one or two of the things I had said might perhaps be partially true.

I then told Yosh about my experiences in Nara. From his demeanor it was clear that I finally had his undivided attention. I began by telling him about the man who sat next to me on the train."

"Was the train full?"

"Not at all, it was half past eight on Saturday morning. There were no other passengers in the carriage."

"The fact that his reserved seat was the aisle seat next to your window seat pretty much proves that Watanabe arranged for him to sit next to you."

"I'm certain of that."

"You say he introduced himself as Suzuki. After he introduced himself, did he give you his card or perhaps show you some other form of identification?"

"No. Why should he?"

"Because Suzuki is the most common Japanese last name. When he told you that his name was Suzuki, it was like an American telling you that his name was Smith. Did Suzuki ever mention his first name?"

"No. We never got on first-name terms."

"Okay. Please continue."

"You saw that Inspector Watanabe's note mentioned the temples of Nara. Once Suzuki told me that the purpose of his visit was to visit temples, I asked him if he would take me along with him. Bad mistake."

"Why?"

"Because the whole trip seemed to be an exercise in trying to get me to lose my temper."

I listed the many stratagems that Suzuki had utilized to anger me.

"But why would anyone want to do that?" Yosh asked. "I assume that he was carrying out Watanabe's orders. But why Watanabe would instruct Suzuki to do that is entirely beyond me. This makes about as much as sense as everything else in this case, that is, it makes absolutely no sense at all!" Yosh smiled grimly. He paused for a moment, and then asked, "And what else happened to you in the six days you've been in Kyoto?"

"Well, on the first morning the cashier turned out to have the wrong gender and gave me the wrong change."

Yosh didn't bat an eyelid at my strange pronouncement—the letter from Inspector Watanabe had altered everything for the former policeman. He waited for me to explain in detail, which I did.

"Again I'm baffled. This may or may not have anything to do with the big-ticket items, the hold-up and the shooting. Has anything else happened?"

I told Yosh about the shoes that disappeared and mysteriously reappeared. I even mentioned the abortive trips to the Kyoto Noh Theater and the GoGoGo Club, as well as the visit to the Big Bell Temple the previous day and the page advertising the Kyoto Craft Emporium that someone had pushed under my door that I'd ignored. When I'd finished, there was silence again, but this time it was a comfortable silence.

"Mr. Thompson," Yosh said, "I pride myself that I'm an honest man. And I'm going to speak openly. I've no doubt that you believe every word that you've said. You, too, are an honest man, and it shows.

"On the other hand, I was in the San Francisco Police Department for nine years, and I've been running this business for eight years, and in all that time I've never heard anything remotely like what you've told me. We have two possibilities. The first is that you're the victim of some sort of conspiracy that's so complex that I can't even begin to understand what's happening. The second possibility is even less pleasant. Please forgive my frankness, but you've already hinted more than once at the possibility that you imagined some of the events that you've described to me this morning.

"Here's the best that I can do under the circumstances. First, I need to determine whether you're being tailed. I want you to go back to your hotel and have lunch in public there. I seem to recall that there's a coffee shop in the lobby. Try to get a table where everyone who passes through the lobby will see you sitting there. Then, take a taxi from your hotel to a popular and public tourist attraction. Have you seen Nijo Castle? From the outside it looks like that castle that you see in every samurai movie, but it's most interesting inside. Go there. I'll arrange to have one operative waiting at Nijo Castle before you arrive, and another will follow you there in a taxi. My people are very skilled, and you won't notice that they're tailing you. Don't try to find out if anyone else is following you—that's the job of my operatives. Also, my people are licensed to carry weapons, so don't worry about being shot at again by the bad guys, whoever they are. From now on you're safe.

"Second, I want to investigate every aspect of what you've told me. I'll send a team to Nara, and a second team here in Kyoto will visit all the places you mentioned and ask questions. I know you want answers quickly, but this approach will be expensive. Is that a problem?"

"Give me your bank details, and I'll phone my secretary in New York and tell her to wire you any amount you require. She's in my office from nine o'clock every morning, New York time, that is."

"Thank you, but that won't be necessary. I'll give you an itemized bill when I want the funds, and you can pay me then."

That remark was most reassuring. Few sensible businessmen will extend credit to someone they believe to be mentally unstable—the risks of non-payment are far too great.

Yosh asked me to come back to his office at about half past five. "Take a leisurely tour of the castle. I know you'll find it very interesting. Don't forget to visit the extensive gardens. I assure you that they're worth visiting at any time of the year, but they're especially lovely now, in the cherry blossom season. Stroll around. Give my operatives time to determine with certainty whether or not you're being followed. Then go to a nice bar, have a relaxing drink or two, and come back here."

CHAPTER THIRTEEN

I followed Yosh's instructions to the letter. I walked back to the Mikado Hotel and went to my room and relaxed with a book in one of the comfortable armchairs. I felt certain that, by the time I returned to his office, Yosh would have solved the mystery. At noon I collected my guidebooks and the map of Kyoto I'd bought in New York, took the elevator back to the lobby and walked straight into the coffee shop. I asked the hostess for a table from where, as I told her, I could see my friend when he came into the hotel.

She obligingly took me to a table overlooking the lobby. From there anyone who was trying to tail me could see me. I placed my guidebooks and map prominently in a pile in one corner of the table to ensure that someone who was interested in my movements would realize that I was about to go touring.

I ate a leisurely lunch, ending with a huge slice of triple chocolate cake that rivaled the products of the best patisseries in Paris. It was so delicious that I just had to have a second slice. Then I walked slowly toward the main exit to the street and asked the doorman to get me a taxi. Following Yosh's orders, I didn't look around the lobby as I passed through. I also didn't glance around to see who else was standing under the portico of the hotel waiting for a taxi.

Before getting into the taxi I asked the driver to take me to Nijo Castle. I did this in a loud and clear voice, to make it easy for anyone trying to tail me. Perhaps I was overdoing it, but I wanted to be certain that even an incompetent tail wouldn't lose me. Then, in the taxi I stared straight ahead. I made no attempt to see if I was indeed being tailed—that was the job of Yosh's troops.

When we arrived at Nijo Castle I got out of the taxi as slowly as I dared, again to make things easier for any tail. Then I bought an entrance ticket and strolled through the main gateway. Yosh was right—the castle looked as if Kurosawa had built it on the sound stage of one of his samurai movies. The gateway was built in such a way that you have to turn sharply left and then sharply right after passing through, in order to slow down any attacking force that managed to break down the gate. There were no exits from the route, so watchers would have no problem following me.

Then I thought for a moment. There weren't too many visitors to Nijo Castle at that time; few were foreigners and none had my build. Furthermore, the roadways and paths inside the castle walls were wide and there were few obstacles to an uninterrupted line of sight. In other words, if one of the bad guys had managed to follow my taxi to the castle, he couldn't possibly lose me. I decided to relax and enjoy myself.

First, I decided to visit the shogun's palace. In addition to the expected fittings—beautiful screens, exquisite wall paintings, and the like—there are hidden guard chambers and another so-called nightingale floor that squeaks if anyone walks on it, thereby alerting the guard to any sort of surprise attack. What surprised me was the almost total absence of furniture. Then I realized that everyone other than the shogun sat on the ground; small tables could be brought in for food; and bedding was stored in closets and placed on the floor at night. There was no need for furniture. The floor of the palace is laid with tatami mats, and visitors have to remove their shoes before entering. It should go without saying that on this occasion I didn't have the slightest fear that my shoes would be stolen.

After seeing everything in the palace, especially the truly exquisite artwork, I retrieved my shoes and walked through the shogun's superlative garden. The palace grounds and buildings seem to go on forever. I crossed the moat and found an extensive walled terrace. Beyond this were battlements and another moat. I continued slowly, relishing the spring gardens and forgetting, at least for a moment, that the real purpose of my visit here wasn't sightseeing but rather for Yosh's operatives to determine definitively whether or not I was being tailed.

I spent two delightful hours at Nijo Castle. Then I walked out through the gateway and hailed a taxi.

Again following Yosh's instructions, I asked the driver to take me to a nice bar. The one he chose for me was all red leather and brass rails. I found myself a booth and enjoyed a few whiskey sours. Punctually at 5:15 p.m., I left the bar and took a cab back to Golden Gate Services.

Again his secretary ushered me into Yosh's office. Yosh got up from behind his large desk and smiled broadly. "I've lots of good news. Unfortunately, I also have some bad news."

We sat down, settled ourselves, and Yosh began to speak.

"The first piece of good news is that you're definitely *not* being followed. My operatives tailed you from the time you left this building until you returned, and they're absolutely certain that you're not being followed.

"The second piece of good news is that your story checks out completely. With the greatest of respect, your build ensures that people don't forget seeing you. It was therefore extremely easy to get confirmation of just about everything you told me this morning. Let me consult the various reports I've received to make sure that I've omitted nothing."

Notwithstanding that remark, at no time during the interview did Yosh even glance down at the pile of papers in front of him, let alone read through any of the numerous reports on his desk. His memory was clearly prodigious.

"A waitress confirms seeing you at breakfast that first morning, but she couldn't recall anything to do with cashiers. Another waitress told us about your noodle meal before you walked along the Philosophers' Pathway, and the pottery shop owner confirms that you called the police from his shop. However, my people couldn't locate anyone who observed the hold-up.

"You were seen sitting on the veranda at the Silver Pavilion Temple two mornings ago, but no one recalls hearing a shot. When you rushed out in such a hurry, you made an impression on a number of employees, including two gardeners and a ticket taker.

"The monk in black near the big bell recalls your asking him which fork in the path to follow in order to visit the brass bell.

"The woman at Ryoan-ji remembers your asking about your shoes outside the temple, but recalls nothing else about your visit. We were even able to locate a chambermaid who remembered seeing your shoes standing outside the door of your room that afternoon and wondering what they were doing there.

"The team at Nara similarly confirmed every detail of your movements. It wasn't too hard for them to find both of the train conductors as well as the two bus drivers, and also the waiter who served you lunch. In addition, they spoke to the woman who sold you your admission tickets to the Shinto shrine that you couldn't visit because of the wedding, and even the seller of the pornographic T-shirts remembered seeing you. The only item for which no confirmation could be found was your visit to the exhibition of ritual drums and seventeenth century paintings, but that's hardly of critical importance.

"Here is the overall situation: Wherever we've been able to verify your story, every single detail without fail has checked out completely and accurately. Unfortunately, we've been unable to find any proof, one way or the other, regarding four key points: the wrong change; the hold-up on the Philosophers' Pathway; the shot fired at you at the Silver Pavilion Temple; and the return of your money. In other words, where we could check, we found that you were telling the truth in even the smallest particulars. For those other four items, we've found no evidence either way. Nevertheless, let me state categorically that I believe your story in every detail."

I told Yosh that I was most relieved to hear that.

Then he continued. "However, the news is not all good. First, we haven't been able to locate Mr. Suzuki. The description you gave fits too many men. The people in Nara who saw you with him were able to give a good description of you, but they hardly noticed your companion.

"Suzuki is just one part of the puzzle. What's more serious is that we've been unable to obtain any information that would help explain the things that have been happening to you."

I didn't like the way that the conversation was going.

"But you've just said that you believed everything I told you."

"Yes, I do, I really do. But the problem is that no one today learned anything above and beyond what you'd already told me this morning. And that's why I'm helpless.

"You described in some detail what happened to you this week. You're an extremely intelligent man; yet you were unable to make any sense of any of it—that's why you came to see me. I'm highly experienced in both police work and private investigation, but all the events that puzzled you made no sense to me, either."

"Are you saying that you can't help me?" I asked.

"In one sense, I think that I've been of great service to you. Now you know for a fact that you're not imagining things, and that should prove to be immensely comforting to you.

"But I can't help you to understand or explain what's been happening to you. I'd dearly love to instruct my men and women to keep searching and asking questions while you run up a huge bill. But I live my life as honestly as I can, and I can tell you that if I ordered any additional activities of that kind I'd be stealing money from you."

I thanked Yosh for his candor. Then I asked him, "What do *you* think is going on?"

"I don't have the faintest idea. This morning I suggested to you that perhaps you were the victim of a conspiracy. I don't have a clue who is behind this conspiracy or what his or her objective is. In fact, I don't have the slightest sliver of evidence that there even is such a conspiracy. But a conspiracy is the only explanation that I can propose, as unlikely as it sounds.

"Your hotel recommended me because I have an enviable record as a discrete and successful private investigator. I've had very few failures. Unfortunately, your case is one of them.

"When all the various expense accounts have been filed, I'll be able to determine the total cost of today's activities. If they exceed $5,000 I'll send you a bill for the difference. If not, I'll refund you the balance, notwithstanding our agreement that the money you paid me was a non-refundable deposit. I feel bad about all this, though not as bad as I know you feel!"

He accompanied me to the door of his office.

"I wish you the very best of luck. If anything else happens, anything at all, no matter how minor it may seem to you, you come straight back here, and I'll see if I can uncover what's going on. But I'm not too hopeful. Good-bye!"

Yoshio Goto smiled sympathetically. We shook hands, and I left.

As I walked the two blocks back toward the hotel, I suddenly felt that all my troubles were over. I realized that what really had been bothering me wasn't the strange events in themselves, but rather the fact that they had caused me to doubt my own sanity. I'm not proud of my body, but I'm very proud indeed of my brain. In retrospect, for the past few days I'd been living with the continual fear that I'd lost my mind. After all, it's been conclusively shown that some forms of mental illness are hereditary. I still had no idea whether paranoia was hereditary or not, but it certainly seemed possible. Accordingly, my family medical history seemed to indicate that, at the very least, I had a predisposition to paranoia.

I should have realized that I wasn't going crazy earlier that morning when Yosh had suggested that I was perhaps the victim of a conspiracy. If that was the only interpretation of the facts that a highly experienced private investigator and former detective in the San Francisco Police Department could suggest, then I was clearly being rational when that explanation had come to me, too.

The real question was: Was there indeed a conspiracy and, if so, who was behind it and why? But I decided to try to forget all that for a while, and go out and celebrate. I decided to eat at a French restaurant, partly because I love *haute cuisine*, and partly because I wanted to discover how a top Japanese chef would modify classic French cooking for local palates and tastes.

The concierge who had put me in touch with Yosh was seated at his desk. I thanked him for recommending Yosh and then asked him to suggest a French restaurant. He assured me that the best French restaurant in Kyoto, Chez Gaston, was on the mezzanine floor of the hotel. I decided to take his advice.

From the time I walked into Chez Gaston until I staggered out, slightly drunk, some four hours later, I had to keep reminding myself that I was in Kyoto and not in Paris. The only concession to Japan was that a few of the waiters were Japanese—there wasn't even a Japanese version of the menu or the extensive wine list. Chez Gaston was French sovereign territory on the mezzanine floor of a Kyoto hotel. I'd walked into Chez Gaston expecting to eat a meal that was a fusion of the best of French and Japanese cuisines. I walked out wondering why the eponymous Gaston—if indeed there was such a person—was even aware of the fact that the Mikado Hotel is situated in Japan.

Every aspect of the restaurant had revealed a deep understanding of food and wine and how they should be served. The glorious meal reminded me of our honeymoon in Paris. As a result, I was thinking fond thoughts of Nikki as I opened the door of my room.

The red message light on the telephone was blinking. I played the message. Yosh's voice was businesslike, almost brusque: "Please come to my office tomorrow morning at ten." That was all.

Suddenly I was very sober indeed. The wonderful mood that my evening at Chez Gaston had brought on was completely gone. All my worries had returned. It was back to the trenches again.

CHAPTER FOURTEEN

"What have you discovered?" I asked Yosh when we met in his office the next morning.

He ignored my question. "When did you last have any contact with Inspector Watanabe?" he asked.

"Inspector Watanabe? What has he got to with it?"

Again he ignored my question.

"When did you last have contact with him?"

"I've had contact with Inspector Watanabe exactly twice in my entire life. The first time was last Thursday, after the hold-up on the Philosophers' Pathway. The second time was the following afternoon when I received his note and the train ticket to Nara. Why? What's happened?"

Yet again he ignored me. "You definitely had no contact with him yesterday, then?"

"I've just told you. I've met him once and only once, and I've received one and only one note from him. I have no intention of ever meeting the man again, and any future tickets of any kind, for the train or otherwise, will be tossed out at once. Why?"

"And Suzuki, or whatever his real name is? Have you had any dealings at all with him since your trip to Nara on Saturday?"

"No, of course not. If I ever see him coming toward me, I'll immediately cross the street to avoid him—I'd rather be run over by a beer truck in the middle of the road than meet Suzuki on the sidewalk. Now would you *please* tell me what's going on?"

Finally he stopped asking questions and responded to my query.

"Last night I got home at 7:30. As I walked into my apartment the telephone was ringing. I ran to pick it up. It was Inspector Watanabe."

I was horrified. "What did he want?"

"He asked me why you decided to take a walk on the Philosophers' Pathway last Thursday."

"Why on earth would he want to know that?" I asked.

"That's hardly the issue, is it?" Yosh said.

"It's very much the issue, as far as I'm concerned. That man all but called me a liar to my face. Now he calls you to ask you a totally irrelevant question. What's he up to?"

"Again, that's not the main issue. Think for a minute. You came to see me yesterday morning and again yesterday late afternoon. Watanabe called me about an hour after you left the second time. Just how did he know that you'd consulted me yesterday?"

My mouth dropped open. I was completely and utterly astonished. I was so badly shocked that I was unable to speak.

Yosh, however, had no problems with continuing the conversation. "I think we need to go over your interactions with Watanabe and Suzuki again. Then I need you to tell me exactly who knew about our meeting yesterday."

For half an hour I answered Yosh's questions. Finally, Yosh looked me straight in the eye, and asked, "Do you think that Inspector Watanabe is part of this conspiracy?"

"Certainly not. The only reason that I've let you go on about this mysterious cabal that's so busily conspiring against me is because neither of us, as yet, has been able to come up with a more likely explanation. I'd very much like not to believe in conspiracy theories—they remind me much too much of my sister Eloise. But until we come up with a better alternative, let's assume that there's some vast evil conspiracy at work in Kyoto and that I'm a target of these vile malefactors. It's highly unlikely, but it's possible. However, there's no way that you could convince me that Watanabe is part of this hypothetical conspiracy."

"Did he make such a good impression on you, then?"

"No, quite the contrary. But I'm basically an optimist, and I have to believe that there's a rational explanation for what's happening to me. That's why I came to you, to help me find out what really is going on. If Watanabe is part of the conspiracy then we'll never be able to uncover the truth. Accordingly, I have to believe that the detested Inspector Watanabe wears a white hat."

"Interesting. I've come to know Watanabe well since I came to Kyoto eight years ago. As I told you, he handles most of the cases involving foreigners. Many of my clients are English-speaking, and, as a result, I have had lots of contact with Seiji Watanabe. Unlike you, I've a very high opinion of him, and it's for that reason that I agree with you that he isn't part of the conspiracy I've suggested.

"On the other hand, I know from personal experience that Watanabe is extremely clever and can be very devious indeed. I've no doubt that he set up the train meeting between you and Suzuki. The question is: Why?"

Neither of us knew the answer to that.

"We've been talking for nearly an hour," Yosh said. "There's a coffeehouse around the corner. Let's go for some java and when we come back, maybe we'll understand more."

The coffeehouse was typical for Japan—small and exceedingly well appointed. After all, with coffee costing more than $12 a cup, the owner of a coffee shop could afford to use fine cups and silverware. The shop was decorated with deep red tiles and chrome rods, an unusual combination that was most effective. As we seated ourselves at a corner table the owner gave us each a traditional hot towel, then brought us glasses of ice water. Yosh ordered for both of us. The owner scooped freshly ground beans into two French presses and placed them in front of us. The coffee was superb; in fact, I never had anything other than excellent coffee all the time I was in Kyoto. I ordered a second cup, and Yosh did, too. The owner prepared the second cups just as meticulously as he had the first.

While we drank our coffee, I asked Yosh why he'd come to live in Kyoto.

"I'm a second generation Japanese-American. My parents were born in San Francisco, but they viewed themselves as Japanese first and Americans a distant second. We spoke only Japanese in the home.

"When I started to date, my parents made it clear that I was to marry a woman not just of Japanese ancestry, but also one who shared their view of the prime importance of Japanese culture. But each time I introduced them to my current girlfriend, the next day they would call me with the same complaint, 'She's too American.'

"Finally, I went to a Fourth of July barbecue at the home of a fellow SFPD detective and met Miko. She was a Japanese graduate student at Berkeley who had come to the United States to get a Ph.D. in Genetic Engineering. We started dating, and after eighteen months, we were married. Then Miko got her degree, and announced that we should now leave for Japan.

"I managed to persuade her to take up a three-year post-doctoral fellowship at Stanford, but toward the end of the fellowship she again announced that it was time to go home. Much to my amazement, my parents vehemently opposed her—being Japanese first and American second was fine for them until it meant that their only child and any future grandchildren would be living six thousand miles away. Eventually I realized that I loved my wife more than my parents, and we left for Japan where Miko had been offered a job at Kyoto University. I started Golden Gate Services, and life was blissful.

"Then our marriage started to fall apart. Somehow, life in Japan put stresses and strains on our daily existence that weren't there when we lived in California. I suggested marital counseling, but Miko wouldn't hear of it. And a few months later, we divorced.

"Meantime, my business was thriving. As a former U.S. police detective I attracted lots of work from visiting English-speakers like you, and the idea of a former San Francisco police detective appealed to many Japanese, too. I haven't had a holiday in years. The only reason I was able to see you on such short notice is that the client I was supposed to see yesterday morning got a bad case of the flu over the weekend and postponed her appointment. Anyway, with business booming, I saw no reason to return home.

"Yes, I used the word 'home.' For me, San Francisco is home, for my American-born parents, Japan is home. How about that?"

It was interesting to learn more about Yosh and his background, but the conversation wasn't leading us toward a solution to the puzzle. I suggested that we return to his office and get back to business. Yosh readily agreed.

As soon as we were comfortably settled in his office, Yosh tackled the latest piece of the puzzle, Watanabe's phone call to Yosh's home.

Yosh started in his usual methodical way. "You explained that you had no contact whatsoever with either Watanabe or Suzuki once you left Suzuki at Kyoto station on Saturday afternoon. Accordingly, the only way that Watanabe could have found out that you visited me is that he's put a tail on you. The tail saw you walking to my office, and Watanabe then deduced that you came to see me about the hold-up. The problem with that theory is that you're definitely not being tailed. I'm absolutely sure of that."

"Then how did Watanabe find out that I'd consulted you?"

"I don't have the faintest idea. But it's worse than that. The purpose of his call wasn't to ask me why you chose to take a stroll on the Philosophers' Pathway. Instead, Watanabe called me last night to tell me that he knew that you'd consulted me. Worst of all, I think he wanted me to know that he knew that I'd no idea how he knew."

Yosh and I had previously agreed that Watanabe wasn't part of the conspiracy, but I wanted to be sure whether or not Yosh was now suggesting that he'd changed his belief that Inspector Watanabe was on the side of the angels.

"Are we back at conspiracy theories again?" I asked, as politely as I could.

"No, that's not what I'm saying. There are two separate activities going on here. First, there are the bad guys who, for some reason, are doing strange things to you that we can't explain. Second, there are the police. Watanabe, aided by Suzuki, is trying really hard to find out what's going on. In the course of his investigations, he discovered that you consulted me yesterday. The best guess I can come with is that the purpose of his call was to let you know through me that he's investigating the hold-up."

"You know," I said, "I feel like the proverbial blind man looking for a black cat in a dark room, only there are two cats in the room, the bad guys and the police. Let's face it, neither of us has the faintest idea what the conspirators are up to, and neither of us has the remotest clue regarding Watanabe's activities."

Yosh sighed. "I guess you're right. We've been talking all morning, and we're as much in the dark as we were before we started. I'm sorry to have wasted your time, but at least you now know that Watanabe called me last night. I'll get in touch with you if anything else happens, and I'm sure that you'll do the same for me. Here is my card. This number will reach me at any hour of the day or night."

I put the card in my wallet out of politeness. I was certain that this was the last time that I'd have any contact with Yosh.

CHAPTER FIFTEEN

I walked to the street corner that was on the direct route back to my hotel. The green man lit up to indicate that pedestrians could now cross the intersection. I didn't see any traffic driving along the street in front of me, and I started to cross the road. I'd forgotten that traffic in Japan drives on the left-hand side of the road and therefore I didn't look behind me and see the beer truck coming toward me and turning left across my path. At the last minute, I saw the massive vehicle in the corner of my right eye and I jumped backward as far as I could. The side of the truck brushed my right sleeve, but I wasn't hit. The attempt to kill me had failed.

I stood at the side of the road, panting from exertion and relief. Then I took stock of the situation. Was this really an assassination attempt, or was it just possible that the truck driver simply hadn't seen me? That was unlikely unless he was legally blind. Was he perhaps not looking? That was possible. But then, anything was possible.

I carefully analyzed the speed and the path of the truck and then suddenly there was no doubt in my mind: The driver of the beer truck had deliberately tried to kill me on behalf of the mysterious conspiracy that Yosh had put forward as the only possible explanation for what had been happening to me. It wasn't that a tired Japanese beer truck driver saw the green traffic light but overlooked the green man as I tried to cross the intersection. The fact was that I'd had a lucky escape from a botched-up murder attempt. The question was: What should I do about it? I had three choices: I could go to Inspector Watanabe, I could go back to Yosh's office or I could do nothing.

Despite Watanabe's sudden interest in the hold-up as evidenced by his phone call to Yosh at his home the previous evening, I decided against reporting the attempted murder to the police. There were only a handful of pedestrians in the vicinity, and no one seemed to have noticed anything. Also, I hadn't taken down the number of the truck because I was too busy trying to save my life. In fact, I couldn't even remember the brand name of the beer painted on the side of the truck. That meant that there was no point in contacting Inspector Watanabe.

I also decided not to tell Yosh about it. The incident would just fuel his burning belief in the conspiracy he'd conjured up to explain the mysterious goings on. I had to admit that I couldn't come up with a better explanation than his, ridiculous as it was, but that didn't make his theory any more correct or any more palatable to me. The more I thought about it, the less I could accept his idea of a large-scale conspiracy directed against me. The major reason why I rejected his theory was that neither Yosh nor I could come up any motivation for it—there was just no reason why some group of conspirators in Kyoto should be treating me this way.

Having rejected alternatives one and two, I concluded that the best thing to do was simply to file the incident away for a while. Maybe it would make more sense if and when other incidents could be explained, always assuming that I could stay alive long enough for the mystery to be solved. I'd always hoped that I'd live to a ripe old age, but after having been assailed by bullets and beer trucks, my hope was merely to live long enough to get back to New York.

After lunch I decided to visit the National Kyoto Museum. My guidebooks spoke highly of the Buddhist art there, and I thought that seeing the various religious statues in the museum would make up for the many disappointing temples I'd visited. The challenge was how to get to the museum without being hit by another truck and how to see the various exhibits of interest to me without getting shot at.

One guidebook indicated that the Royal Claremont Hotel was across the road from the museum. I asked the doorman to call me a taxi. Only when I was safely inside with the doors shut against eavesdroppers did I ask the driver to take me to the Royal Claremont Hotel. When we arrived at the imposing hotel, I walked into the lobby and sat down as if I was expecting to meet someone. After a few minutes I got up again, left the hotel, and crossed the street to the National Kyoto Museum.

The museum consists of two large buildings at right angles to one another, both fronting a large grassed courtyard. The building on the right looked Victorian. The style somehow reminded me of Kyoto police headquarters, an edifice that brought back unhappy memories. The building on the left was insipid and featureless, but because I didn't associate it in any way with Inspector Watanabe, I decided to begin my tour of the museum there.

The museum turned out to be every bit as good as the guidebooks had indicated. The archaeology halls gave an excellent description of early civilization in the Kyoto region. Next came two pottery halls. I was interested to note that the Chinese pottery exhibited there was far superior in every way to the Japanese pottery on display and wondered why that was. Then I found myself in an area where paintings were exhibited. The works were really fine indeed and I congratulated myself on my decision to go the museum that afternoon.

I moved from there into the calligraphy section. I was about to inspect an interesting looking ancient scroll more closely when a Japanese woman in a business suit rushed up to me.

"Are you Mr. Thompson," she asked in a heavy accent.

"Yes, I am. What's the problem?" I asked somewhat defensively. After all, I was thoroughly enjoying the museum and wasn't too pleased at being disturbed in this way.

"I'm sorry but your wife has been injured in an accident and has been taken to Kyoto Hospital." She handed me a piece of paper on which was written "Nike Tomson, Kyoto Hospital."

I was speechless with shock. The woman pointed in the direction of the exit, and I rushed out as fast as I could. As I hastened across the grass, I realized what must have happened. Nikki had returned from Stockholm without telling me to surprise me. But somehow she'd been injured on her way to the hotel and was being treated in the Kyoto Hospital.

I crossed the large courtyard and clambered into a waiting taxi. "Kyoto Hospital," I said, "and hurry."

The driver looked at me. "Kyoto has many hospitals. Which hospital do you want?"

I handed over the piece of paper the woman had given me. The driver read it and repeated, "Which hospital?"

"Kyoto Hospital," I responded, somewhat sharply.

Fortunately the driver's English was good. Slowly and clearly he enunciated, "Which Kyoto Hospital?"

Suddenly I realized what the problem was. Either the person who had called the museum or the person who had taken the message hadn't been explicit enough. Kyoto is a city of more than a million people, and surely had many hospitals. I had visions of myself traipsing from hospital to hospital desperately trying to find Nikki.

Then I recalled that in New York accident victims are taken to the nearest hospital with an emergency room. Every ambulance driver knows which hospitals are on call twenty-four hours a day to handle emergencies. Perhaps Kyoto had a similar system—it didn't seem particularly likely that every hospital or clinic would have the necessary facilities and staff. So I said the driver, "Take me to the Kyoto Emergency Hospital."

The driver understood what I was getting at; I could see that. However, to my extreme annoyance he asked, "Which emergency hospital?"

Angry as I now was, this made sense. There was surely more than one.

"The nearest one, and please hurry!"

This was easier said than done. It was now about 3:30, and the Kyoto rush hour seemed to have begun. As I've mentioned before, traffic in Kyoto is never light, but at rush hour it locks up the streets. We finally arrived at a large building that looked like a hospital, and the driver dropped me at the sign marked "Emergency Room."

I rushed inside and asked the first person I saw, "Where can I find Nikki Thompson?" She shrugged to indicate that she didn't understand and called across to another woman who I assumed was a triage nurse. The nurse walked up to me and asked in English, "Can I help you?"

"I received a message that my wife, Nikki Thompson, has been injured in an accident and has been taken to hospital." I showed her the piece of paper I'd been given at the museum. I then took out one of my cards, which showed the correct spelling of 'Thompson.' I crossed out my first name, wrote Nikolina (Nikki) above my name and handed the card to her.

"One minute, please." She walked over to a central desk area that had a number of computer screens and keyboards. She seated herself in front of one of the computers and began to type.

The "one minute" became two, then five, and then ten. The nurse kept typing into the computer but didn't seem to be getting satisfactory responses. Then she called a colleague over to assist her, and the two of them tried together to obtain the information they wanted from the computer. I assumed that the problem was that the names of patients had to be entered in Japanese characters, and it was unclear to them how to transliterate the foreign name Thompson.

Finally, after about fifteen minutes, the nurse came back to me. Her face was deeply apologetic. "I'm sorry, I've searched diligently, but your wife isn't in this hospital."

"Is there another hospital to which she might have been taken?" I asked.

"Yes, there are a number of other emergency hospitals here. I'll write their names down on a piece of paper for you, and you can show them to the taxi driver."

She went back to the desk and wrote for a few moments. "There are four other hospitals that you can try. The nearest one is at the top of the list."

I thanked her and rushed out of the emergency room. Fortunately I found another taxi waiting near the spot where the first taxi had dropped me. I showed him the nurse's list and pointed to the top name. He nodded, and off we went.

By now the traffic rivaled New York rush hour on a rainy day. At one point the taxicab didn't move for at least fifteen minutes. I knew that there wasn't anything that I could do and that I should just sit back and relax, but the thought of Nikki lying injured in a hospital in a foreign country where she probably couldn't communicate clearly with the doctors or nurses totally drove from my mind any attempts to stay calm. I grew tenser and tenser—I was ready to scream. Then the traffic eased suddenly, and we were able to move about twenty-five yards before we were again in total gridlock. It took over an hour to reach the second hospital, even though it couldn't have been more than two miles from the first one.

This time, a doorman who couldn't speak English met me at the door of the emergency room. He escorted me to a man in an immaculate white uniform. From then on it was dèja vu all over again except that it took at least twenty minutes of diligent effort on the part of the staff to be certain that Nikki wasn't at that hospital, either. The nurse came over to me.

"I'm afraid that your wife isn't in the hospital. Who told you that she was here?"

I began to tell him the story, when suddenly I realized something that should have occurred to me when I first received the message. I'd told nobody that I was in the Kyoto National Museum. In fact, I'd taken every precaution to avoid being followed. So, how had the caller who had left the message known that I was there? Yosh's conspiracy was only too real. I had arrived at the only possible explanation of how "they" had known that I was in the museum.

I started to feel faint. The nurse immediately grabbed me and called for help. After all, I weigh far too much for one person to support.

I don't remember too much about the next few minutes, but when I recovered consciousness, I found myself lying on a bed with a different nurse taking my blood pressure. He looked worried. Next to him stood a physician.

I assured them both that I'd exhausted myself trying to locate my wife who had been taken to the hospital, and that I'd soon be fine. They didn't seem too convinced of my self-diagnosis or prognosis. The physician insisted that I lie down for at least half an hour after which she would re-examine me and decide what should be done next. In America, a patient can discharge himself at will, even against the strongest advice of the medical staff. But here I had the feeling that I'd be forcibly restrained if I attempted to leave the emergency room without the full consent of the doctor. And from the look on her face, I was absolutely certain that her consent wouldn't be forthcoming.

The doctor said, "You must rest now," and moved on to the patient lying on the next bed. I took out my wallet, found Yosh's card, grabbed my BlackBerry and dialed the twenty-four-hour number. The phone rang and rang. Long after I'd given up all hope of a response, Yosh answered. I told him everything that had happened, stressing that no one could possibly have known where I was.

"I'll call all the emergency hospitals and find out about your wife. I'll also call the police to find the details of the accident. Just relax until I call you back. Please give me the exact spelling of your wife's name, and I'll take care of everything. I'll call you back as soon as I can."

I lay on the bed. I was wide awake, but through my brain raced a vision of Nikki lying in a hospital bed wondering what had happened to me, unable to understand why I wasn't at her bedside.

But worse was to come. Twenty minutes later Yosh called me back. "I'm not quite sure how to interpret this, but here are the facts. Your wife isn't in any of the area emergency hospitals. Also, none of the accidents that were reported in the last twenty-four hours involved a foreigner."

"But that's impossible. I've the note here. It says that Nikki is in Kyoto Hospital."

Yosh spoke very gently and slowly. "The fact that someone calls a museum and instructs the person who answers the phone to locate you and tell you that your wife has been in an accident and is now in Kyoto Hospital doesn't prove that your wife has been in an accident. It also doesn't prove that she's now in a hospital. Your wife is most likely still in Sweden with her sick mother."

I nearly lost consciousness again, but Yosh was right. I'd been the victim of a cruel hoax.

"Here's what to do. Rest for a while until you feel better, then get discharged from the hospital and take a cab to your hotel. I'll meet you there. In the meantime, I'll get an assistant to help me call every single hospital in Kyoto to confirm once and for all that Nikki isn't there. Another assistant will call Kansai International Airport. It's hard to get information about passengers, but I have a friend who may be able to tell us whether or not Nikki passed through Osaka airport today. That wouldn't be conclusive, because she could have arrived at Narita Airport in Tokyo and then taken the bullet train—if Kansai proves negative we'll contact Narita. These are just precautionary measures to reassure you. Personally, I'm 120 percent certain that Nikki is still in Stockholm, and the members of the conspiracy or their agents are at work again."

I followed his advice. The physician was visibly reluctant to let me leave, but she examined me carefully and had to admit that there was no medical reason to keep me any longer. I paid my bill using a good proportion of the money that the hold-up artist had returned, and took a taxi back to the Mikado Hotel. I was truly angry. What was happening to me was bad enough, but the cabal had no right to involve Nikki in this affair.

CHAPTER SIXTEEN

Yosh wasn't in the lobby when I got back to the hotel, so I went up to my room. As I unlocked the door, I suddenly realized that I could check if Nikki was still in Stockholm by phoning her there. And then I remembered that this might wake her mother. But clearly this was an emergency. But would Nikki see it that way? Would she be furious with me for disregarding her explicit instructions? I decided that—for the first time ever—I would disobey Nikki. I phoned her.

After two rings, I heard a recording in Swedish. I waited to the end, hoping that an English translation would follow, but the message was repeated in Swedish. Hoping that perhaps I had dialed the wrong number, I hastily tried again. Again I heard the Swedish message. I don't speak one word of Swedish, but it sounded to me like "This number is out of order."

What bad luck, I thought. The one time that I really have to speak to Nikki, her iPhone is out of order. But was it really out of order? Or had the Swedish agents of the conspiracy somehow disconnected her phone? I decided to wait until Yosh came—perhaps he would have news of Nikki.

It was nearly midnight, and I hadn't eaten since lunchtime. I'd no idea whether or not Yosh had managed to have dinner while he was trying to locate Nikki, so I called room service and ordered for both of us. Yosh arrived at the same time as two waiters pushing trolleys laden with food and drink.

The waiters set up the meal. When they finally left, Yosh turned to me.

"First things first. The good news is that, as I told you, Nikki is definitely not in any hospital in Kyoto—every single call proved negative. Also, today she's not passed through either Kansai International Airport or Narita. Most reassuring of all, I called the police again and they confirmed that there have been no accidents involving foreigners reported in Kyoto in the last twenty-four hours. So, let's eat and drink, and try to solve your mystery."

We piled our plates high from the serving dishes on the first trolley, filled one another's glasses with beer, and dug in. Yosh weighed nearly as much as I did, but—like Oddjob whom he resembled so closely—most of his weight was muscle, not fat. It was clear that he was enjoying his meal as much as I was, but after a few minutes of contented munching he spoke.

"Sorry to spoil your meal, but I think we need to talk while we eat. Tell me everything that happened leading up to your visit to the museum."

"Well, after the truck driver tried to kill me—"

Yosh immediately interrupted. "What truck driver? You never said anything about this. Is that why you were in the hospital?"

I quickly explained what had happened when the beer truck nearly ran me down outside his office that morning. Then I added, "There are two ways of looking at the incident with the truck driver. The way I see it—and I'm pretty certain that I'm right—is that the members of the conspiracy knew that I was visiting your office. Heck, Inspector Watanabe knew all about my meeting at your office yesterday, so why shouldn't the bad guys have known about today's visit? So they parked a beer truck around the corner, hoping that someone deep in thought would not look behind him before he crossed the intersection. As I started to move forward, the truck driver accelerated and tried to kill me.

"The other way to look at it is to put it down as an accident. After all, over the years haven't you had plenty of near misses, both as a driver and as a pedestrian? I reluctantly have to admit that this could have been one of those occurrences that could happen to anybody from time to time. However, it happened just three days after the gunman shot at me at the Silver Pavilion Temple, so I'm pretty certain that this, too, was an attempt to kill me."

Yosh had been methodically demolishing a thick juicy steak of marbled Kobe beef smothered in a rich mushroom cream sauce. Reluctantly he stopped eating so that he could reply.

"I've just realized something. There's a most peculiar aspect of the murder attempt at the Silver Pavilion Temple that we've overlooked up to now. You were sitting on the veranda of the Silver Pavilion Temple when you heard a shot coming from behind you. You were completely unprotected. There was nothing between your back and the glass window of the pavilion, which was five or ten yards to your back. The gunman in the pavilion had an easy shot.

"But what happened? Nothing! You said that you didn't hear a bullet zip past you or thud into the wooden veranda. And there was no broken glass, either."

"What are you saying?"

"I'm saying that this was a mighty strange murder attempt. The gunman is in a room behind you. Through a window he aims a gun at your back, then fires. But where does the bullet go? Even if the gunman closed his eyes before shooting at you, at the very least the glass of the window would have shattered.

"In other words," Yosh continued, "There was no bullet. The gunman must've fired a blank. What happened at the Silver Pavilion Temple wasn't attempted murder, but instead an attempt to terrify you, one which succeeded beyond the perpetrator's wildest dreams. It even fooled me up to now.

"But the incident with that beer truck was quite different. If you hadn't jumped back in time, you'd be dead. Even if you'd jumped back but not quite far enough, you would have been badly injured. The incident with the beer truck was totally different than the 'shooting' at the Silver Pavilion Temple." With a grin of triumph, Yosh drained his beer glass and returned to the last of his steak.

Remembering the Japanese custom, I quickly refilled Yosh's glass. I thought for a second or two. "Yosh, there was something else not quite right about the shooting at the pavilion. I know that I wasn't hallucinating. I definitely heard a shot but, as I told you, no one else seemed to notice anything."

Now it was Yosh's turn to think. "I've no idea. Let's move on to the museum incident."

"Fine, but there's dessert, coffee and liqueurs on that other trolley. Let's first help ourselves, and then we can analyze what happened today."

We settled down with our plates filled with a variety of cakes, and turned to the next issue.

Yosh spoke first. "You told me over the phone that you took a cab to the Royal Claremont Hotel, you sat in the lobby for a short while, and then you walked across the street toward the museum."

"Correct."

"Once again we have a number of possible explanations, none of them particularly plausible. One is that someone followed you first to the hotel and then to the museum. I know you weren't tailed yesterday, and I see no reason why you were tailed earlier today. So I'm going to reject that one. A second possibility is—"

I rudely interrupted him. "Isn't it possible," I asked, "that the opposition spotted your operatives yesterday and called off the tail? As a result, your people completely convinced you that I wasn't being followed, and you didn't assign anyone to me today. Once I was unprotected by your staffers, the agents of the conspiracy resumed tailing me."

My suggestion bewildered Yosh. He even stopped chewing his mouthful of dessert. There was complete silence in the room. Then he started chewing again, perhaps to help him think. Finally he spoke.

"I've been so stupid, so utterly stupid. Of course that's what happened. They obviously have hired top men and women, personnel who can spot a tail a mile off. They realized that my people were following you at Nijo Castle, either to protect you or to determine whether the opposition was following you. As a result, they left you alone. However, once my operatives were withdrawn, the bad guys resumed tailing as usual. You didn't notice anything because you don't have the skills and experience to detect an expert in the art of following."

Yosh paused and took a deep breath. I could see that something was troubling him.

"This puts me in a really difficult situation. On the one hand, it's my duty to protect you. From that viewpoint, I should arrange for my people to follow you twenty-four hours a day. But if I do that, the opposition will do what they did at Nijo Castle, that is, they'll do precisely nothing. And they'll continue to do nothing until you go back to New York. In all probability, you'll never ever find out why these strange events have occurred. In fact, a better option for you would be to return to New York right away. You can phone Nikki in Stockholm and tell her to fly straight home as soon as her mother is better.

"The other alternative is to leave you unprotected. I'm certain that they don't want to kill you—the gunman at the Silver Pavilion Temple had every opportunity to shoot you but fired a blank instead. It's my professional opinion that you wouldn't be in physical danger on your own, other than dropping dead from a heart attack if they pull another stunt like the phone call to the museum."

"But what did they hope to achieve by that phone call?" I asked. "Were they just trying to tell me that they have me under surveillance? If that were the case, they could have simply called you, the way Inspector Watanabe did the other night. Alternatively, they could push an envelope under my bedroom door that contains photographs of me taken at various places. That would certainly be more than enough to convince me that I'm being tailed."

"All I can think of is that they're trying to terrify you. They scared you with the gunshot at the Silver Pavilion Temple, didn't they? And they scared you enough with the hospital story for you to lose consciousness. Fortunately, you had the forethought to faint in an emergency room, which shows just how smart you are." He grinned as he raised the last piece of cake on his plate to his mouth with a fork that seemed so small in his huge hand.

"I think we've covered everything that needs to be covered at this time. Now the choice is yours. You can fly back to New York right away, or you can take the risk of staying here, unguarded, in order to find out what's happening."

I thought for less than a millisecond before I shook my head firmly. "No, I won't take the easy way out. You know that basically I'm a coward. Heck, I was even prepared to use innocent schoolchildren as human shields at the Silver Pavilion Temple. You might even say that I'm a despicable coward. But I'm an intensely curious despicable coward. If I go back to New York now, I'll never know what was behind these strange incidents."

"I thought you'd say that. Anyhow, thanks for the great dinner, but it's time for me to go home. Let's both get as much sleep as we can during what's left of the night. We can't afford to be tired when weird events like these are happening all the time."

After he left, I went straight to sleep. And then the nightmares started. First, came the usual one, being chased down the endless wide street lined with high walls. I eventually managed to wake up to find my heart pounding and sweat pouring out all over my body. Finally, I calmed down enough to get back to sleep.

Hardly had I fallen asleep for the second time when the same nightmare recurred. Again I was being chased down that long street with the high walls on both sides. It was almost like watching an instant replay during a sports telecast. Again I had to force myself awake to stop the nightmare, and again my heart was hammering away and my body was drenched with sweat.

I read a newspaper for a few minutes to try to relax. I suddenly felt exhausted. I turned out the light and tried to sleep again.

Sleep came quickly, and so did a totally different nightmare. This time I was standing in front of large table. Behind the table stood fourteen people wearing black clothes with black hoods over their heads. A fifteenth person, presumably a leader, wore a red hood and stood at the front of the crowd. Then they seated themselves at the table, seven to the right of the leader, seven to the left. The leader of the conspirators stood up and removed his red hood. It was Yosh.

I sat bolt upright in bed. If my dream was in any way accurate, the best thing I could do would be to rush to catch the very next plane straight back to New York. But was it possible that Yosh was the head conspirator? For some reason I'd instinctively trusted Yosh from the beginning, and it was inconceivable to me that the man was anything other than what he seemed to be. But at the same time, it was at least possible that Yosh was the organizer and instigator of all the weird events that had been happening to me since I arrived in Kyoto. By consulting Yosh, I'd walked straight into the lions' den.

I took a deep breath and then deliberately put out of my mind the possibility that Yosh was in any way connected to the conspiracy that he appeared to think was so real. I turned on the TV and watched CNN International for half an hour. Then I tried to sleep again.

I dropped off as my head hit the pillow. There were no more nightmares.

CHAPTER SEVENTEEN

The next morning I was woken, yet again, by the telephone next to my bed. I picked it up expecting to hear the voice of the gunman asking me, in his fake American accent, why I hadn't visited the Kyoto Handicraft Emporium as ordered. This time, however, the caller was a man who mumbled something in Japanese and hung up. I assumed that what he said was the Japanese for "Sorry, wrong number."

Having braced myself for the gunman, I was now wide-awake, even though it was only 6 a.m., so I got out of bed to retrieve the newspaper. As I think I've already told you, each morning the hotel left a copy of the *Japan Daily Bulletin*, an English-language newspaper, outside my door. A bellhop neatly folded the newspaper in half, placed it in an off-white coarsely woven cloth bag and hung it from the outside doorknob, a pleasant touch. That morning, however, when I picked up the bag and took out the contents, I saw that a sheet of white paper had been placed on top of the *Daily Bulletin*. Written on the paper in Nikki's handwriting were the words:

Heian Shrine
at 12
Nikki

She'd used a pen with a really thick nib and black ink, but there was no doubt in my mind that this was Nikki's handwriting. I nearly fainted again. Yosh had assured me that there was no possibility whatsoever that Nikki could be in Kyoto. Yet here was a note from her, delivered via a somewhat unexpected route.

And why had a note from Nikki been delivered with my morning newspaper? That answer was clear: She wrote because couldn't phone me. That meant that she'd been kidnapped, and had bribed one of her captors to smuggle out a note. And the note she'd written using a pen with an exceptionally wide nib had been placed in the bag containing my morning *Daily Bulletin*.

I needed to calm down quickly. My thoughts were paranoid ravings, not the rational ideas of a successful CPA. If Nikki had indeed been kidnapped—which was as unlikely a supposition as any of the other truly ridiculous ideas that I'd come up with that morning—why would her note be delivered this peculiar way? No, there was clearly a much simpler explanation, but what?

Then another thought struck me. Perhaps I'd been mistaken; perhaps the handwriting was a forgery. In other words, someone (presumably a member of the conspiracy) had tried to copy Nikki's handwriting. I'd fallen right into his trap and believed that Nikki had written the note, just as I'd believed the previous day that Nikki was lying injured in a Kyoto hospital.

I picked up the sheet of paper again and examined it more closely.

Heian Shrine
at 1

There was absolutely no doubt in my mind at that moment that I was going crazy. Now the note was printed, not handwritten. The time of the appointment had changed from noon to one o'clock, and the note was now unsigned—the place where Nikki's signature had been—or perhaps, where I'd imagined Nikki's signature had been— was now completely blank.

The connection between Nikki and the note had disappeared without a trace. As a result, the question of how the note had travelled from Nikki to the cloth bag containing my newspaper was now moot. However, there was now a new question that was truly terrifying: How had the note metamorphosed? The reason that the question was so terrifying was simple: The obvious answer was that I was hallucinating. I missed Nikki so much that I *saw* her handwriting in a printed note and her signature where there was none. But that wouldn't explain the other part of the riddle: Why had the time of the appointment at the Heian Shrine changed from noon to one? Was that also part of my hallucinations?

I decided to take a shower to try to clear my mind. I luxuriated in the hot water and then dried myself off with a thick Egyptian cotton bath sheet. I dried what was left of my hair using the hair drier that the hotel also conveniently supplied and started shaving. And as my razor touched my chin, the penny dropped. The note had been written with disappearing ink.

You can go into any shop that sells supplies for stage magicians and buy various chemicals that can be used to write words that appear or disappear. Most of the chemicals are sensitive to heat. In some cases, if you apply a hot iron to the page, words that previously were there will now disappear. Other chemicals work the other way round—heat causes words to appear. Yet other chemicals are sensitive to acids or alkalis. For example, if chemicals of that sort have been used and you rub the paper with lemon juice, letters will materialize or dematerialize.

Now I understood how the trick had been played on me. To begin with, the second message had been printed on the sheet of white paper, probably using a computer and a laser printer. Then, someone had taken a broad pen, filled it with black disappearing ink and written a message on top of the printed letters, imitating Nikki's handwriting. Then, the writer added a two after the one, making the time of the appointment noon, and finally added a passable imitation of Nikki's signature. Then he had heated the sheet of paper and placed it in the cloth bag. Somewhat later, I fetched the newspaper and read the message on the sheet of paper. As the minutes passed, the paper cooled. The disappearing ink duly disappeared, revealing the printed letters underneath. All I had to do was to apply a hot iron and "Nikki's handwriting" would reappear.

I went to the closet. I took out the ironing board and set it up. I plugged in the iron. The indicator light failed to come on. I tried a different electrical socket. Again nothing. So I picked up the telephone and asked the operator to tell housekeeping to send another iron to Room 1507 without delay. Then I calmly resumed shaving.

I felt marvelous. The vicious people who had carried out the hospital hoax the previous day were now trying to play another nasty trick on me, but this time I was on to them. Maybe now I'd discover something about the secret conspiracy that had sent me from hospital to hospital and was now trying to send me, for some reason, to the Heian Shrine.

I suddenly realized that I'd overlooked something important. The perpetrators had heated the sheet of paper to reveal the handwritten letters. When I took the *Japan Daily Bulletin* out of the cloth bag, the sheet of paper placed on top hadn't seemed particularly warm, but maybe they'd applied the heat to the letters themselves, not to the part of the paper where I'd held it. After I'd read the handwritten message the sheet of paper cooled down and the disappearing ink had accordingly disappeared. All this was fine, but if I'd slept a few minutes longer, the paper would have cooled sufficiently for the handwritten letters to disappear before I went to fetch the *Daily Bulletin*. How could the conspirators have known when I was going to wake up?

Then I understood the telephone call to the "wrong number" that had woken me earlier that morning. They'd heated the handwritten letters, placed the sheet of paper in the cloth bag on top of my *Daily Bulletin* and then used a cell phone to call my room to wake me. When I fetched the newspaper, the disappearing ink would still be warm enough for the handwritten letters, apparently penned by Nikki, to mask the printed letters. After a few minutes the page cooled to room temperature and the invisible ink duly disappeared. The good news was that, as soon as the second iron had been delivered, I could reheat the page and the handwriting would reappear.

I finished shaving and applied my favorite aftershave lotion. As I was patting it on, there was a knock at the door. I looked through the peephole. There stood a bellhop, brandishing an iron. I opened the door and took the iron from the bellhop. I asked him to wait while I tested the second iron. This time the light came on.

Now I waited for the iron to heat up. They say that the watched pot never boils, but the indicator light of that iron eventually did go out. Rubbing my hands with glee that at last I was going to turn the tables on the vicious conspirators who had ruined my trip, I picked up the sheet of paper and placed it on the ironing board. As I put it there, I glanced down at the words, which now read:

𝕳𝖊𝖎𝖆𝖓 𝕾𝖍𝖗𝖎𝖓𝖊
at 2

It was a good thing that I hadn't yet picked up the hot iron or I'd have dropped it from sheer shock. Not only had the type font mysteriously changed to Gothic, but the time of the appointment was now yet another hour later.

Then I realized that the conspirators were being very clever. They had used not one but two different disappearing inks to get me really worried. But the iron would show them up, of course. I placed the paper on the ironing board and applied the iron for a few seconds.

Nothing happened.

I took the iron and applied it more firmly to the sheet of paper, holding it far longer than should have been necessary to reveal the secret writing. But the disappearing ink stubbornly refused to reappear. Fortunately I had the sense to unplug the iron before I collapsed onto the bed in a state of panic. The conclusion was inescapable. This wasn't an instance of disappearing ink used by a practical joker. Three pieces of paper were involved, and the perpetrators—I couldn't bear even to think the word "conspirators," let alone say it aloud—had somehow entered my bedroom twice to switch papers. The second time I'd been in the bathroom, so all they needed was a passkey, but how had they managed to switch the first and second pieces of paper while I was still in the bedroom? There was, of course, still another possibility, but I wasn't yet willing to concede that I'd become mentally unbalanced.

With shaking hands I opened my wallet and took out Yosh's twenty-four-hour number. It was now a quarter to seven in the morning, and I assumed that he was still at home. Yosh answered the phone on the second ring. As succinctly as I could I told him what had happened.

"Get dressed, take the message with you, go downstairs, and I'll meet you at the main entrance of the hotel in fifteen minutes."

He was true to his word. Exactly on time a white Nissan Fuga drew up under the portico at the front of the hotel. I got into his car.

"I'm going to take you to a friend of mine who runs a chemical laboratory. She's going to examine that paper and tell us what's going on."

We drove to an older part of town with artisan shops of various kinds. We parked in front of a nondescript door and got out. Yosh knocked on the door, which bore no name. We heard someone walking down a long hallway and then the door unlocking. There stood a short woman with long black hair worn in a braid down her back, wearing a sparkling white laboratory coat. She ushered us along a narrow hallway into what I can only describe as the most sophisticated laboratory I've ever seen. The exterior of the building looked as if it hadn't been painted for at least fifty years but no expense had been spared on the laboratory itself.

"This is Dr. Yamada," said Yosh. "She is the top forensic chemist in Kyoto. Even the police lab experts consult her on hard cases. Give her the paper, she'll give us the answers we need."

I handed the paper to Dr. Yamada.

"Do you want this back?" she asked me in heavily accented English.

"If you photograph it, that'll be good enough for me," replied Yosh. "Is the paper of sentimental value to you, Oliver? I gather that it will be easier to test it if we allow parts to be destroyed in the course of the analysis."

"Go right ahead!" I said. "I'll do anything to get to the bottom of this. If it means that you have to destroy the entire piece of paper, be my guest."

"Thank you. Yosh, I'll call you as soon as I have some answers."

We walked back along the hallway. As Dr. Yamada opened the door for us I noticed that the inside of the door was lined with steel. It seemed that the laboratory handled sensitive materials and Dr. Yamada wanted to be sure that anything left in her keeping would be safe. The old wooden building in which the laboratory was housed looked like a fire trap, but I was sure that Dr. Yamada had taken adequate precautions against fire, too.

Yosh and I walked to the car. "Have you had breakfast?" Yosh asked. "If not, let's go to your hotel. I want to see first-hand where the incident with the cashier took place."

He paused and then continued. "I also want to sample this breakfast buffet that you've been touting so highly. Let's eat and then we'll call Dr. Yamada and see what she's found out. There's no point discussing what happened this morning until we've learnt from her what's on that paper."

We returned to the Mikado Hotel and went to Le Lac des Cygnes restaurant for the breakfast buffet. After we'd both eaten our fill, Yosh and I walked over to his office building, leaving his car in the hotel parking garage. We settled down in his office and Yosh called the chemist. The conversation was lengthy, and I could sense that Yosh wasn't at all happy. He put down the phone and turned to me.

"Dr. Yamada is absolutely adamant that the paper has no chemicals of any kind on it, other than from the sweat on your hands and things like that. She also confirms that heating the paper with the iron couldn't have destroyed any chemicals that the bad guys had used. The bottom line is that neither 'disappearing ink' nor any other chemicals were applied.

"There are two possibilities. Either you're hallucinating, which I believe is unlikely, or the bad guys somehow twice gained access to your room, which is extremely worrying. Also, we need to discuss whether or not you propose to visit the Heian Shrine."

"Would I be safe there?"

"It's a hugely popular attraction, despite the fact that it's not original—it's a 1895 replica of the imperial palace that was built around the year 800 and destroyed about four hundred years later. As you may know, Kyoto was the second capital of Japan—the Emperor ruled there from 794 to 1868. You'll no doubt be greatly amused to hear that Nara, the other city you love so much, was the first capital. The problem, of course, is that no one really knows exactly how the Kyoto imperial palace looked in those days, so I've no idea how accurate a replica the Heian Shrine is. Anyhow, the big attraction is the garden, which is truly fabulous at all times, especially today with the cherry blossoms in full bloom. The place is likely to be crowded."

"Good. I think I need to visit the Heian Shrine, but at what time? The first note said noon, the second note said one, and the note that Dr. Yamada analyzed said two."

"I'm not sure that it matters. If the time were at all critical, they would've ensured that the same time appeared on all three sheets of paper. I suggest you arrive after noon but before two. It's a really popular tourist site, and I'm sure you'll be safe. If the conspirators pull another stunt comparable to their 'Nikki is in the hospital' joke, just don't fall for it."

"I won't. I know their style by now, and I'll watch out for their tricks."

"That's easy for you to say. However, I suspect that they succeeded in panicking you with the ever-changing messages this morning. If I were you, I'd be extremely wary, and I wouldn't take anything at face value."

I thanked Yosh for his advice and left his office. On my way back to the hotel I suddenly realized that, in the very last part of our conversation, Yosh had referred to the source of the threatening incidents as "they." In other words, Yosh now really believed in the existence of some large-scale conspiracy that was responsible for all the otherwise inexplicable events. He'd referred to them as if there were no doubt at all in his mind that "they" existed. On the one hand, this was a major blow to me, because it meant that Yosh had essentially given up all hope of even trying to solve the mystery. On the other hand, at least I knew for certain exactly what Yosh was thinking, and accordingly I had some idea of the extent to which I could or couldn't rely on him in the future.

I'd also referred to the perpetrators as "they." Nevertheless, I still had some vestige of hope that, despite the mystifying nature of the many unpleasant and frightening things that had happened to me during the past few days, in the not-too-distant future I'd somehow be able to come up with a comprehensive solution to the puzzle that would make a lot more sense than Yosh's explanation of a cabal that apparently was conspiring against me for no apparent rhyme or reason whatsoever.

When I reached the Mikado Hotel I went to my room to see if there had been any further messages of any kind pushed under my door regarding the

Heian Shrine. There were none. I next consulted *Japan for the English-Speaking Tourist* for a good restaurant close to the Heian Shrine; there was no way that I'd enter the lions' den on an empty stomach. Then I put my guidebooks and map into my messenger bag and took a taxi to the restaurant for lunch. The tempura meal that followed was truly excellent.

But great as the meal was, it was not enough to put aside my fears of a large-scale murderous conspiracy. My courage totally failed me. Instead of walking to the shrine, I hailed another taxi, and returned to the Mikado Hotel.

CHAPTER EIGHTEEN

The next morning, the phone once again awoke me. This time, instead of the armed robber calling me at 4 a.m., Nikki had called me at seven. I was instantly awake.

"Darling, it's so good to hear your voice," I said. "Are you all right now?"

Then I remembered that Nikki hadn't been in an accident, nor had she been hospitalized. Before she had a chance to reply, I quickly added, "How's your mother?"

"She's much better, thank you. I think I'll be able to rejoin you in Kyoto in two or three days' time. I miss you so much."

"What time is it in Stockholm now?"

"It's midnight. Oliver, darling, tell me, have you been sulking in your hotel room, or did you go out and see the sights?"

"I've been touring. It's been most interesting."

I decided not tell Nikki of my many misadventures. There was no point in frightening her unnecessarily. There was nothing she could do while she was in Stockholm, and her mother's illness gave her quite enough to worry about. When she was once again back with me in Kyoto I could decide how much, if anything, to tell her about what had been happening to me.

"Darling, where are you going to tour today?" Nikki asked.

"Well, I'd thought of visiting the Kiyomizu Temple, or would you rather that I waited and we can visit it together when get here?"

"No, I absolutely insist that you go. If you like, we can see it again together. Oh, my mother is calling. I must go. I love you so much. Bye!"

And the line went dead. It was the first time that I'd had a proper telephone conversation with her since she had flown to Sweden—such a delightful change from the one-sided Nikki-grams she usually delivered, although by the end of the call she'd reverted to type.

***

The taxi drove up the long narrow street lined with small food and souvenir shops and deposited me in front of the Kiyomizu Temple. I could quickly see that the vast temple complex in front of me was on a higher elevation than where I now stood—it looked as though there was going to be plenty of large-scale walking in my immediate future, especially uphill walking. I slowly climbed toward the main entrance, wondering whether to go on or simply to declare a truce and go back to the hotel. Then I remembered that I'd promised Nikki that I'd visit the Kiyomizu Temple that day, so I gritted my teeth and continued onward and upward.

In front of me I saw a pretty young Japanese woman wearing a navy blue polyester suit and holding up a cardboard sign that read, "Official Guide, Kiyomizu Temple."

I slowly approached her and asked, "Is there a way I can visit the temple without too much walking?"

"I'll take you around," she said. "There's much to see. My name is April."

On the one hand, "There's much to see" is exactly what I didn't want to hear. The day was warm and somewhat humid. I was still grossly out of condition, despite the exercise that Suzuki had inflicted on me in Nara. After all, one day of walking can't make up for decades of living the life of an overstuffed couch potato. On the other hand, "I'll take you around" sounded wonderful. If only she'd been with me on the Philosophers' Pathway when I was robbed by the gunman, Inspector Watanabe would have had to take me seriously.

Then I wondered what the opposition would do when they saw that I was with April. They had not tried anything at Nijo Castle when they realized that Yosh's people were protecting me; maybe the whole morning would be wasted because I'd accepted April's offer. I was about to tell her that I'd prefer to visit the site on my own when I realized that there was a considerable difference between my being accompanied by an official guide and my being protected by trained operatives. Accordingly I thanked April warmly and told her that I looked forward to visiting the temple with her.

She led me up the hill to the temple gateway, a large imposing structure, essentially a complete building with the front and back walls missing. In front of us was a three-story orange pagoda. April explained that the entire wooden pagoda had been built without a single nail. Past the pagoda there was a glorious view of the whole of Kyoto laid out below us. Despite my earlier misgivings about climbing around the temple grounds, this panorama made it all worthwhile.

After I'd drunk my fill of the view, April explained to me that the temple is dedicated to Kannon, an eleven-faced goddess of mercy who has the power to bring about an easy childbirth. Unfortunately, April went on, the Main Hall was closed for repairs, but she would show me the Jishu Shrine behind the Main Hall instead. The fact that the Main Hall was closed came as no surprise to me—I'd yet to visit a temple that was open to the public as described in my guidebooks—and I was willing to accept the Jishu Shrine as a substitute.

April explained that Jishu is a Shinto shrine dedicated to Okuninushino-Mikoto, a god of love and marriage. I found it to be a most unusual place because it was the only shrine in Kyoto where I saw explanatory signs in English. April first showed me the racks holding *ema* votive plaques. These wooden plaques with pictures and writing are letters to the god requesting that one's wishes be granted. You buy a plaque and place it in a slot. Then, on the first and third Sunday of every month, the chief priest of the shrine prays that your wish will be granted. I asked April to find a votive plaque for a long and happy marriage, which I duly bought and placed in the slot.

She then took me to a statue of Okuninushino-Mikoto. Next to the life-size bronze statue was a smaller stone statue of a large rabbit, the messenger of the god of love and marriage. The symbolism was pretty obvious, even to me. By this time I was panting from the exertion, but April insisted on showing me two stones about ten yards apart.

"If you can walk from the one stone to the other with your eyes closed," April explained, "Your love wishes will come true without fail."

Well, I thought, it certainly doesn't hurt to try. I stood with my back to the one stone, closed my eyes, and started off for the second stone. April stopped me as I was about to trip over a statue on the other side of the stone plaza. I was so far off-target that the thought crossed my mind that my marriage was in real trouble.

Next, April wanted to show me the Kiyomizu Temple from the side to enable me to appreciate the origin of the expression "jumping from the veranda of the Kiyomizu Temple." This expression, she explained to me, means being about to undertake some bold or daring adventure. Despite my protestations, we walked from the Jishu Shrine to the gardens on the south side of the Kiyomizu Temple. Finally, we approached a gap in the trees. April wanted to point something out to me, but I insisted that we first sit down for a few minutes on a convenient stone bench so that I could catch my breath. The combination of heat, humidity and exercise was taking its toll. Finally, I indicated that I was ready and able to see the next item on her agenda, and we both got up from the bench.

April led the way back to the gap in the trees and pointed toward the temple complex. As I peered through the gap, I could see the three-story orange pagoda at the entrance to the Main Temple. "Do you see the base of the pagoda?" April asked. "Now look a little to your left…"

Her voice trailed off as she suddenly saw what I saw. There was a narrow ledge that formed part of the otherwise steep mountainside to the left of the pagoda and about five yards below it. Between the ledge and the pagoda the ground rose steeply, so steeply that it was impossible to see the ledge from the temple grounds, only from the side where we stood. On the ledge two men were fighting. One man moved stiffly. Even at that distance I could see that he was badly hurt. The second man punched the first man two or three times, and then he rushed toward him and pushed. The first man tumbled off the narrow ledge toward the ground hundreds of yards below. The second man then clambered along the ledge and disappeared from our view.

From where we stood, the large trees prevented us from seeing where the body of the first man lay, but, from the height of the ledge from which he was pushed, there could be no doubt whatsoever that the first man was dead.

"Wait here!" April said. "I'll call the police and report the murder."

The word "police" brought back unhappy memories of Inspector Watanabe, but at least he wouldn't be able to pin the murder on me. April and I had witnessed the fight together from a cliff top at least two hundred yards away from the ledge, so my alibi was thankfully unbreakable. Even better, April had witnessed the murder with me and would report it to the police herself. This time there was no way that Inspector Watanabe could insinuate that I was making up the whole story.

I watched April as she ran back to the Main Temple and from there toward the orange pagoda. She disappeared from view as she reached the steep slope that led down to the gateway. There was no point in my standing in the heat when there was a shady bench a few yards away. I returned to the bench to wait for April to return once she'd told the police what had occurred.

After fifteen minutes April hadn't returned. I wondered what had happened to her. After thirty minutes I became worried. After forty-five minutes I was greatly concerned. And after a full hour had gone by and April still hadn't come back, I was in a state of full-blown panic for the second time in two successive days.

I got up from the bench and followed the path along which April had run. In New York City, by this time there would have been yellow police tape around the pagoda to allow the investigation to proceed unhindered. There would have been TV crews filming the area and interviewing bystanders. Most of all, there would have been an air of excitement all around.

However, as I walked as fast as I could through the grounds of the Kiyomizu Temple, the atmosphere was as totally calm as before. It was as if nothing whatsoever had happened. Unending streams of schoolchildren carried on flowing into and out of the temple complex, and worshippers continued to walk up to statues and say their prayers. Buddhist monks went on strolling purposefully through the area, and tourists kept on taking photographs of everything and anything. It was clear that no one was yet aware of the fact that a murder had been committed an hour before on the ledge just below the orange pagoda.

What had happened to April? Had the killer intercepted her and killed her, too? This was unlikely, because April had run along the major thoroughfare through the temple grounds. More seriously, April surely had a cell phone. Why didn't she call the police right away, and stay with me until the police came?

I was in a quandary. What should I do? If I called the police, what would I say, even assuming that the person who answered the phone understood English? Eventually I realized that I had two choices. I could take a taxi back to my hotel and forget about the whole thing, or I could take a taxi to police headquarters and tell Inspector Watanabe what had happened. My inclination was to go straight back to my hotel, of course, but what would happen when April told her story? I'd surely find myself in jail for failing to report a murder. So, I waited at the entrance to the temple complex until a taxi arrived with tourists, then I asked the driver to take me to police headquarters.

We soon arrived at the imposing stone building. It looked even less like a police station than before. I wondered if perhaps it had been the head office of a major trading house or possibly even a large insurance company. I paid the driver, climbed up the steps and entered the building. There was a woman sitting at a desk to my left. I showed her my passport and asked to see Inspector Watanabe. She picked up the telephone and spoke for a few seconds. Then she called over a man in uniform who escorted me along the same route as previously to the same interview room.

The ashtray had been cleaned, but the smell of cigarette smoke still permeated the room as before. I sat down on the chair opposite the wanted poster to wait for Inspector Watanabe.

Perhaps I was reading more into the situation that I should have. Nevertheless, it was my impression that the inspector wasn't too pleased to see me but hid his irritation as best he could. As succinctly as I could I told him what had happened. I stressed the fact that April had been with me and that she'd therefore been a witness to the murder. He just nodded, and left the room.

A few minutes later he was back. He looked worried.

"Your guide April didn't report the murder. Also, no ambulance has been dispatched to the area below the Kiyomizu Temple today. Let's go there."

We took a back route out of the building to where a car and driver were waiting. With siren blaring, we raced to the temple complex. During the entire trip Inspector Watanabe spoke into his cell phone. It sounded as if he was switching rapidly from one person to another. Sometimes he listened, but most of the time he barked commands. It seemed to me that a large proportion of the Kyoto police force was being mobilized.

As the car neared the top of the steep street leading to the entrance to the temple, I pointed out where the taxi had dropped me. Watanabe shouted something into his phone, then told the driver to stop. The inspector and I got out of the car. Then the driver started speaking into the microphone that was plugged into the police radio mounted on the dashboard.

"Here was where the taxi dropped me," I explained, pointing to the spot again. "I crossed here, and here was where April was waiting."

Standing at almost the identical place was a Buddhist monk. His colorful robes and headdress contrasted strongly with the simple navy blue polyester suit that April had worn. Inspector Watanabe bowed most respectfully to the monk and had a lengthy conversation with him. The monk then walked through the gateway and entered the temple complex.

Inspector Watanabe turned to me. "Come, let's sit on this bench. There's a lot for us to talk about."

We walked over to a wooden bench just beyond where the monk had stood.

"Do you recall the words on April's sign?" he asked.

"The first line said 'Official Guide' and the second line said 'Kiyomizu Temple.'"

"How big was the sign?"

I was about to point out that, with a dead body lying below the ledge, the size of the sign was totally irrelevant. But I held my tongue. There was no point in trying to argue with Inspector Watanabe— no point whatsoever.

"The sign was about twelve inches by about six inches."

Watanabe nodded. "Was it a plastic sign?"

"No, it was thin cardboard. I know that because after she'd introduced herself to me she folded the sign and put it in her handbag."

"Was it a hand-lettered sign?" the inspector continued.

I was becoming increasingly irritated with this line of questioning, but I again I didn't say anything. Instead I replied as calmly as I could, "The letters could have been printed on a computer; the cardboard was pretty thin."

"Was she wearing a name badge?"

I pondered the question. "I don't think so."

Then I remembered. "No, she was definitely not wearing a name badge, because I recall during the tour seeing April standing next to a schoolgirl in a navy blue sailor suit. I thought it was amusing that they were both in navy blue uniforms, and then I noticed that only the student wore a name badge."

"How much did she say she'd charge for her services as guide?"

"Nothing. From the way she spoke, I assumed that her services were included in the admission fee."

"The senior monk who was standing here has stated categorically that the temple does not employ official guides. Occasionally a monk will be asked to show a visiting dignitary around the temple complex, but there are no full-time guides employed here. Even if there were, the rules of the order would require all such guides to be men. There's no way that the temple would ever employ a woman as an official guide.

"Next, we Japanese are a proud people with a long heritage. It's extremely rare for one of us to adopt an English first name. No, it isn't unknown. But I can't recall the last time that I heard of a Kyoto resident, other than a prostitute, who told a foreigner that her name was April or the like. In fact, even someone born abroad of Japanese ancestry who returns to live in Japan will almost always adopt a Japanese first name and use it at all times, even in dealings with foreigners.

"That leads to another idea. Is there any possibility that this wasn't a Japanese woman? Could she have been Korean, say, or Indonesian?"

"I really have no idea." I said. "To me, she seemed Japanese."

Now I could contain myself no longer. "Why are you asking all these questions about April? April has nothing to do with it. A murder has been committed, a murder witnessed by two people, and you're concentrating on one of the witnesses, ignoring both the killer and the victim. What's going on?"

He ignored my outburst completely. It was as if I'd said absolutely nothing at all. Calmly he continued to speak.

"My initial deduction was that this April is a scam artist of some kind. Here in Kyoto there are a number of universities, and students volunteer as guides in order to improve their English. They don't charge for this service, but you have to pay their expenses, such as transportation, entrance fees and meals.

"I don't believe that April was a volunteer student guide. I first thought that she was going to escort you all over the temple complex, then demand a huge fee for her services. Because the two of you hadn't previously discussed money, you wouldn't have had a leg to stand on. Her amateurish sign, lack of official nametag and the use of a foreign name all support this theory.

"Then I learned in the car on the way over here that no shake-down activities of that kind have been reported either to the police or to the monks of this temple. On the other hand, a tourist who has been cheated this way is often too ashamed to report to it to anyone. Also, the language barrier is very real. Most tourists would have no idea how to find someone in authority who could speak English sufficiently well to understand their complaint and act on it.

"However, before this April could shake you down for a large sum of money, you and she witnessed a murder. April could hardly report the murder to the police, because her unofficial guiding activities would immediately come to light. After all, she had no way of knowing whether an earlier victim had reported her, and contact with the police might well lead to a lengthy jail term. Then, when she saw the murder, she just ran away.

"That would explain everything that has happened up to now. Oh, good, here comes Detective Sergeant Takahashi. I've been waiting for his report."

A plainclothes officer came running up to us. Watanabe rose from the bench, excused himself, and listened to Sergeant Takahashi's report. When he returned to the bench his eyebrows were already at half-mast. By now I knew what this meant, and I braced myself for trouble.

"The sergeant has inspected the ledge where you said the fight took place, as well the slopes below the ledge where the body would have fallen. Three other detectives assisted him. All four are exceptionally competent. One of the things I was doing on the phone as we drove over here was to order those four detectives to come here to the temple and investigate the crime.

"First, there are indications that someone walked on the ledge not too long ago, but only one person, not two. Had there been a fight, there surely would have been footprints of two different people. Second, there's absolutely no sign of a body lying on the slopes below the ledge or, for that matter, of a body having been there earlier today and then removed. Third, there's no evidence of a body having fallen down the mountainside. There are no broken branches or even twigs, no stones have been dislodged, and there are no marks in the sand from a body that rolled after someone had pushed it off the ledge.

"Fourth, there's no evidence whatsoever of the existence of this mysterious 'April.' In fact, not only is there no evidence that she exists, but neither the police nor the monks of this temple have ever received any reports regarding the presence of an unofficial guide."

His eyebrows slowly continued to rise.

"Now we come to the 'murder' you reported. Just like the 'armed robbery' on the Philosophers' Pathway, there's absolutely no evidence of any kind that it ever happened. Quite the contrary in fact. There's no way that two people can fight on a grassy ledge and leave only one set of footprints, and a body hurtling down a mountainside can't vaporize into thin air.

"Now you will return to your hotel. If you contact me again, I'll have you arrested for filing a false police report." He gave me the very briefest of bows, turned his back to me and strode off.

Fortunately a taxi was dropping off passengers at the temple entrance as he spoke, and I was able to leave the temple area immediately. My mind was totally unable to comprehend what was happening to me. Yosh had assured me that everything I said to him had been verified and that I was the most honest client he'd ever had. Now Inspector Watanabe was telling me that absolutely nothing I'd said could be verified, quite the contrary in fact. I'd witnessed a murder that hadn't taken place in the company of a guide who didn't exist. There was only one explanation: I'd gone crazy.

But much worse was to follow.

CHAPTER NINETEEN

I unlocked the door of Room 1507 of the Mikado Hotel in Kyoto, turned on the light and stepped inside. The first thing I saw was Yoko Azuma's body lying in my bed. She was still wearing her navy blue bellhop's uniform, including the perky cap, but her blood had flowed all over the pillow as well as the sheet and floral bedspread that covered her. Even her cap was smeared with blood. I rushed out of the room as fast as I could. As I reached the bank of four elevators, one arrived. The doors opened and two elderly Japanese women, resplendent in silver and peacock blue kimonos, slowly exited. I pushed past them into the elevator and slammed my fist on the button for the lobby. The women didn't even glance back at me.

As the elevator began to descend the fifteen floors, I realized that this would mean a third interview in a week with Inspector Watanabe. I didn't relish the prospect.

The image of the dead girl in my bed haunted me. As the elevator doors opened, I could see that the lobby of the Mikado Hotel was crowded. I rushed toward the front desk as fast as I could. On my left, a line of dozens of smartly dressed men and women waited for an elevator to take them to a wedding reception in one of the ballrooms. I pushed through them, and also through the line of businessmen waiting patiently to check in. I caught a glimpse of the general manager of the hotel, Mr. Mori, about to enter the room behind the check-in counter, and shouted across to him.

"Yoko Azuma is dead—her body is in my bed!"

The Japanese highly prize the ability of not showing any emotion. Mr. Mori had demonstrated that skill to me on a previous occasion, and now had no problem in demonstrating it again.

"Why, Mr. Thompson, how good to see you again. How are you today?"

I repeated, "Yoko Azuma is dead—her body is in my bed!"

Mori didn't bat an eyelid. "Come," he said, "Let's go up to your room and see."

He walked around the check-in counter, put a friendly arm on my shoulder and firmly walked me to the bank of elevators. The long line of waiting wedding guests moved back, making room for Mori and me at the head of the line. After a few seconds, an elevator arrived. The doors opened. Out walked two American tourists, festooned with cameras. Behind them, pushing a laden luggage trolley, came Yoko Azuma.

There was no sign of blood anywhere on her bellhop uniform, even her perky cap was clean and crisp as always. And the happy grin was back in place.

Exiting the elevator at the Mikado Hotel, Yoko Azuma bowed deeply and respectfully to her boss. Mr. Mori returned her bow. Then she saw me and bowed, not quite so respectfully. She then put her arm against the door of the elevator to prevent it from closing to allow Mori and me to enter. Despite the long queue, no one else joined us in the elevator.

We rode in silence to the fifteenth floor. We walked to my room, and I inserted my card into the electronic lock of Room 1507. I walked in. Mori closely followed. The room was exactly as I'd left it, but with just a few important differences. The bed was empty, there was no blood on the pillow, there was no blood on the sheet and there was no blood on the floral bedspread.

***

"Please repeat what you saw when you entered the room, Mr. Thompson," said Inspector Watanabe. Mr. Mori had called the police and they had received instructions to take me to the inspector. We were once again in the small interview room at Kyoto Police Headquarters. I'd been sitting there for over an hour.

"I've already told you twice what happened."

"Please tell me again."

"I unlocked the door of this room, I stepped inside, and saw Yoko Azuma's body lying in my bed."

"How could you see her in the darkness?"

"I told you, I turned on the light."

"No, Mr. Thompson, you mentioned nothing about lights before."

"I unlocked the door," I said through gritted teeth. "I switched on the light. I walked into the room. I saw the body of Yoko Azuma lying in my bed. She was dead."

"How did you know she was dead?"

"She was pale like a dead person, and there was blood everywhere on the bed and on her cap."

"But you've just seen Yoko Azuma for yourself, here in this very room. She didn't seem at all dead to me, and I couldn't see any blood on her. Also, there's no blood anywhere on your bed. She also denied entering your room at any time other than the first day when she carried your luggage into your room. How do you explain this?"

"I can't explain it any more than I can explain the murder at the Kiyomizu Temple or the armed robbery on the Philosophers' Pathway. But all three crimes happened."

"Mr. Thompson," said Inspector Watanabe with exquisite politeness, "I understand from Mr. Mori that you're waiting for you wife to rejoin you. I'll have you driven back to your hotel, and you will stay in your room until your wife returns. You will then have twenty-four hours to leave Japan."

He gave the briefest of bows, then left.

In the taxi back to the Mikado Hotel, I decided that I'd die happy if I never saw Inspector Watanabe, Mr. Mori or Yoko Azuma again. To that list I added the Mikado Hotel and the city of Kyoto.

Unfortunately, I had to go back to the hotel to await Nikki's return from Stockholm.

Standing at the hotel entrance was Yoko Azuma, perky cap, happy grin and all. And behind the front desk was Mr. Mori. I put on the best face I could manage under the circumstances and returned to Room 1507. I tried to sleep but, for obvious reasons, sleep eluded me. I opened the refrigerator and liberally sampled the well-stocked bar. The only effect was that I got drunk, but remained wide-awake. How I wished that Nikki would return.

Finally, I dropped off to sleep.

CHAPTER TWENTY

I lay on the bed, just staring into space. I'd been doing so for nearly two hours since awakening. Then my BlackBerry rang. It was Nikki.

"Darling, I'm in Osaka, at the Shinkansen platform at Kansai International Airport. I'll be with you in an hour and a half. I can't wait to see you again! Oh, I have to board the train. Bye!"

And the Nikki-gram ended. I looked at my watch. It was just after 10. By the time that Nikki arrived, it would be 11:30 a.m. Kyoto time or 4:30 a.m. Stockholm time. I decided to have Nikki's favorite food waiting for her. I called room service and ordered a large pot of Beluga caviar to be brought to Room 1507 at exactly 11:30 a.m., together with a bottle of 1985 Dom Pérignon champagne.

As I hung up, there was the sound of someone trying to open the door. I'd bolted it and as a result the electronic key didn't work. But who could this be? Neither Nikki nor the caviar could possibly arrive for another ninety minutes. In any event, the hotel staff would knock before trying to unlock the door. I got up from the bed and looked through the peephole. To my total surprise, I saw Nikki, and next to her the familiar navy blue of a bellhop's uniform. She certainly had needed to buy clothes in Stockholm, and the bellhop must have brought up her new suitcases laden with her many Swedish purchases, which she no doubt would now proudly show me.

I opened the door with joy. There stood Nikki. Her face was grim. On her right was Fred, my brother-in-law, wearing a navy blue blazer. They were both wearing gloves. Without saying a word, Nikki pushed me into the room. As Fred followed her and closed the door, she took a silver-gray gun out of her Gucci handbag. I've no knowledge of guns and couldn't identify it in any way. But I did notice that it had a silencer.

As at our very first meeting, I was rendered totally speechless.

"Lie down on the bed," she ordered.

Not only could I not speak, I couldn't move.

"Lie down on the bed." Her voice was louder this time.

I was rigid with fear. Fred and Nikki maneuvered me onto the bed. Then Fred sat down in one of the comfortable armchairs with which the room was furnished. Keeping the gun pointed firmly at my head, Nikki shifted the other armchair until it was only a yard from me. Then she sat down, too, and started moving the gun ever closer to my head.

"Nikki, darling, what's going on?"

Fred spoke up. "We're going to kill you, then place the gun in your hand and make it look like a suicide. After all, you and everyone else know that you've gone crazy. Suicide is the only answer."

Nikki hissed, "Shut up, Fred!"

"No, I won't shut up. I'm going to tell him everything. I want him to suffer, just like he's made me suffer. For eight years this man has humiliated me. He sends me those legal documents he's drafted, with each page bearing the header "DRAFT" to ensure that there's no risk that the Bar Association will charge him with trying to practice law. I then have the ultimate humiliation. I am allowed to make precisely one change to each document—I use my word processor to remove the one-word header. Then I print out the document, and mail it to him with a cover letter that makes it clear that I'm responsible in every way for the document. I'm not even allowed to send an account to the client. This selfish bastard decides how much the work is worth, based on the number of hours *he* spends on it, and charges the client accordingly, in my name. At least I'm allowed to deposit the checks in my bank account after he's forwarded them to me."

Had it not been for the gun that Nikki was pointing at my head from a distance of about a foot, I'd have mentioned that, thanks to me, Fred had an income of about $250,000 a year with no expenses in return for less than an hour's work each week. However, the presence of the gun, replete with silencer, made me considerably more conciliatory than I otherwise would have been.

"Fred, I never made you suffer—"

"You will listen, and you will not interrupt. If you interrupt just once more, we'll kill you," Fred said. This didn't seem like much of a threat, because clearly they were going to kill me anyway, but listening and not interrupting seemed a good thing to do at the time.

"I'll begin with the item that's going to hurt you the most," Fred said. "For the past two years, Nikki and I have been lovers."

I was so flabbergasted by this revelation that I forgot that I'd be killed if I interrupted and I said, "But, but—"

Nikki knew exactly what I was trying to say. She said to Fred, "Oliver here had the greatest difficulty in deflowering me on our wedding night. There was no possible doubt in his mind that I was a virgin. My dear husband, however, is so sexually naïve that he's not even heard of the plastic surgeons in Switzerland who 'restore virginity,' especially for brides of rich Arab men."

Turning to me, she went on. "You kept asking me how a virgin could possibly be so sexually knowledgeable, and then you thought that it was part of the curriculum at my Swiss finishing school. The very idea of those prim and proper Swiss teachers even mentioning sex was hilarious, let alone providing instruction in the techniques I employed that night, but I couldn't explain all that to you, of course. Now do you understand?"

I nodded.

Fred asked Nikki, "Did his sexual performance ever improve to the point where you no longer had to fake it?"

Nikki laughed a truly nasty laugh. "The issue never arose because, soon after the honeymoon, my dear husband totally lost his sexual urge. Darling, did you ever wonder why you lost your urge?" There was no love in the word "darling."

I said nothing, and Nikki continued.

"Soon after I hired Alexandre, I told him that you were HIV-positive but that you refused, point blank, to use a condom. I obtained a supply of cyproterone acetate, and I told Alexandre that, to save my life, he should slip a large dose of the drug into one dish in every meal, thereby rendering you impotent. It was always the dish that was most laden with fat and cholesterol, the kind of food that I never touch but that you can't resist. And the more food you ate, the fatter you got, and the more cyproterone acetate you ingested. Yes, there certainly are women who are turned on by grossly fat men, but I assure you that I'm not one of them, never mind what I told you when I took you to lunch at Guido's that first day I met you. Fat is a major sexual turn-off for most women, including me, but in your case, the more fatty food you ate, the more you turned yourself off.

"That was why Alexandre always stayed in the kitchen. As a fellow male, he couldn't face you while knowing that, by lacing your food with cyproterone acetate, he'd rendered you totally impotent."

Now it was Fred's turn again. "Let's tell him what we did to him in Kyoto."

Before I could say anything, Nikki spoke. "You're going to tell us that we weren't in Kyoto because I was in Stockholm. I wasn't. My mother lives in Palm Springs, and, as far as I know, she's in the best of health and has been for years. Fred flew to Kyoto five days before you and I did, leaving a note for dear Eloise that was plausible enough for her not to go looking for him for another week or two. She thinks that Fred is in New York putting through that big deal that'll make them rich beyond their wildest dreams. By the time that Eloise wakes up to the fact that Fred isn't in New York and, in fact, will never return to her, he and I will be safely in the Caribbean, where we'll live on your money for the rest of our lives."

I had to interrupt. "But what about the prenuptial contract?"

"Well, what about it?" replied Nikki with a humorless laugh. "The prenuptial contract was worded exactly the way you wanted. It dealt with what would happen to our respective assets in the event of a divorce. But there isn't going to be a divorce, darling. You're going to commit suicide, and your ever-loving widow is going to inherit hundreds of millions of dollars of your money, perhaps more. You were even stupid enough to draft your own will and send it to Fred. Of course, Fred immediately informed me of its contents. You were so in love with me that you left everything you own to me. What a fool!

"Actually, ever since we've been married, I've been trying to kill you. The rich food, remember? *Haute cuisine* doesn't seem to have much effect on the French, perhaps because of the red wine they drink. But when I first met you, your arteries were already lined with gobs of yellow fat, and I've done everything I could to thicken the layers of fat to the point where the coronary arteries clog and you get a terminal heart attack, or where an embolus from the carotid artery causes a fatal stroke. I hired the best chef available at the time and paid Alexandre a princely salary—from your income, of course. There was true poetic irony in you paying for your own death through your disgusting overeating.

"The really funny part was when your doctor so astutely connected your total lack of sexual urge to your uncontrollable craving for food, but then proceeded to refer you to that psychiatrist whom you refused to consult because you won't discuss sex with a woman. What's so hilarious is that she wouldn't have started any psychotherapy until she'd excluded all physical causes. That's right, she would've done what your dear Doctor Arthur Buller overlooked. She would've ordered a complete physical examination, including blood work, which surely would've shown up the cyproterone acetate. Of course, Fred and I couldn't let that happen because you were our future meal ticket. But thanks to your adolescent sexual outlook, you refused to see her. You just went on eating Alexandre's superb food in ever increasing quantities, getting fatter and fatter as you ingested more and more cyproterone acetate. Just look at Fred, see how slim and muscular he is. Can you imagine any woman wanting to sleep with you rather than with Fred? You always mocked Eloise for having married Fred. But which of you had a better sex life: you or Eloise?

"Now, where was I? Oh, yes, Fred flew here five days before we did. He rented a furnished apartment diagonally across the road from the Mikado Hotel and, yes, every time I called you it was from the apartment, from a Japanese cell phone that Fred acquired soon after he arrived here. It's extremely unlikely that there'll be any sort of police investigation of your suicide. But in the unlikely event that your dear friend Inspector Watanabe investigates what will seem to be in every way a routine suicide, he'll learn that, despite what you said to him and Mr. Mori, you received no phone calls from overseas. Yes, he'll discover the calls I made to you on our Japanese phone, but there's no way that he can connect that phone to Fred or me—Fred bought it through a local intermediary.

"Your dead body will soon be discovered by your loving wife who will be utterly heartbroken. In the extremely unlikely event that the good inspector actually looks into the matter, he'll discover that your wife never flew to Stockholm, let alone flew back from Stockholm. He'll conclude that, no matter what you told him, the idea that I'd been in Stockholm was also a figment of your over feverish imagination or, more likely, part of the many delusions from which you so clearly suffered before you put this gun to your head and fired. You'd obviously realized that there was no hope that you'd ever be able to lead a normal life again and therefore, in a fit of depression, you decided to end it all in a luxury Kyoto hotel room.

"But there'll be no investigation. In Japan, committing suicide is considered an honorable act, and what could be more honorable than for one of the most brilliant CPAs in the world to kill himself when he realizes that he's lost his reason?

"On the other hand, it's undeniably true that, when an American citizen dies in a foreign country under unusual circumstances, especially if he's very rich, the American embassy insists on an police investigation. In some cases, top investigators are even flown in from Washington, D.C. But your loving wife will quickly have you cremated and your ashes scattered on the Sea of Japan—no way will we allow Eloise to organize an autopsy back in America. I'll rent a fancy launch, drape it in black, sail out into international waters and scatter your ashes there. I'll tell Eloise that, as an expert on offshore trusts, you always wanted to be buried offshore."

Nikki paused for a moment to give a loving look to Fred, and then continued.

"Oliver, I know with absolute certainty that there won't be any sort of inquiry into your 'suicide.' Too many people can attest that you've gone stark staring crazy, too many important people."

At that point I knew with equally absolute certainty that I was going to die very soon. Nikki was going to shoot me by placing the gun against my head and firing. She'd then put the gun into my right hand, and she and Fred would leave Room 1507. Eventually someone would find me, probably Nikki, and the verdict would be obvious: suicide while of unsound mind, with Inspector Watanabe providing overwhelming evidence of insanity.

Suddenly, I realized that there was a weakness in their scheme. I remembered reading somewhere that there's a chemical test that can prove, beyond all doubt, whether or not someone has recently fired a gun. Even, I thought, in a country with as high a suicide rate and as low a murder rate as Japan, the police would make every effort to be certain that a suicide was exactly that, and not a murder in disguise. They would definitely check my right hand and discover that I hadn't fired the gun.

This revelation, however, didn't solve the problem of not getting murdered in the first place. If I pointed out the weakness in their plan to the murderous duo, they would put the gun into my hand and then force my fingers to pull the trigger. Nikki, I knew, was amazingly strong, whereas I was a 450-pound weakling. With Fred to tip the balance, there was no question that they could compel me to shoot myself. The question was how to avert any sort of shooting at all.

My first reaction was to play for time. I asked Nikki, "How did you get hold of the gun?"

As Nikki started to reply, Fred cut across her. "The day I arrived here in Kyoto, I contacted my former client, the yakuza cocaine smuggler Matsuko Hirohito. He's so grateful that my legal brilliance saved him from fifty years in a high security prison that he's willing to do anything for me, including procuring the gun Nikki is holding. He also sold me the phone Nikki used, and the cocaine I used to bribe Yoko Azuma. Yoko's cheery smile masks a major drug habit. In return for a big baggie of cocaine she was willing to do anything."

Suddenly, I saw it all.

"Your one-time stepfather, James Dragonhead, he didn't die of an accidental drug overdose, did he? You killed him by giving him a drug mixture that was a lot stronger than he was expecting. No, I'm wrong. You added something to his cocaine, something deadly."

Nikki smiled proudly. I knew I was on the right track.

"You killed him in order to inherit the Dragonhead Family Trust. Once you turned twenty-five, you no longer had any income from your grandfather's trust. You thought that the Dragonhead Family Trust contained tens of millions of dollars, money that you and Fred could live on for the rest of your lives. Once you had control of the Dragonhead Family Trust, your financial problems would be over for good. Fred could immediately leave Eloise for you—there wouldn't be a need to conduct a clandestine affair any longer. But when you contacted the trustees, you received a rude shock; the trust all but was insolvent. Am I right?"

Nikki had continued to smile, and now she nodded. "When it comes to money," she said to Fred, "There's no one in the whole wide world who's smarter than Oliver here." There was no sarcasm or bitterness in her voice, nor any pride in having selected so clever a husband. Nikki was simply stating a fact.

"Having failed to net the Dragonhead millions," I said to Nikki, "you and Fred decided to go after the Thompson millions. In the meantime, you had to have money to live in New York—that hotel you stayed in before we got married is pretty expensive. And I think I know who paid for that hotel. It was Fred, right?" I didn't wait for a response from either of them. I knew I was correct.

"And where did Fred get that money from?" I continued. "It must've come from the $250,000 I arranged for him to have each year. I pay him that money in order for him and Eloise to live in comfort in Philadelphia, but he seems to have used rather a large chunk of it for you to live in luxury in New York. That 'big deal' that Eloise told me that you, Fred, were working on was just a cover for your visits to the love nest that, indirectly at least, I was paying for. Nikki, the irony is unbelievable. I sent money to Fred for him and Eloise to live together without financial worries, but the money was used to enable you and Fred to cheat on both Eloise and me.

"And here's another idea, Nikki. Once we were married, I gave you your own American Express Centurion card and told you to use it to your heart's content. Remember, I arranged for the charges on that card to be paid each month sight unseen directly from my bank, because I didn't want you to think that I was prying into the way you spent my money. But if I'd looked, I'm sure I'd have found huge monthly charges for a suite at some luxury hotel where you and Fred could rendezvous while I was at work, or perhaps you rented a super luxury apartment because that would be more discrete. In fact, I bet you took an apartment in the same building as your good friend Elisabièta, to ensure that if you were seen entering or leaving the building, you had a superlative cover story."

This time it was Fred who smiled. "Nikki was right. You really are unbelievably smart when it comes to money."

"Yes, Fred, I'm so smart that I've paid for my own murder. My money was used to pay for your air ticket to Japan and for the rental of the furnished apartment across the road from this hotel. I paid for all of your Kyoto expenses. Worst of all, I paid for the baggie of drugs that you bought from Matsuko Hirohito to bribe poor Yoko, and may have killed her."

"And we even used your money to pay Matsuko for this gun, and that's what we're going to use to kill you."

There was a sudden silence, and I realized that I'd been too clever. I'd arrived at a point where everything had been said. There was nothing more for them to do except kill me.

Then I remembered the Beluga caviar and champagne that I'd ordered.

CHAPTER TWENTY-ONE

I looked at my watch. It was eleven o'clock. I spoke up.

"There's just one problem with your plans. In about thirty minutes, room service will be here with a large pot of Beluga caviar and a chilled bottle of champagne. I told them to deliver the order at 11:30 a.m. when my wife was arriving, in order for her to have her favorite food on her return to Kyoto." That last part wasn't true, but there was no way for them to know that.

"So what?" sneered Fred. "Are telling us to kill you quickly, before the caviar arrives? Or are you worried that the noise of the shot will cause the caviar to collapse, like a soufflé? Don't worry, that was why we brought a silencer. The police will no doubt think that you were considerate and bought the silencer to be sure that you wouldn't disturb the other guests, but the real reason is that you didn't want to harm the caviar." He and Nikki proceeded to chortle.

"Wait a minute. You and Nikki have forgotten one thing. Inspector Watanabe will testify that I undoubtedly suffer from delusions, but that I utterly believe in the truth of those delusions. He'll certainly testify that, if I ordered my wife's favorite meal in the belief that she'd arrive at 11:30 a.m., there's no doubt whatsoever that I was certain that my wife was coming at 11:30 a.m. In other words, whether or not Nikki was really coming at that time, the inspector will state that, to the best of his belief, I was totally certain that my wife was arriving at that time. Why on earth would I kill myself before she arrived? If that happened, there'd unquestionably be real doubts about my death, for that and the other reason."

"What other reason?" Fred asked. He sounded interested, for the first time.

I ignored his question, and proceeded. "If the police suspect foul play, they'll surely pass their suspicions on to the American authorities. And if the New York State Probate Court decides that it's likely that Nikki was somehow involved in my death, she won't get one single, solitary red cent. Remember, according to New York State law, a murderer can't benefit from his or her crime. Yes, you could file suit in a New York State court to try to force the Probate Court to pay you your inheritance, but that would trigger a full-scale American investigation of my 'suicide,' the very last thing either of you can afford. After all, the cocaine has probably killed Yoko by now, and the murders of Yoko and James Dragonhead will be linked, followed by a realization that I was murdered, too. Accordingly, every penny of my money will go to Eloise, which will make you very happy, Fred."

The thought of Eloise inheriting hundreds of millions of dollars while he and Nikki at best starved on a beach in the Caribbean—and at worst rotted in a jail in Japan or America—clearly infuriated Fred, but he said nothing.

"Here's the situation," I explained. "If you kill me before the caviar and champagne arrive, you won't get any money, and you'll almost certainly be convicted of murder for the two reasons I've given. But if—"

"What two reasons? What's the second reason?" Fred interrupted.

Again I ignored him. I wanted him to be uneasy.

"On the other hand, once the room service waiter arrives, I'll tell him I'm being held at gun point, and that'll be end of that. But if you let me go now, nothing will happen to you."

"No, we'll just be convicted of two murders and conspiracy to murder," said Fred.

"On whose evidence? Inspector Watanabe won't listen to me. Yoko is either going to die or she'll have to deny everything in order to avoid a long prison sentence for drug use, because the Japanese authorities penalize druggies very heavily.

"It's certainly true that you've committed murder and armed robbery and shoe theft, and the way you've been brandishing that gun and threatening to kill me with it is highly illegal, I'm sure. But there's no evidence against you other than what you've told me now, and here in Japan no one is going to believe a word I say about anything. Also, I doubt if the Bahamian police are going to be interested in opening an investigation into your stepfather's death when you two are living on an island with no extradition treaty with the Bahamas, especially if you change your names, as I'm sure you both will."

Nikki, who had been quiet for the past few minutes, finally spoke. "Fred, he's right. How can we be convicted of anything? The only crimes we can be charged with are the things we did here in Japan. If we let him go, the only risk is what might happen here. It won't be possible to charge us with armed robbery. There were no witnesses. The only person who knows anything about it is Oliver. And if my darling husband tries to communicate with the police, he'll be put in contact with Inspector Watanabe who is utterly convinced that Oliver is mad. The good inspector wants to lock Oliver up for filing three false police reports. If he sees Oliver again, he'll either jail him, deport him, or both.

"With regard to Yoko, she's probably already dead, and there's nothing to tie us to the drugs. But even if she's alive, there's nothing for her to gain and everything for her to lose by going to the police. After all, she'd have to admit that she's a cocaine addict and that she took part in her 'murder' in this room yesterday. I'm not sure what the charge for that would be, but I'm sure that Inspector Watanabe will find some felony or other. And, from what I've heard, a Japanese prison isn't a holiday resort. I think we should let him go. We're about to leave Japan in any event. Dear Oliver will also leave Japan just as soon as he can, and the matter will be closed."

I was about to compliment Nikki on her logic when Fred snarled, "What a great idea! So we let Oliver fly back to New York. Within one hour of his arrival he'll change his will, and one hour after that he'll file for divorce. If his clogged arteries let him live until the divorce is final, the prenuptial agreement comes into play. You'll get nothing, so we'll get nothing. And if he dies before the divorce is final, you'll certainly inherit nothing under his new will.

"Rubbish," Nikki said. "New York State law requires a husband to leave a third or a half or some such fraction to his widow."

"Not if he has good cause not to, and I'm sure that he'll leave enough evidence with his new lawyer that'll make it impossible for you to challenge the will. Furthermore, we can be certain that he'll tell Eloise everything, probably by telephone from the plane, and she'll immediately divorce me. She may be paranoid, but she definitely won't tolerate adultery on my part. I'll have no income, you'll have no income. It's true that two can live as cheaply as one, but not if both have zero income and zero assets."

"Just a minute," I said. "If the only reason you want to kill me is to have enough money to live in comfort together in the Caribbean for the rest of your lives, I'd be delighted to give you ten million dollars or whatever you need. One of you can open an account in a Kyoto bank. I'll send a fax to Miss

Dixon in my office in New York—you obviously won't let me phone her—and she'll wire the money to your new account. It may take a day to organize everything, but the three of us can eat and sleep in this room until you have your money and can transfer it to an offshore bank account. Then we can all leave Japan."

While I was talking I could see that Nikki thought that this might work, and was prepared to discuss my proposal to see if we could settle all the details to our mutual satisfaction. But when I finished speaking I glanced at Fred. It was all too clear that, unlike Nikki, money wasn't the driving factor behind his actions. Years of humiliation as my tame lawyer had taken their toll. I'd despised Fred so much that I hadn't realized that he was a human being with feelings, and now he wanted his revenge. Nikki had physically emasculated me with cyproterone acetate, but I'd emotionally emasculated Fred from the time Eloise had married him some eight years ago. Each time he received a document marked "DRAFT," he felt utterly humiliated and denigrated. And my cruel remark to him to stop him boasting about the Matsuko Hirohito case couldn't have done me much good. My legal chickens were now coming home to roost.

I realized that Nikki was thinking rationally but Fred was reacting to his emotions. Nothing I could say or do would prevent him from killing me, but perhaps I could postpone the inevitable until a miracle occurred. So I tried again. "If you kill me before the champagne and caviar arrive, then you'll certainly be convicted of murder. Why not at least wait until room service arrives?"

"Despite what you think," Fred said, "I'm not a total idiot. As you yourself pointed out, when the waiter arrives, you'll yell out, 'Help! Help! They're going to kill me! They have a gun! Help!' and that'll be the end of our plans."

"Wait a minute," Nikki said. "There's a way out. We'll march Oliver into the bathroom and gag him with a towel. You stay with him, keeping the gun pointed at his head. He said that room service knows that the caviar and champagne are for his wife's arrival, and what could be more natural than for his wife to be in the room to sign for the food and drink? Once the waiter has left, we can decide what to do. We can still kill Oliver or we can let him go. Both our options are still open."

"You fool," Fred hissed, "Once you sign for the food, there'll be evidence that you were here."

"So what? I'm *supposed* to be here. I never left Kyoto. After the 'suicide' I can tell the police that I asked Oliver for a divorce, and the double loss of his reason and his wife was enough to push him over the edge. If anything, it strengthens the suicide."

I could see that Fred wasn't totally convinced, but he was prepared to play along. "Okay, let's get him into the bathroom."

Fred and Nikki levered me off the bed, fastened my hands together behind my back with one of my neckties, and frog-marched me to the bathroom. They made me sit on the floor of the shower compartment. Nikki put a face cloth into my mouth, and Fred tied it in place with a hand towel. They wanted to make very sure that, when the waiter arrived, I couldn't utter a sound. Fred then stood in the middle of the bathroom, pointing the gun at my head. Nikki left and shut the door of the bathroom.

Surprisingly soon there was a knock on the door, and Nikki went to open it. Through the bathroom door I could hear the sound of two trolleys being wheeled into the room. I heard nothing for a short while, and then I heard two pairs of footsteps walking toward the bathroom door.

Suddenly the bathroom door flung open, and Detective Sergeant Takahashi, dressed in a waiter's uniform, threw himself across the room at Fred. Taken completely by surprise, Fred let the gun fall. Through the open door I could see the second room service waiter observing the one-sided struggle. He was a short, dapper man with a nondescript face except for a pencil moustache that seemed to come straight from a Late Late Movie made in the 1930s.

As soon as he was sure that I was safe, Inspector Watanabe rushed to handcuff Nikki. Uniformed police poured into Room 1507 until it started to look like the crowded stateroom in the Marx Brothers' classic *A Night at the Opera*. Two policemen led Nikki and Fred away in handcuffs, and a third policeman walked behind, carrying the gun in a plastic evidence bag.

Once the criminals were safely under arrest, two uniformed policemen gently untied me, helped me to walk from the bathroom to the bedroom and then used sign language to suggest that I lie on the bed until I felt better. I lay there for a few minutes, panting. All the policemen had left.

Suddenly, there was a knock on the door and a familiar voice called out, "Don't get up, I have a key."

Inspector Watanabe accompanied by Detective Sergeant Takahashi walked into the room, both smiling broadly, both still wearing their waiter's uniforms.

"May we sit down?" Watanabe asked.

"You saved my life. The very least I can do is to invite you to sit down," I said.

They duly occupied the armchairs that had been vacated by Nikki and Fred just a few minutes earlier. I tried to say something to Inspector Watanabe but, yet again, I was rendered speechless.

CHAPTER TWENTY-TWO

Realizing that I was too emotional to speak, Inspector Watanabe took the initiative.

"I'm sure you're wondering how we knew that you needed rescuing."

I nodded.

"I'm afraid that, in order to answer that question, I'll have to tell the story from the very beginning, otherwise nothing in this strange tale will make any sense. Please interrupt me if anything is unclear."

Again I nodded.

"I first met you soon after you claimed you'd been held up at gunpoint on the Philosophers' Pathway. There were no witnesses, and there was no evidence of any kind to back up your story. My reaction—and I apologize for it—was to conclude that either you'd made up the whole story or you were insane. Either way, I saw no point in taking the matter any further. It only occurred to me afterwards that you had no money to get back to your hotel. I assume you used your credit card to get money to pay for a cab?"

I was just barely able to nod.

"I think you've met my father-in-law, Asahi Suzuki, MD, retired head of the Osaka Hospital for the Criminally Insane and one of Japan's best-known psychiatrists."

All I could do was gasp.

"The previous evening at dinner I told my father-in-law about an interesting case that had come up that afternoon. An American tourist had complained that he'd been the victim of an armed robbery on the Philosophers' Pathway but there was absolutely no evidence of any kind to back up his story, which had many unusual features, to say the least. It was my opinion that the robbery hadn't occurred, but I couldn't fathom the American's motive for reporting a crime that had never happened.

"My father-in-law was as fascinated with the case as I thought he'd be, and we sat up much later than I'd intended discussing various aspects of the incident and poking holes in the various theories that we constructed to try to account for the many strange elements of the case. He asked if he could meet you. When I pointed out that there was no way that I could sanction that officially, he suggested the stratagem of the train ticket to Nara. He was certain that you'd take the bait, and he looked forward to spending the day with you.

"American tourists to Japan are usually wealthy, because the airfare alone is about twice the cost of a ticket to Europe, so it was likely that you could function well in business and make a good living. In fact, you appeared to be quite wealthy—for example, I happen to know that your American Express Centurion card is an invitation-only card with an annual fee of $2,500.

"However, Dr. Suzuki's hypothesis was that, no matter how well you function under normal circumstances, under pressure you'd behave strangely. He believed that you'd made up the story about the armed robbery as a consequence of being under extreme pressure of some sort.

"So, Dr. Suzuki wanted to put you under pressure. There were three obvious ways to do that. The first was to force you to take physical exercise. That's why you were made to walk everywhere. Second, when the distance was too far to walk, he insisted that you use public transportation rather than the cabs to which you're accustomed. And third, he made sure that you were given food that you probably wouldn't like. That green tea ice cream was truly awful, wasn't it?" and he grinned to show that he hoped that there were no hard feelings.

"Contrary to what he'd anticipated, Dr. Suzuki was amazed to see how well you reacted to pressure. In fact, while you were gamely eating that fish-and-rice abomination, he suddenly changed his mind about you, and he became convinced that you genuinely believed that you had been a victim of a hold-up. However, he had to stay in character. That was why the afternoon was a repeat of the morning—unending walks from boring temple to boring temple, paying admission fees to sites you couldn't enter, and ghastly food. The XXX-rated pornographic T-shirts were shown to you in order to introduce sex into the equation. You can think of those T-shirts as Japanese Rorschach inkblots!

"However, when you refused to enter the Nara National Museum, it was clear that he'd overdone it and you were totally exhausted. He did his best to look after you on the trip back to Kyoto and was really concerned that he might have done you some physical harm. In his defense, he's been a psychiatrist for over forty years, and he does tend to concentrate on the mind and forget about the body." Again he grinned, this time probably in the hope that I'd forgive his father-in-law for nearly killing me that day.

"When he came back to our apartment, he told me that, in his professional opinion, you were utterly truthful and largely impervious to pressure. As a consequence, he'd deduced that you genuinely believed the armed robbery had taken place exactly as you'd described it to me last Thursday. Unfortunately, this did not help matters in any way; I still didn't know whether the robbery had actually occurred, or whether it was a figment of your imagination.

"Sunday was my day off. I spent most of the day thinking about the case. Monday morning I decided to meet with you unofficially, that is, in your hotel. Now imagine my surprise. The unmarked car in which I was being driven had almost reached the Mikado Hotel when I saw you entering the building in which Yoshio Goto has his office. I shouted to my driver to stop, and I stayed in the car until I could see that you were safely in the elevator. Then I rushed into the lobby. When I saw from the display that the elevator had stopped on the floor on which Yosh has his office, I realized that you were seeing a private detective to get the help that the police wouldn't give you. I called Yosh that evening in order to ask him whether he believed that the hold-up had actually taken place, when I suddenly realized that I couldn't do that without telling him about my father-in-law's role in the matter. I quickly asked Yosh why you'd decided to take a stroll on the Philosophers' Pathway, and hung up. I handled that part of the investigation really badly.

"Yesterday you came to see me to report a murder you'd witnessed at the Kiyomizu Temple. After what I learned from my father-in-law, I knew that you thought that you'd seen something that had appeared to you to be a murder. However, when we investigated the incident in depth, the situation was identical to the hold-up. First, there was no sign of a murder having taken place. On the contrary, the evidence pointed to the fact that there had been no murder of any kind. Second, April had disappeared, and as a result there were no witnesses.

"One possibility was that you were hallucinating. Another was that you were the victim of some plot, but by whom and to what end? Again I couldn't help you in any way. I felt terrible that again there was nothing I could do, and I handled my guilt by treating you really badly. I apologize deeply and ask your forgiveness for my rudeness. I hurt you unnecessarily, but at the time I could see no alternative.

"Then came the incident with Yoko Azuma. You reported that she, too, had been murdered and that she was lying in your bed, only to discover that she was alive and well, and there was no sign of blood—or of Yoko, for that matter—in your bed. You may have seen my friend Yosh's favorite movie of all time, the James Bond movie *Goldfinger*. There's a line in that movie: 'Once is happenstance. Twice is coincidence. The third time it's enemy action.' This was the third time, and now I was going to find out once and for all whether or not you were suffering from paranoid hallucinations, or whether some evildoers were behind it all.

"Mr. Mori, the manager of this hotel, had explained to me the circumstances of the latest incident. I decided that the best way to proceed was to call you in for questioning. While you were in the car on the way to police headquarters I went to the magistrate on duty and obtained permission to tap your telephone and also to send technicians to install a hidden microphone in your hotel room while you were with me at police headquarters. That was why I interrogated you numerous times, each time covering the same set of facts. I was trying to give the technicians as much time as possible to install the microphone in a such a way that you wouldn't notice anything."

Inspector Watanabe walked to the other side of the bed, took out a Swiss Army knife, and unscrewed the front panel of the radio. He reached inside and took out a small microphone connected to a pair of twisted green wires. I sat up, looked into the radio cavity and saw the wires disappearing into the wall of the next room.

"We won't need this any more," the inspector said as he sliced through the wires with his penknife and put the microphone and knife into his jacket pocket.

"Now you understand why I ordered you to stay in your room until your wife arrived and then leave the country within twenty-four hours. As long as you were in Room 1507 we could listen from the next room, Room 1505, to everything that was going on in here. However, once Nikki had arrived, there was no reason for you to stay on in Kyoto, and for your own safety I wanted you back in New York as soon as possible. Yes, as a policeman my primary aim was to find out if the three incidents had actually occurred, and if they had, who was behind the crimes. But in the total absence of any clues or any witnesses, the most prudent thing to do was to get you out of our country as quickly as I could.

"When your wife and brother-in-law arrived, the listeners in the next room realized that something really serious was going on. After all, your wife had pulled a gun on you and was threatening to kill you. They contacted me at once, and I rushed to the hotel with Detective Sergeant Takahashi, with the siren of our car blaring all the way. We arrived just as you started talking about the champagne and caviar. You were good. In fact, you were very good.

"As you continued your spiel, Takahashi and I used the phone in the next room to commandeer a set of waiters' uniforms. Then we instructed room service to bring your order immediately to Room 1505 where we were monitoring the situation in order to use the two trolleys as a subterfuge to enter Room 1507 at any time. Of course, a SWAT team was standing by with weapons. If there had been any risk that Nikki would kill you before the food arrived, they would certainly have burst in with stun grenades and tear gas. But, thanks to you, everything seemed to be going so well that I decided to play it as a waiter rather than ask the SWAT team to release you. Once you'd been moved to the bathroom, Fred and Nikki were separated, and that seemed a good time to make our move. The rest you know, I think.

"Is there anything else you'd like me to tell you about?"

I had only one question. "What will happen to Nikki?"

"As you know, we Japanese are law-abiding people. Occasionally something terrible happens, like the Japanese Red Army in the 1970s or the sarin gas terror attacks of the Aum Shinrikyo sect in 1995, but by and large our islands are crime-free, notwithstanding our one hundred thousand yakuza, members of organized crime syndicates. Also, as I think you know, we have extremely strict gun-control laws and we don't look kindly on people like Fred who commit armed robbery or women like Nikki who have every intention of shooting their husbands. We also don't like people who murder a bellhop by adding poison to the drugs they supplied her. I'm sorry to have to tell you that Yoko Azuma is dead. But I believe we have enough evidence to convict both your wife and your brother-in-law of her murder. The penalty is life in prison without the possibility of parole.

"We'll prosecute your wife and your brother-in-law to the maximum extent of the law. The fact that they are visitors to our country won't result in a lighter punishment, nor will they be permitted to serve their lengthy sentences in America. It will be a long, long time before either of them gets out of prison here in Japan, in fact it's unlikely that they'll ever be released.

"I also know that it will be a long, long time before you'll be able to forgive Nikki for what she's done to you, perhaps never. I am very sorry."

Then Inspector Watanabe rose to his feet. So did Detective Sergeant Takahashi who hadn't said a single word the entire time. They both shook hands with me, and left the room.

I wept.

CHAPTER TWENTY-THREE

Nikki hadn't killed me, but, as a result of the day's happenings, I felt as if I was no longer alive. Significantly, although I'd eaten nothing the entire day, I wasn't hungry. Bearing in mind the major role that food plays in the life of a man who weighs 450 pounds, that should give you some idea of the magnitude of the blow to my very being.

Toward nightfall the phone rang. It was Yosh. "I'm in the lobby. May I come up?" he asked.

I wanted to say that I just didn't give a darn either way, but Yosh had been really kind when I'd tried to locate the hospital to which the "injured" Nikki had supposedly been taken, so I said, "Yes, if you wish."

When he knocked, it wasn't easy to force myself to get off the bed and walk to the door to let him in, but somehow I managed it.

Yosh greeted me. I was doubly surprised to see that he looked awful, first because I was amazed that I still had the ability to observe others and be concerned about their welfare, and second because

I was the one who now had no wife and no life, not Yosh.

I invited him to sit on one of the armchairs. I moved the other armchair back from where Nikki had placed it, and sat opposite him on the other side of the table.

"Have you had dinner yet?" he asked.

"I haven't had breakfast yet," I replied.

"Come now, food lovers like you and me have to keep our strength up. Let me take you to my favorite restaurant. I guarantee you that you'll enjoy it."

"Thank you, but I'm not hungry. And even if I were, there's no force on earth that would get me to leave this room."

"Do you have any objection to my ordering a room service dinner for myself? I also haven't eaten all day."

"Go ahead," I said. I didn't add that I wished that he'd go away and leave me to my misery. But despite the deep pain that I felt, I simply couldn't hurt Yosh.

Yosh picked up the desk phone and dialed room service. He gave a series of instructions in Japanese and then paused, presumably to have his order repeated. Then, instead of hanging up, he gave a second set of instructions and again listened for a while. Finally, there was a third set of instructions. He listened a third time and then hung up. I had no idea what was going on.

We sat in silence for a few minutes. Yosh had a friendly smile on his face. I felt drained, and again I wished he'd go as soon as he'd eaten his meal and preferably a lot sooner than that.

There was a knock on the door. Yosh rose to his feet and opened the door. A waiter wheeled in a trolley containing two large ice buckets, each containing three large bottles of Kirin lager. The lower shelf of the trolley contained a mammoth platter of sushi. It seemed a lot of food, even for a man of Yosh's appetite. Then the waiter laid two places, one for him and one for me, put the sushi platter in the middle of the table and placed an empty plate in front of each of us. He opened two bottles of lager and poured half of one bottle into my glass and half of the other bottle into Yosh's glass. Then he bowed to each of us and left.

I sat there, stunned. "Come, eat!" Yosh said.

"I'm not hungry," I said, as politely as I could.

"What's that got to do with it?" Yosh asked, proving once and for all that you don't have to be Jewish or a mother to be a Jewish mother.

Reluctantly I took a piece of sushi, a sip of beer and then another piece of sushi. Pretty soon the table was bare. I sat back, replete.

Again we sat in companionable silence. There was another knock on the door. "Round Two," Yosh said. "I couldn't decide if you wanted French food and wine, or Japanese food and *sake*, so I ordered both. And don't forget to leave room for dessert—that's Round Three."

We helped ourselves and started eating.

"By the way, just in case you think all this food is to cheer you up, you're wrong. It's to cheer me up."

"Cheer *you* up? Why do *you* need cheering up?"

"Until today I had a reputation as a respected private investigator. Now I'm wondering whether to find another line of work. Perhaps I should open a Weight Watchers Clinic."

I couldn't see what he was getting at, so I just went on eating. It seemed the easiest response.

"You came to see me with a problem. Strange things were happening to you. But instead of following Rule A, I invented a conspiracy."

"What's Rule A?" I asked, without bothering to swallow first. The yakitori food was superb, and I knew he was going to tell me even if I didn't ask.

"As every policeman and every ex-policeman knows, Rule A is *cherchez la femme*, as we say in Japanese. If a married man is in trouble, nine times out of ten his wife is behind it, and the tenth time it's his girlfriend. But did I follow Rule A? No, I did not! Instead I had to create a conspiracy. After nine highly successful years as a detective on the San Francisco police force and eight even more successful years running my own private investigator business here, I decided that a vast conspiracy was a more likely explanation than a woman. And, oh, what a far-reaching, global conspiracy it turned out to be!

He took a deep drink of *sake*, snorted at his stupidity and attacked his food again.

I refilled his cup. "C'mon, be fair to yourself. Nikki and Fred were unbelievably clever. They staged crime after crime without witnesses and without leaving any evidence."

"That's precisely what should've made me suspicious that a woman was behind it all. Women are infinitely craftier than men, especially woman criminals. Instead of inventing a vast male conspiracy, I should've remembered *cherchez la femme* and looked for your wife.

"And that would've been trivially easy. I would've tried to track her down in Sweden. The first step would've been to find out which flight she'd taken from Japan to get to the bedside of her 'sick mother.' When it became clear that she'd never left Japan, everything else would've quickly snapped into place."

"Yosh, we all have 20/20 hindsight. Stop torturing yourself. She fooled me, she fooled you, she even fooled Inspector Watanabe and his clever father-in-law, Suzuki."

"Don't talk to me about Suzuki," Yosh groaned. "Remember what I told you about Suzuki being a false name. I was even blind to the possibility that he might really be named Suzuki, just as there are people in America who really are named Smith. No, I'm giving up the detective business."

"You're just drunk."

"I came here with my mind made up before I started drinking. And I'm not drunk. Yet. But I soon will be if you'd kindly stop making stupid remarks and let me concentrate on my drinking."

"Tomorrow you'll feel better."

"Will you feel better tomorrow?" The question was blunt. In fact, it was way, way below the belt, but Yosh had a valid point.

"Okay," I said, "let's make a deal. After this Nikki affair, I'm giving up my offshore trust business, for the same reason that you want to give up your detective business. We've both been made fools of, big time, and we're both too proud to overlook it.

"Tomorrow I'm flying back to New York. Come with me. Together we can go into some other business. As I think you know, I've more than enough money to underwrite anything we choose to undertake together. Do you have any unfinished cases that your assistants can't adequately complete?"

Yosh shook his head.

"Fine, it's a deal, let's get good and drunk tonight, and tomorrow we'll find something worthy of our talents."

Round Three soon arrived, complete with liqueurs, and we both soon collapsed into a happy stupor.

CHAPTER TWENTY-FOUR

Transcript of an interrogation of Prisoner
4519-83R Nikolina Thompson, born Stenqvist
("Nikki") and Prisoner 8395-345Q J.
Frederick Wagoneer ("Fred"), conducted by
Inspector Seiji Watanabe, Kyoto Police
("Watanabe"), in the presence of Detective
Sergeant Takahashi, in Kyoto Prison, 20
Higashino-Inoue-cho, Kyoto.

Watanabe: Prisoner Thompson, Prisoner
          Wagoneer, you have both been
          convicted of the crime of murder
          of Yoko Azuma. The penalty for
          murder is life in prison without
          the possibility of parole, but the
          judge is prepared to give you both
          a twenty-five-year sentence and to
          drop the other charges, including
          attempted murder and armed
          robbery, in return for a full and
          truthful confession. Are you
          prepared to confess?

Nikki: Yes.

Fred: Yes.

Watanabe: In particular, we want full
          information about your accomplices

in Kyoto. Are you prepared to give that information?

Nikki: I will tell you everything I know.

Watanabe: Prisoner Thompson, describe what happened after you arrived in Japan. Do not omit any details.

Nikki: Oliver and I landed at Kansai International Airport. We took the bullet train to Kyoto station. We took a taxi from there to the Mikado Hotel. When our taxi arrived, Fred was watching from a furnished apartment across the road that he'd rented when he arrived in Kyoto five days ahead of us. He'd also acquired a Japanese cell phone that we used for communicating with Oliver.

As soon as he saw us, Fred sent the first text, the one stating that my mother in Sweden was ill. I'd prepared it in Swedish some days previously and given it to Fred to take with him to Kyoto. I rushed out of the hotel into a waiting taxi, apparently on my way to the airport to fly to Sweden, but the cab actually took me across the road to the apartment Fred had rented.

I also brought along a recording of the standard TeliaSonera announcement stating in Swedish that the number you have reached is out of order. I loaded this onto my cell, just in case Oliver disobeyed my orders and tried to phone me in "Sweden."

Fred: I want to talk about the breakfast cashier. In the five days before Nikki and Oliver arrived, I spent as much time as I could in the Mikado Hotel so that if the staff saw me there, they would think that I was a guest. The first morning I woke early, and I decided to have breakfast in Le Lac des Cygnes as soon as the restaurant opened. The restaurant manager gave me totally wrong change. Unlike Oliver when the same thing happened to him, I made a big scene. In order to prevent the scene from getting any bigger, the restaurant manager explained to me that the cashier's child was ill and that was why she had not yet arrived that morning. None of the waitresses were prepared to try and work the cash register, so the manager himself had to stand in for the cashier until she finally arrived. The problem was that, as Oliver later discovered, that particular manager is no good at computing change, and knows nothing about credit cards or charging meals to rooms.

The manager explained the situation to me while repeatedly asking me politely to lower my voice. As he spoke, I noted the extension number on the telephone next to the cash register. Then, on Nikki's first morning in Kyoto, I was seated in the lounge area leading to the entrance to Le Lac des Cygnes restaurant, my face shielded by a Japanese newspaper.

I made a hole in the paper to enable me to see Oliver arriving for breakfast, but he didn't even glance my way. As soon as he was seated, I went to the house phone around the corner from the restaurant and dialed the cashier's

extension. When she answered, I read
from a piece of paper that contained,
transliterated, the Japanese for "Your
child is very ill. Return home at
once." The cashier was, understandably,
so distraught that I doubt that she
even realized that the caller wasn't
Japanese. She dashed out of the
restaurant in a panic. And that was how
we arranged for Oliver to be given the
wrong change at breakfast.

Watanabe: How did you arrange the hold-up on
the Philosophers' Pathway?

Nikki: I sent Oliver a text, apparently from
Stockholm, telling him to visit the
Philosophers' Pathway, and off he
went. Up till then, whenever I said,
"Jump!" his only response was, "How
high?" There hadn't been a single
request of mine that he didn't
immediately carry out. I'd no doubt
whatsoever that he'd visit the
Philosophers' Pathway as soon as he'd
finished reading my text.

Fred: I waited behind the tree for ages for
Oliver to arrive—I later learned that
he'd spent a long time eating. Then I
heard him coming down the path. As he
passed the tree I stepped out and stuck
the gun in his back. He fell for the
story about "my friend" hook, line and
sinker.

Watanabe: How did you know where he kept his
wallet?

Fred: Nikki told me.

Watanabe: How did you obtain the gun? (Fred
does not answer.)

Watanabe: Prisoner Wagoneer, I repeat, how did you obtain the gun? If you do not tell me, you and Prisoner Thompson will spend the rest of your lives in Abashiri Maximum Security Prison.

Fred: And if I tell you, the yakuza will have me killed in prison.

Nikki: He bought it from a grateful former client, a drug smuggler named Matsuko Hirohito.

Watanabe: Prisoner Wagoneer, is this correct?

Fred: Yes.

Nikki: That was why Fred decided to travel to Kyoto. We were getting impatient, because Oliver was showing no sign of dying from a stroke or a heart attack. In New York we had no way of acquiring a gun, but Fred knew that Matsuko would do anything for him. That was why we decided that we would both go to Kyoto, to enable Fred to obtain a gun and, hopefully, find a way for us to use it without getting caught.

Watanabe: Why did you send Oliver to the Noh Theater and the GoGoGo Club?

Fred: Our intention was to ensure that as many people as possible saw Oliver acting strangely. The kind of people who attend Noh performances are important people, the kind of people who are credible when they stand up in court and testify that Oliver sat by himself at the very back of the auditorium in the worst seat in the house, when much better seats were available at the same price. They would also express amazement that, unlike almost all foreign tourists, Oliver chose to watch Noh rather than Kabuki. We'd hoped that Oliver would arrive early and be seen by more people, but at least some theatergoers saw him.

Watanabe: Surely you realized that the box-office clerk would tell us that he sold Oliver's ticket to you and not to Oliver? Once I'd found out who had bought Oliver's ticket, the trail would lead straight back to his wife and her boyfriend.

Fred: We didn't buy Oliver's ticket. We went to the box office together to buy a pair of the best seats in the house, apparently for ourselves. Then Nikki asked the clerk to show us which number on a ticket represented the row number and which was the seat number. While this was going on, I carefully studied the seating plan and found the seat where we wanted Oliver to sit.

We then went to a paper shop and bought purple paper with a color and a texture that, to our eyes, was indistinguishable from that of the two tickets we'd bought. Many computer printers these days can scan and make copies, including the one I'd brought with me from Philadelphia. We made the appropriate changes to one of the tickets and then xeroxed the doctored ticket onto the purple paper we'd bought—copying can hide almost all signs of tampering. That meant that

there was no way anyone could tie us to
the purchase of Oliver's ticket because
we never bought it; we forged it.

I was standing at the window of the
traditional crafts shop across from the
theater and I saw Oliver arrive. And
when the foyer finally emptied I snuck
into the auditorium, dropped the
envelope into his lap and rushed out
into the street, knowing he could never
catch up with me.

And I'm sure that everyone at the
GoGoGo Club noticed him. First, Oliver
is vastly obese. Second, he was
probably the first person ever to go to
that club wearing a navy blue pinstripe suit. Third, knowing Oliver as I
do, I'm certain he scurried around,
methodically covering every square inch
of the club in the hope of seeing
someone he recognized, which meant that
everyone in the place must've seen him.
After Oliver's suicide, you would've
had no trouble finding dozens of young
people who would attest to the strange
behavior of the grossly fat gaijin who
came to the club without a partner,
then proceeded to carefully inspect
everyone in the club.

We sent him to the Chionin Temple and
its big bell for the same reason. The
sight of him assiduously searching that
vast complex would surely be implanted
on the memories of many visitors.

Watanabe: How did you arrange for the theft
of Oliver Thompson's shoes at
Ryoan-ji?

Fred: The night before Oliver lost his
shoes, we were in the bar across the
road from the Mikado Hotel, downstairs
from our apartment. There were five
Japanese college students there, seated
at a table next to ours. I had an idea.
Nikki had given me a number of eight by
ten photographs of Oliver. I rushed up
to the apartment, took five of the
photographs and returned to our table
in the bar. When there was a pause in
their conversation, I introduced myself
to the students under a false name. I
offered each of them ¥50,000 on the
spot if they would each go the next day
to a different major temple and, if
Oliver arrived there, steal his shoes
while he was inside. The person who
brought me his shoes would get an
additional ¥50,000. Now, $500 is a lot
of money for a student, and that was
why they were willing to accept my
explanation that this was a practical
joke that I wanted to play on my
business partner.

I told them that I'd be back at the bar
at a specific time to pay the reward if
one of them managed to take the shoes.
Much to my delight, at the agreed time
one of them came into the bar carrying
a plastic bag containing the stolen
shoes. He'd waited for nearly two hours
at Ryoan-ji before Oliver arrived. A
few seconds after Oliver reached the
temple veranda, his shoes were gone. I
paid the student the promised reward,
then I walked across the street to the
Mikado Hotel, took the elevator to Room
1507, and left his shoes where Oliver
found them, outside the door to his
room.

Watanabe: And what happened at the Silver Pavilion Temple? There was an early morning phone call in which the whispering gunman tried to sound like an American. Was that you masquerading as a Japanese pretending to be an American?

Fred: Yes. And I set off that firecracker.

Watanabe: What firecracker?

Fred: I realized that it would be truly stupid to fire a gun inside the Silver Pavilion Temple. I arrived at the garden ahead of Oliver, even though I knew he'd come an hour early. When I saw him arrive, I entered the pavilion itself, despite the "No Unauthorized Entry" sign. If you act with sufficient authority, people believe you have the right to go anywhere. I hid in the Men's Room for about half an hour. Then I entered the room that overlooks the veranda where Oliver was sitting. I'd brought with me a loud firecracker that I set off. No one took any notice because firecrackers are often set off as part of Japanese religious rituals, but Oliver interpreted it as a gunshot exactly as he was supposed to, and he ran off like a chicken with its tail feathers on fire.

Nikki: And while Fred and Oliver were at the Silver Pavilion Temple, I entered Oliver's room using the electronic key that I'd been given at check-in. I placed the envelope containing the hold-up money and the ATM receipt on the table and left the way I'd come, in the service elevator. I certainly didn't want to bump into Mr. Mori or

one of the receptionists.
Fortunately, no one saw me.

Watanabe: Oliver was nearly hit by a beer
truck. How did you manage that?

Nikki: What beer truck?

Fred: We had nothing to do with a beer
truck. But if a beer truck had struck
him, it would've saved us a lot of
bother, and we wouldn't be sitting here
in Kyoto Prison.

Watanabe: How did you know that Oliver was
in the museum?

Nikki: Fred and I were angry that we'd lost
two days. For some reason, Oliver
left the Mikado Hotel early on
Saturday morning and came back late,
and then he did it again on Tuesday
morning. When he left the hotel early
on Wednesday morning as well we
reckoned we'd lost yet another day
and we decided to console ourselves
with a nice lunch, expecting that he
wouldn't be back until late yet
again. The best restaurant in Kyoto
is in the Royal Claremont Hotel.

After the meal I walked to the powder
room to freshen up, and on the way I
saw Oliver sitting in the lobby. I
rushed back to Fred. He paid the bill
at once, and as we left the
restaurant we saw Oliver leave the
lobby and walk across the street to
the museum. It didn't take us long to
come up with a plan that, we hoped,
would put so much strain on him that
he'd drop dead from a stroke or a
heart attack.

Watanabe: How did you get the writing on that paper to change without using disappearing ink and heat?

Nikki: There were two pieces of paper involved. We printed the first message on the first piece of paper using Fred's laptop computer and printer that he brought with him from Philadelphia, and then I wrote the second message on top of his message with a thick pen using disappearing ink. Fred went up to Oliver's room soon after 5:45 a.m. when the bellhops distribute the newspapers. Fred had spent a lot of time in the hotel, so they thought he was staying there, and the Mikado Hotel is so vast that no one can possibly know all the guests. Fred snuck into a large linen closet right next to Oliver's room. As soon as the newspaper was in the woven cloth bag on the door handle of Oliver's room and the bellhop who had delivered the papers had gone up to the next floor, Fred plugged in the iron he'd taken with him (having checked during an earlier visit that there was an electric socket in the closet), and heated the letters of my message with the iron. My handwriting appeared, masking the printed letters. Fred snuck out of the linen closet, slipped the piece of paper into the cloth bag containing Oliver's newspaper and retreated back into the linen closet. Using his iPhone, he called Oliver's room. When Oliver answered, Fred said something and hung up. What did you say to him, Fred?

Fred: There was a label on a sheet with the name and address of the manufacturer in both Japanese and English characters. I just mumbled the address. Then I waited for Oliver to take a shower.

Watanabe: But how did you know that he'd take a shower next?

Nikki: I lived with Oliver for about six months, and he's totally predictable. After he gets up, he gets the newspaper, and then he showers and shaves. All Fred had to do was to wait for the sound of running water, carefully emerge from the linen closet, listen outside Oliver's door to be sure that his shower was still running, sneak into the room using my key, replace the first sheet of paper bearing the first two messages with the second sheet of paper bearing the third message, the Gothic-looking one, and sneak out again.

The one risk was that Oliver might bolt the door again after he opened it to take the newspaper into his room, but we reckoned that he'd be so frightened when he saw the sheet of paper on top of his newspaper that he'd forget to bolt the door. Luckily for us, we were right.

The object of the exercise was to convince Oliver that he was going crazy as he watched the message on the sheet of paper keep changing—we didn't care whether or not he went to the Heian Shrine.

Watanabe: And how does April fit into this, and what actually happened at the Kiyomizu Temple?

Fred: April is the name that I asked her to use. She's a student at Kyoto University, a volunteer tour guide. I don't remember her real name. I met her through the Kyoto Travel Center in the Kyoto High Rise Building; they organize tours with student guides. The five students in the bar had accepted the explanation that I wanted to play a joke on my business partner and "April" was equally willing to accept the same story. I paid her ¥50,000 in advance to pretend to be an official guide. She was to take Oliver right through the Temple, ending at the gap in the trees from which he witnessed the murder. I instructed her to wave in the direction of the three-story orange pagoda when she arrived with Oliver at the preselected spot, and I told her what I'd do when I saw the signal.

Oliver thought he saw a fight ending in murder. In reality, I'd climbed down to the ledge with a duffel bag containing an inflatable plastic life-sized dummy, a strong but thin rope and a small air pump. I inflated the dummy, fastened a rope to its waist and waited. When I got the signal from April, I "fought" valiantly with the dummy. Finally, I administered the coup de grace and tossed the dummy over the edge. I knew that Oliver's vision isn't too good, even with the aid of his thick glasses, so when April shouted "murder" and, as pre-arranged, ran away, I knew that he'd be totally convinced that a murder had taken place. I clambered along the

ledge in the direction away from him
and, when I was out of his sight,
retrieved the dummy by hauling in the
rope. I then deflated the dummy and
replaced it in the duffel bag together
with the rope and air pump.

Watanabe: How could you know in advance that
Oliver would go to the Kiyomizu
Temple? He told us that going
there was his idea, not yours like
the visit to the Philosophers'
Pathway. There wasn't time to
organize the scheme with April.

Nikki: We'd taken a major risk that first
day in sending Oliver a text telling
him to go to the Philosophers'
Pathway. After all, Oliver might've
displayed it on his BlackBerry when
he went to the police and you
might've put two and two together. It
was our intention before leaving
Oliver's room after his "suicide" to
delete any incriminating texts. Yes,
you could have subpoenaed telephone
company records and obtained copies
of every text he received, but we
were sure that you'd conclude that
Oliver had killed himself and that a
detailed investigation wouldn't be
necessary.

That was why we were unwilling to
send Oliver another text specifying a
tourist venue. Even Oliver might have
become suspicious. And if he showed
it you, you'd soon realize that there
was a nasty pattern. Instead, I
called Oliver. I casually asked him
where he was going, and he said the
Kiyomizu Temple. If he'd said
anywhere else, I'd have suggested

Kiyomizu. Knowing him as I do, he'd
go anywhere I told him and do
anything I asked him to do—the dumb
lovesick fool! We'd made all the
arrangements with April the previous
day, and as a result she was at the
temple waiting for him when he
arrived.

Watanabe: And how did you pull off the stunt
with Yoko Azuma's dead body in his
bed?

Fred: Yoko had a major drug habit. She was
willing to do anything in return for
cocaine.

Watanabe: How did you get the cocaine?

Nikki: Fred bought it from Matsuko Hirohito.

Watanabe: Prisoner Wagoneer, is that
correct?

Fred: Yes.

Watanabe: What did you ask Yoko to do?

Nikki: I told her to come to work with two
of those navy blue uniform caps.
While Oliver was busy with the police
at the Kiyomizu Temple, Yoko, Fred
and I went to Oliver's hotel room. I
had the key and so we had no problem
getting in. Fred and I put white
powder on Yoko's face and poured fake
blood onto her face and cap, being
careful not to put any on her hair or
the rest of her uniform. Yoko got
into Oliver's bed, and Nikki and I
put more of the fake blood on the
sheet and blanket. Nikki and I then
waited in the bathroom—Yoko had

stored an additional sheet, blanket
and pillowcase there. Oliver came in,
saw Yoko lying dead in his bed and
ran for the elevator as fast as his
fat little legs could carry him. Yoko
jumped out of bed, washed the white
powder and fake blood from her face,
changed caps, and took the next
elevator down to the lobby. As soon
as she was out of Oliver's bed, Fred
and I quickly remade it. Then we put
the dirty linen into one of Oliver's
suitcases and left. Yoko came back
later and used my key to retrieve the
"bloodstained" cap, pillowcase, sheet
and blanket. I've no idea how she
disposed of them and neither do I
care. Nor do I care about anything
else.

End of transcript

AFTERWORD

I travelled to Japan to present a paper at a Software Engineering conference. While I was there, I took the opportunity to visit a few tourist sites in Kyoto and Nara. Much of this book is based on my experiences on that trip.

I have described the touristic aspects as clearly as I could. For example, Oliver and Suzuki's excursion to Nara is a reasonably accurate account of my solo visit to that city, down to the food, the wedding and even the Labrador Retriever.

On the other hand, all the commercial establishments in this story, including hotels, banks, theaters, nightclubs, stores, bars, and restaurants, are figments of my imagination, as are the hospitals, guidebooks and phrasebooks. Also, all crime-related issues are totally fictional, including my description of Kyoto Police Headquarters. And none of the characters in *A Matter of Trust* are based, even loosely, on real people.

Cyproterone acetate, sold under brand names such as Androcur and Cyprostat, is a drug that suppresses androgenic activity in the body.